DARK SURVIVOR
REUNITED

THE CHILDREN OF THE GODS BOOK 22

I. T. LUCAS

Also by I. T. Lucas

42: Dark Choices Paradigm Shift

PERFECT MATCH
Perfect Match 1: Vampire's Consort
Perfect Match 2: King's Chosen
Perfect Match 3: Captain's Conquest

SETS

The Children of the Gods books 1-3: Dark Stranger trilogy—Includes a bonus short story: **The Fates take a Vacation**

The Children of the Gods: Books 1-6—includes **character lists**

The Children of the Gods: Books 6.5-10 —includes character lists

---

TRY THE CHILDREN OF THE GODS SERIES ON
AUDIBLE
2 FREE audiobooks with your new Audible subscription!

WONDER

"What are you doing?' Anandur asked as Wonder pulled out her phone and aimed the camera at the appetizers the waitress had just delivered to their table.

"It's for Callie." Taking a quick glance, she checked that no one was looking, then snapped several pictures in quick succession.

The restaurant was a bit fancy but not too much so. The tables were covered with white tablecloths, but there were no candles, and most of the diners were dressed casually. Even if someone caught her in the act, she doubted anyone would mind.

Like little pieces of art, the appetizers were a feast for the senses, and not just the sense of taste or smell. She loved their colors, and the way they were arranged on the platter, with the sauce poured in a meandering pattern around them and several mint leaves scattered around like little trees on a riverbank.

"They look delicious." She opened up the menu and

took a picture of the ingredients. "Callie should add them to her recipe collection."

"I don't think it's okay." Anandur regarded her with amusement dancing in his eyes. "What if recipes are copyrighted? Besides, Callie still has two years of studying to do before she makes up her mind whether she wants to be a teacher or a chef. Until then, she might change her mind about the restaurant business and come up with another idea, or just teach. It would be a waste to spend four years studying a subject and then not use what she learned."

Wonder saw nothing wrong with that. Learning new skills and gaining new knowledge was rewarding in itself, and having several options was always better than having none or just one. "I have a feeling she's not going to wait until she's done, and I also think that learning new things should be a goal in itself. It's not just about getting ready for a job."

Wonder put the phone away and lifted her utensils. "I don't think she is going to change her mind. Callie is excited about it. And as for copying recipes, no one is going to find out what she serves in the village. She can also change them around and make them her own."

Hands hovering over the platter, she hesitated. "It's almost a shame to destroy the display." With a sigh, she scooped a piece onto her plate, cut it in two, and lifted one of the halves into her mouth.

As the flavors hit her taste buds, she groaned with pleasure.

Eyes glued to her lips, Anandur cleared his throat. "How is it?"

Swallowing, Wonder rolled her eyes. "Amazing. It tastes even better than it looks."

"That's one of Kian's favorites. The dude is vegan, so there is no meat in it, which means I would've never ordered it for myself. But once I gave it a try, I was sold." He forked a whole piece and winked. "You can tell Callie I'm eating my veggies."

Anandur was so easy to be with.

After last night, Wonder had expected things to be a little awkward between them, but he was acting as if nothing had happened, or as if it wasn't a big deal.

Maybe for him it wasn't, but it sure was for her.

In one evening, Anandur had officially become her boyfriend and had given her first venom bite as well as her first explosive climax.

Remembering her powerful reaction, a shiver of desire rocked Wonder's body. A girl could get addicted to that, and according to Anandur it was bound to happen if they kept at it.

Though he wasn't sure if the process would start with the bite alone.

Not that Wonder planned on waiting much longer for the rest.

As usual, Anandur had his weird opinions about when and how that should happen. Perhaps he was right about that, but she wasn't going to take his word for it. When they returned to the village, she was going to talk to Carol, who'd made several offers to expand Wonder's education on the subject.

But at least he was showing her a lot of affection, touching and kissing her at every opportunity. Except, to do that without getting all fired up, the man must've been made from solid rock and determination. Every kiss, even to the back of her hand, sent electrical currents throughout her body, flipping the switch on her arousal.

Was Anandur just as affected and only better at hiding his responses?

Wonder had tried to sniff for it, but she was either a lousy sniffer, or the constant touching was not making him as hot and bothered as it was her.

It probably had something to do with experience. She suspected that after nearly a millennium of existence, and gods only knew how many partners, Anandur wasn't as easily excitable. Carol had said something about men getting bored with the mundane and seeking new thrills with the exotic and unusual, naturally regarding herself as the latter.

Last night, though, Wonder hadn't been the only one erupting in an explosive climax. Even though it must've been embarrassing for a male his age, Anandur had been such a gentleman for choosing to ejaculate in his pants and not take advantage of her euphoric state. He could've easily taken her right then and there on the bench, and Wonder would not have minded if he had.

No, actually that wasn't true.

She would've regretted it later. Not because she didn't want Anandur, and not even because she wanted to wait, but because she wanted their first time together to be magical and not a quick romp on a public bench.

Anandur waved a hand in front of her eyes. "If you keep on daydreaming, I'm going to finish both appetizers."

She glanced at the platters, expecting to see only a few pieces left, but she should've known better. Like the true gentleman he was, Anandur had left more than half of each for her.

"You can eat the rest. I want to save room for the main course."

He arched a brow. "Are you sure?"

"Yes."

Eying the platters, he still hesitated. "We can order another serving."

"No need. Please, eat the rest." Wonder put her hand over his.

Eyes flashing with inner light, Anandur sucked in a breath.

That was interesting. How come the small touch elicited such a strong reaction from him? Was it because she had touched him and not the other way around?

Wonder frowned.

When Anandur touched her, she got all excited while he seemed in control. But when she touched him, the effect was reversed.

Evidently, getting touched was more stimulating than touching.

Gods, she was such a novice. This was yet another question for Carol.

"Are you done with the appetizers?" The waitress reached for one of the platters.

"No, not yet," Wonder said.

The woman smiled. "No problem, take your time."

Glancing down, Wonder realized she was still holding on to Anandur's hand and that he needed it to eat. Except, as soon as she tried to pull hers away, he caught it and brought it up to his mouth for a kiss.

Her reaction was instantaneous. His hot breath fanning over her skin followed by the soft brush of his lips sent a bolt of lightning straight to her center.

Wow, she'd actually guessed it right. Being touched was hotter than touching.

Was it like that with all couples? Or was it just them?

Yet another question she needed to ask Carol. At this rate, by the end of their all day long date in the city, she would have an entire list of them.

"I want to ask you something," Anandur said.

"Yes?"

"I know it's a little early for this, but I'm impatient." He rubbed a hand over the back of his neck.

Wonder's breath caught in her throat. In the movies, the guy usually said something like that to the girl before asking her to marry him.

Was Anandur about to propose?

He couldn't be. This outing was their first official date.

He squeezed her hand. "I want to take you to Egypt."

"What? Why?"

"Maybe it will help bring your memories back. Vanessa said that you need to have more experiences. I thought that going back to where it all began might be beneficial."

What the heck? He wanted her to remember Esag?

Up until that moment, Wonder hadn't internalized how terrified she was of regaining her memories. Without making a conscious decision to do so, she wanted to forget the past and concentrate on a future with Anandur.

She didn't want to remember loving someone else who might have abandoned her to die, or who'd left her. And if Esag had died and his death had been the cause of her trauma, she certainly didn't want to remember that and go through the grief of losing a man she loved twice.

It was a cowardly approach, but she had started

building a new life with the clan, and it was a good one. She didn't want to lose it.

She didn't want to lose Anandur.

Wonder shook her head. "I don't understand. Why would you want me to get my memories back? What if I remember loving Esag? Don't you want to give us a chance?"

"Oh, lass, that's exactly why I want you to remember. I want to find him and prove to you that I'm the better man. Otherwise, his shadow will always hover between us."

He leaned forward. "I don't want you to live with what ifs and what could've beens. Hell, *I* don't want to live with that. I want you to choose me, knowing that I'm the one for you and never second-guess it."

Wonder swallowed. "Maybe I'm a coward, but I'm afraid of what the past holds. Perhaps losing my memory was a good thing. It allowed me to start a new life."

"You'll not be doing it alone. I will be with you every step of the way. And just so we're clear, I'm not giving up on you no matter what. Your past isn't going to scare me away. I'm going to fight for you."

Despite his earnest promises, Wonder wasn't sure Anandur would stay by her side if she remembered still loving someone else. No one was that selfless.

On the other hand, there was a good chance that the trip would not bring her memories back. She could have a great time with Anandur and try her best not to remember anything.

Yeah, that seemed like a good plan. It could be like a honeymoon, only before the wedding.

Way to get carried away, Wonder Girl.

Still, the trip could be an excellent opportunity for

7

Anandur and her to get closer. He wouldn't get them separate hotel rooms, right?

Suddenly, Wonder was very excited about going to Egypt.

Except, there was the issue of her job at the café that she didn't want to lose. Also, she didn't have a passport or know how to go about getting one, and plane tickets were probably costly. She had some money saved up, but would it be enough?

"So what do you say, lass, are you in for an adventure?"

"I can't take a vacation. I just started working. It's not fair to Carol."

"Carol managed just fine without you before. She can manage for two more weeks."

"Two weeks is a lot. And I don't have a passport."

"Not a problem. I can have one made for you by tomorrow."

Wonder pulled her hand out of Anandur's and crossed her arms over her chest. "On one condition. I pay for my own plane ticket."

Anandur shook his head. "Not going to happen, so don't even think about arguing. This trip is my idea, and I'm paying for it."

"I have money saved up, and I no longer need it for renting an apartment. I can pay for my own ticket." Crossing her fingers under the table, she wished for what she had to be enough to cover the cost of the ticket. After all her bluster, it would be so embarrassing to ask Anandur to pay for it.

"I'll make you a deal."

The smirk on his face promised that she wasn't going to like the deal he was about to offer.

Wonder narrowed her eyes at him. "What is it?"

"After we are done with lunch, I'll take you shopping, and you can use that money you've saved up to buy yourself some nice things for the trip. I wanted to pamper you and pay for it, but I'm willing to compromise."

No wonder he looked so smug. His version of a compromise wasn't a compromise at all. "That's…"

He put a finger on her lips. "That's the best deal you're going to get. So I suggest you take it."

KIAN

"*I*t almost feels like a vacation." Syssi snuggled up to Kian in the back of the limo.

"I wish it was. Thanks for agreeing to sacrifice our date time for a visit to Ojai."

He still felt bad about asking her to do that instead of taking her out somewhere nice. Syssi had been hinting at wanting to see some musical he'd forgotten the name of, and he wanted to take her, but somehow something always came up. Perhaps she should go with Amanda. If she waited for him, by the time he managed to carve out a few hours for it, the musical would be over.

"It's not a sacrifice. As long as we are together, I don't care what we do. Besides, I want to see what you've done with the monastery."

"I hope you don't mind, but as long as we are there, I want to check on the humans we rescued from the Doomers."

"Of course, I don't mind. How long is the drive?"

"We are almost there. The road to the monastery is off

the next exit. The other place, where we keep the rescued humans, is fifteen minutes or so farther away."

She snuggled closer. "That's a shame. I was hoping for a little more alone time with you."

"We have alone time every night."

"But this is different. It's a mini road trip. We are going to do the necessary rounds, and then you're going to take me to a nice restaurant for lunch."

Kian raked his fingers through his hair. "Yeah, about that. If Vanessa and I are not done by lunchtime, we might have to invite her to join us."

Syssi sighed. "I can't say that I'm ecstatic about sharing you with the therapist, but I'm also interested to hear her observations about the girls' progress. And to tell you the truth, ever since I heard about the humans turned zombies by the Doomers, I've been in a really shitty mood. Part angry and part sad. Sentencing a person to a life of an automaton, stripped of his or her personality, is so cruel. I want to hear Vanessa's opinion on their chances of rehabilitation."

So did he. Kian hoped the clan wouldn't get stuck taking care of a bunch of brain-damaged humans until the day they died. These people needed to go back to their families.

As they arrived at the sanctuary, Bhathian parked the limo on the driveway, right in front of the entry.

Kian got out and held the door open, but he didn't offer Syssi his hand until Brundar circled around and stood guard. The place was secure, surrounded by a tall fence and a camera-monitored gate, but Kian trusted Brundar's instincts more than he trusted technology. One could circumvent equipment, but no one could turn off Brundar's extraordinarily sharp senses.

A moment later Vanessa came outside to greet them. "I'd rather you didn't come inside just yet," she said after the initial hellos had been exchanged. Casting a glance at his bodyguards, she shook her head. "Three males your size are going to freak the girls out. I'll have to send them to the backyard while you tour the place."

"Bhathian and Brundar can stay in the limo."

"I don't know. You're a big guy, Kian, and your stern expression looks intimidating to those who don't know you." She smiled sheepishly. "And those who do know you too."

He was well aware of his resting bitch face, as Anandur liked to call it.

The guy would've been a much better choice for this than Brundar and Bhathian. Even though he was massive, Anandur's charm and easy smile would've done wonders as far as putting the skittish girls at ease. In that regard, Bhathian with his perpetual scowl and Brundar with his cyborg expressionless, deadly demeanor, were probably the worst couple of Guardians to take along on a visit to see a bunch of girls recovering from sexual exploitation and abuse.

Fuck, he should've thought of that and brought Onegus and Arwel instead. The chief was quite a charmer, and Arwel was the least intimidating out of all the Guardians.

"What if I cling to Kian like the loving wife that I am?" Syssi asked. "If the girls see that he is with a woman who loves him, they might be less anxious around him."

Vanessa released a puff of air. "That might work." She

turned to Kian. "Just make sure to smile and look relaxed." She lifted a brow. "Can you do that?"

He did his best, grinning so broadly that his cheeks hurt.

She threw her hands in the air. "Fangs alert. I meant a closed-mouthed smile."

It turned out that Vanessa's fears had been mostly unwarranted.

As they were making the rounds, the looks Kian was getting were the same ones he usually got from women everywhere. There were a few gasps, several oh-my-gosh-look-at-this-guy, and some hushed wows.

He hated it when women ogled him. Usually, his response was a grimace, or worse, a growl, but given the circumstances he made an effort to school his expression into an impassive mask.

Only a handful of girls reacted with fear, their haunted eyes quickly darting away from him and leaving a sour taste in his mouth.

If Kian could've gotten his hands on the scum who'd hurt them, he would've torn their black hearts out of their chests with his bare hands.

"Easy, Kian," Syssi whispered. "You're growling, and your fangs are showing." She squeezed him tighter and kissed his arm.

Dipping his head, he buried his nose in her hair and inhaled her soothing scent. All he needed to calm down was to concentrate on Syssi's voice, the feel of her arm around him, and her scent.

"Thank you," he murmured in her ear.

"Anytime, my love."

"Do you want to see one of the rooms?" the therapist asked.

"If that's okay."

She led them down the hallway and knocked on one of the doors. "Sarah has been with us for several weeks, and she is doing well. She wouldn't mind visitors."

"Come in," the girl called out.

Pushing the door open, Vanessa peeked inside. "I have guests with me, a couple who donates generously to this center. They would like to see one of the rooms. Can they come in?"

"Sure."

On the one hand, the way Vanessa was introducing Syssi and him to the girls made Kian uncomfortable, but on the other hand, it was the most logical and least anxiety-inducing explanation for why they were touring the place.

"What an interesting pattern." Syssi lifted an embroidered napkin. "Did you make it yourself?"

"Yeah. It was one of our arts and crafts projects. I have more." Sarah opened a drawer and pulled out several similarly embroidered fabric pieces to show Syssi.

"You're really talented."

"Thank you." The girl smiled. "I can make you one if you want. You can choose any of these patterns." She spread her work on her bed.

"I like this one." Syssi pointed. "How much are you charging for it?" She reached into her purse and pulled out her wallet. "I think it's customary to pay in advance when commissioning a work of art."

His sweet, sweet Syssi.

Not only was she giving the girl much needed praise

and encouragement, but she was also going out of her way to be friendly. As an introvert, it must've been difficult for her to generate so much extroverted energy, which made him appreciate the effort even more.

The girl lifted a pair of questioning eyes to Vanessa. "Can we do that? Can we sell our projects?"

The therapist put her hand on the girl's shoulder. "Sure thing, Sarah. In fact, Syssi just gave me an awesome idea. We can rent a space in the farmers' market and sell our arts and crafts projects there. I'm sure many of the girls would like to earn a little extra spending money."

Kian had authorized a small monthly allowance for each of the girls. It hadn't been his idea, but he'd followed Vanessa's suggestion when she'd explained the importance of having spending money to the rehabilitation of their self-esteem.

Sarah cringed. "Would we have to be there to do the selling? Because I'd rather stay here."

"Until you feel ready to venture outside this sanctuary, no one is going to make you do it."

Sarah's shoulders relaxed. "I wouldn't mind going if Kri came with us. She can fight off anyone."

Vanessa clapped her hands. "A splendid idea. I'll ask her if she is willing to supervise the booth."

Syssi pulled out two twenties and put them on the girl's work table. "I don't know when I'll be able to stop by again, so when you're done give it to Vanessa for me."

"You've made her day," Vanessa said as they walked outside.

"It was nothing. You're doing an amazing job with these girls."

"Thanks. I do my best, and I have lots of help from many volunteers."

Leaning against the car with his arms crossed over his chest, Bhathian glared at Kian. "I don't know why you even bother taking us with you if you leave us in the limo."

Next to him, Brundar nodded in agreement.

A grimace twisted Kian's mouth. He had one mother, and that was more than enough. He didn't need to get lectured by his bodyguards. "Stop with the hissy fit." He waved a dismissive hand. "It's safe inside the sanctuary. A bunch of girls and a couple of female therapists are not going to suddenly attack me. Your job is to guard the outside and keep an eye on the fence."

"Do you have time for the other place?" Vanessa asked.

Kian glanced at his watch. "Yeah, if we make it short."

She sighed. "You can skip it because there isn't much to see. Other than the chemists, whom your guys took to the keep, the rest of the humans are not in good shape."

Kian pushed his hair behind his ears. "Do you think there's a chance they'll recover? At least enough to be set free?"

"I need more time. The repeated thralling messed up their memory so badly that they can't remember where they are from, and whether they have a family or not. Actually, they don't remember anything from before the warehouse. I don't think I can do anything about that. Instead, I'm working on restoring their cognitive functioning. If they regain that, they can at least start a new life."

"What's the prognosis?" Syssi asked.

"I'm making very slow progress. The problem is that I can't involve any of my human colleagues. It would be hard to explain a large group of people all suffering an inexplicable memory loss."

Syssi frowned. "Why didn't you say something before? Amanda and I can help. After all, we work in a related field. I can probably get several other immortals to volunteer as well. I'm sure not everything needs to be done by professionals."

"Amanda is not a clinical neuroscientist."

"Do you have anyone better?"

RUTH

*R*uth looked at Kian's closed office door and imagined herself knocking on it. Except, her arm was still down by her side, and lifting it to do what needed to be done seemed like mission impossible.

Why was she such a coward?

He'd said to come see him anytime she needed to discuss Nick's transition.

"Come in, Ruth," Kian said.

Crap, how did he know it was her? Did she emit a cowardly scent so potent that it had percolated through the closed door?

Taking a deep breath, she commanded her hand to stop shaking and depress the handle.

"Hi." She walked in but stopped a few feet away from his desk. "I hope I'm not interrupting. You said to come to see you if I needed advice regarding Nick."

Kian closed the file he was working on and pushed it aside. "As I said before, this takes priority over everything else. Come, take a seat." With his soft tone and encouraging gestures, Kian was making an effort to be less intimidating.

Ruth appreciated and hated it at the same time.

Everyone thought of her as the little mouse who was afraid of her own shadow, and, frankly, they weren't entirely wrong. As hard as she tried to work on it, her social anxiety wasn't something she could get rid of by just willing it to go away.

She was getting better at handling people at the café, but Kian was a different story. His intensity still intimidated the hell out of her.

"It didn't work," she said as she pulled out a chair and sat down. "Last night, Jackson tried. We talked about a certain band, and he thralled Nick to forget its name. It worked for a few minutes, but Nick managed to bring the memory back."

"Did you have Bhathian give it a try?"

"I texted him this morning. He called me later and said that his thrall held for about ten minutes. He made Nick forget the list of items Eva asked him to get from the supermarket. Five minutes later, he asked Nick to recite the list. Nick struggled to remember, complaining of a headache the same way he did last night, but eventually he broke through the block."

Ruth looked down at her hands to avoid Kian's piercing eyes. "I don't think we should keep trying. I don't like the headaches he gets each time. It might be a sign that it's harmful to his brain."

"I agree."

Kian's answer surprised her. Ruth had expected him to suggest giving the thralling a break, or to offer to do it himself like he'd suggested before.

Was he canning Nick's transition?

Her heart sank low in her gut. "So what do we do? Give up on Nick?"

"Not at all. I've given it a lot of thought, and I think I have a solution. It's up to you if you want to implement it, though. It's not an honorable approach, but in this case I see no other choice."

"What's your idea?" At this point, Ruth was willing to listen to the most out-there suggestions.

"Nick would have to be induced without his knowledge. Which means without his consent."

She could live with that.

As Kian had said, there was no other way. Nick might get a little angry, like he had about Jackson's supposed hypnotism, but he would get over it. He wasn't the type to hold a grudge, and he was also smart enough to understand why it had to be done like that.

The problem was that she couldn't see a way to implement Kian's suggestion.

"How? It's not like it's a quick injection that can be explained away somehow. Nick needs to fight an immortal male and get bitten."

Kian leaned back and crossed his arms over his chest. "You'll have to slip him a sleeping pill or a potion. Then when he's out, he'll get bitten. He won't remember a thing when he wakes up. Then if he starts transitioning, you'll tell him what's going on. And if not, no harm done."

"I still don't get how you plan to do it. Don't you guys need to get aggressive or aroused to produce venom?"

As far as she knew, venom production required a high level of aggression, which was impossible to induce toward a sleeping guy unless they found a clinically insane immortal male. Except, she wasn't aware of any such clansman. And if Kian was thinking about asking a gay immortal to bite Nick, she doubted the male could get aroused just by looking at Nick's inert body, not unless the guy was into necrophilia.

Yuk.

Besides, Ruth would have a tough time agreeing to that. Nick belonged to her, and she couldn't tolerate anyone having naughty thoughts about him, regardless of their sex or sexual orientation.

"You're right. Most of us need provocation to bite another male. Fortunately, I know one guy who can produce venom and elongate his fangs on command."

It was as she had feared.

With a resigned sigh, Ruth closed her eyes and nodded. "It's going to be very difficult for me to have someone ogle my Nick. But I guess that's the only way."

"Ogle?" Kian sounded surprised.

"Yeah. I know it's possessive and silly of me, but I can't help it. It doesn't matter if the naughty thoughts belong to a female or a male. I don't want anyone getting excited by looking at Nick while he is sleeping. I don't think he would appreciate it either. I know I wouldn't. Biting him without his consent is bad enough, but this feels like an even greater violation."

Kian regarded her as if she had several screws missing. "What the hell are you talking about? There is nothing sexual about one male biting another. It's an act of aggression. I'm sure you're aware of that."

Ruth's cheeks weren't the only thing that was heating at an alarming rate. Suddenly, she was covered in sweat.

Had she misunderstood?

"I thought that since Nick couldn't fight anyone while he was asleep, the only way a male could produce venom was if he got aroused by looking at him."

Kian's broad shoulders began shaking, and a moment later he burst out laughing. He even banged his fist on the table. "I'm sorry, Ruth, but imagining Brundar ogling Nick is just too much."

"Brundar? Anandur's brother?"

"Do you know any other Brundar? Yes, that Brundar. He can produce aggression without any provocation."

That was a revelation. Ruth didn't know the Guardian well, but he seemed to have no emotions at all. Except, he was a mated male now, to a female, thank the merciful Fates, so perhaps things had changed for him.

"Is it a newly discovered ability?"

"Not really, but I didn't know about this until recently. The guy isn't the sharing type."

"He was one of those who tried to induce Roni's transition." And he hadn't been successful. In the end, Kian had done it, which wasn't very confidence-inspiring. But at least she had nothing to fear as far as ogling went.

"I've already talked with him about Nick. He said that it's not a sure thing. He never had to summon aggression toward an unconscious male without anything triggering it immediately before, like participating or at least witnessing a fight. It's going to be doubly tough to do so to an unconscious guy that he feels no animosity for. On the other hand, Brundar had no problem summoning his fangs for Roni, and he likes the kid, so I don't think it's going to be a problem."

Crap. If Brundar failed, they were back to square one. Roni had been fully conscious and probably scared shitless, which might have helped trigger Brundar's predatory instincts.

"How am I supposed to bring Nick to Brundar?"

Kian tore a piece a paper from his yellow pad, scribbled something on it, and handed it to her. "Here is Brundar's number. I told him to expect an invitation from you. He knows he will have to come to your house. Invite him and Callie to dinner, preferably along with Sylvia and Roni, whom Nick already knows. It will look less suspicious to him if you invite people he knows together with a new couple he doesn't."

Folding the piece of paper into a square, Ruth tucked it inside her wallet. "Thank you. I really appreciate your help."

Kian pushed to his feet and walked around to give her a hand up, which was a good thing since her legs felt like wet noodles.

"I'm glad to help in any way I can. If I could summon aggression on command, I would induce Nick's transition myself. But, unfortunately, it's not an ability I possess."

WONDER

*W*onder peered at the suitcase Amanda had packed full of beautiful clothes for her when she'd arrived. Now it lay open and empty on her bed, waiting for her to fill it up again.

The best thing would be to just put everything back in, add a few toiletries, and she'd be ready for the trip. After getting used to wearing Amanda's fancy designer stuff, Wonder had a hard time putting on her old clothes, or even the few new items she'd bought when Anandur had taken her shopping. They were fine for work or for hanging around the house but not for taking on a romantic trip.

Amanda had spoiled her, and now she was stuck desiring things she couldn't afford.

But hey, with Amanda supplying her with her discarded wardrobe items, Wonder could get by with never spending a dime on apparel again. The only things she would have to buy were panties, bras and shoes. And socks.

In fact, she felt bad about troubling Magnus with going

to the shelter and packing her old things. Her purse and her laptop were all she really needed. He could've left everything else behind.

"Knock, knock." Amanda pushed the door open. "Are you done packing yet?"

"I was just about to start." Wonder pointed at the empty suitcase. "But I don't know how many outfits I need, or which ones are better for Egypt's hot and humid weather."

"I can help." Amanda put two small-sized shopping bags on the bed. One was white, the other pink, and both were stuffed with paper.

"What's in there?" Wonder asked.

"A little present for the trip. You can take a peek." She sat on the bed and crossed her legs.

Curious, Wonder picked up the white bag and reached inside. At first, it seemed like there was only tissue paper in there, and she thought Amanda was pulling a prank, but after digging a little deeper, her fingers touched lacy fabric. She fished one item out and then another, letting them dangle from her fingers.

"What's that for?"

"Isn't it self-explanatory? A bra and matching panties. I remembered you didn't like the thong and got you some with better backside coverage."

Right, Wonder thought as she examined the items. The panties were more than a string in the back, but not by much. "Thank you. These are very pretty." Just not practical.

"It's a bridal set. I saw it at the store and just knew I had to get it for you. The white is going to look awesome with your dark coloring. So sexy." Amanda smirked. "Save it for a special occasion." She added a wink.

Embarrassed, Wonder looked away. Were her intentions so transparent?

They were flying out less than forty-eight hours after Anandur had offered to take her to Egypt, and since he'd taken care of all the travel arrangements, including hotel reservations, she wasn't sure whether he planned on them sharing a room or not.

But it was likely that he had. Which meant that they'd be sharing a bed. Wonder had absolutely no problem with that. In fact, she was looking forward to it.

A vacation in a nice hotel was the perfect setup for a magical first time. It was going to be like a honeymoon, just before the wedding instead of after.

Clutching the flimsy undergarments to her chest, Wonder smiled wistfully as she fantasized about wearing them for Anandur.

"That's not the only set I got you. Keep digging," Amanda interrupted her musings. "And you need to try on the bras. The salesgirl assured me that they would all fit because they are made from stretchy fabrics."

"You shouldn't have," Wonder said.

Nevertheless, she attacked the two shopping bags with renewed enthusiasm, upending them over the bed and spilling out the tissue together with the additional three sets of bras and panties.

"Wow, Amanda, thank you." She lifted one after the other. "They are all so pretty. I feel sexy just knowing that I have stuff like that."

Bracing on her forearms, Amanda leaned back on the bed. "That's the idea. It's time to transform Wonder Girl into Wonder Woman."

"Hi, girls, can I come in?" Syssi poked her head through the open door.

"Please do," Amanda invited her. "What did you bring?"

Syssi's shopping bag was much bigger than Amanda's. If she had panties in there, they must've been grannie sized.

"I brought a few necessities." She sat on the bed next to Amanda and put the bag in her lap. "A portable cappuccino maker." She pulled out a box. "And two bottles for filtering water. You can't trust water quality in Third World countries." She pulled out two more boxes.

Amanda lifted a brow. "You know that you're obsessed, right?"

"About what?"

"Cappuccinos. I'm sure Wonder and Anandur can survive without them for a week."

"They can, but why should they?" Syssi reached inside her bag and pulled out a box of coffee capsules. "That's all there is to it." She arranged the boxes next to each other. "That doesn't take too much space, and the water bottles are a necessity."

"Thank you." Wonder took the boxes and put them in the suitcase. "You forget that I lived there for half a year and drank the local water. It was fine."

Syssi waved a hand. "That's because you had nothing to compare it with. When you go back, you'll taste the difference. I can promise you that."

Probably.

Water quality hadn't been the only good thing Wonder had gotten so used to that she was taking it for granted.

Nine months ago she was all alone, scavenging for food and hiding under a black garment that had covered her from head to toe leaving only her eyes exposed. Now she

27

was part of a clan, living in a luxurious home, and contemplating wearing sexy lingerie that was more for show than for coverage or any other practical use.

Talk about change.

"Hey? How come no one told me there is a going-away party?" Carol walked in, holding a shopping bag in her hand.

Syssi patted the spot next to her on the bed. "It seems we all had the same idea. Isn't it amazing?"

Carol lifted the bag. "What idea? All I have here are two travel adaptors. No one ever remembers that the electrical outlets are different in every country, and then they are stuck with no way to charge their phones."

"That's a very practical gift. Thank you." Wonder added the two boxes to her suitcase. "Is it customary to buy people gifts when they are going on trips?"

Her three new friends exchanged sheepish looks.

"Not really," Carol admitted. "I just thought you'd need adaptors. That's all."

Syssi shrugged. "And I was only concerned with water quality and staying caffeinated."

Amanda chuckled. "Well, it seems that I was the only one who thought about the fun part and brought the necessary supplies for that."

"What did you get?" Syssi asked.

"Would you care to show them, Wonder? Or would you rather model for us?"

5

TURNER

"You'll have to forgive me," Sylvia said. "Today you'll be eating my cooking, and unfortunately I'm not my mom."

Turner was a bit surprised. Every time Bridget and he had been invited to Sylvia and Roni's for dinner, Ruth had prepared everything.

Roni smiled and offered his hand to Bridget. "Don't worry, people. A steak is a steak. Now that I have my own backyard and a kickass grill, I'm the king of grilling." He offered his hand to Turner. "Come outside, and I'll show you my new baby."

"Is there anything other than steaks to eat?" he heard Bridget ask.

"I'll show you what I made," Sylvia said. "Tell me if it's edible. Roni is not reliable as a taster since he'd eat anything and lick his fingers."

Turner followed the hacker out through the sliding living-room doors. Over the past month, the kid had ordered and sent back several portable grills. He'd probably got another one of those.

Preferring the real thing, Turner was building a proper barbecue grill in his and Bridget's backyard. It was a long process, since he was learning how to do everything from scratch and his free time was limited. But then he had eternity to learn new skills and had every intention of acquiring them one at a time.

It rocked to be an immortal.

Most of the other clan members were wasting their incredible potential, sticking to the one thing they'd learned to do as young people, instead of exploring the possibilities and becoming experts in multiple areas.

Apparently, character traits didn't differ much between humans and immortals. Or maybe it had to do with neural pathways, as Bridget had explained. Once the brain specialized in doing a particular thing, the other areas atrophied.

For adults, especially older ones, it was difficult, often even off-putting, to pick up and learn something new. Not everyone was driven by Turner's kind of determination to excel at everything he touched and master as many skills as he could.

Turner was quite sure that he'd never tire of learning new skills and acquiring more knowledge, and the implication of that was quite mind-blowing given his practically endless lifespan. It was possible that at some point he would acquire the total of human and immortal knowledge.

If that wasn't as close as it got to being a god, then he didn't know what was.

He was smart enough to keep his musings to himself,

though. Having a god complex was not going to fly well with a sensible and practical person like Bridget. She would probably suggest therapy.

"Here it is." Roni pointed at an odd egg-shaped contraption.

"That's a grill?"

Roni puffed out his chest. "It's much more than a grill, but I'm still learning all its tricks. I think I mastered the steaks. Wait until you taste them." He smacked his lips. "Delicious."

For someone who loved to eat as much as Roni did, it was a wonder that the kid was still so skinny. It seemed genetics had as much impact on a person's metabolism as eating habits, if not more.

Turner stuck his hands in his back pockets. "I did some digging around about your grandma."

"Oh, yeah? I thought you forgot about it." Roni pulled the plastic cover off the raw steaks and grabbed a pair of tongs.

"I didn't forget. But between the transition and putting together the rescue operations, I didn't have time. I still don't, but I promised you I'd take a look."

Roni placed four steaks on the grill. "Did you find anything?"

"Maybe." Turner smoothed his hand over his new hair. "I had one of my people snoop around. Did you know that your grandma won a quilting competition?"

"No, I didn't. But how does it help us to find her?"

"She must've been good to win first prize. My guess is that she enjoys quilting to this day, and I wouldn't be surprised if she enters competitions."

Roni flipped the steaks to the other side. "And you

think we can find her by checking the winners of quilting competitions?"

"My next step is to dig into those. Unfortunately, quilting doesn't get much news coverage. What I found are pictures of the winning quilts, not the faces of the quilters."

"I'm sure they have the names next to them."

"They do. But your grandma is a careful lady. I doubt the name she gave is the same as the one on her current driver's license."

Roni sighed. "How many of those competitions are we talking about? She could be anywhere. For all we know, she might be in another country. Which, by the way, I bet she is. Otherwise, William's facial recognition program would've found her new driver's license."

"She might have worn prosthetics for the driver's license picture."

"Right. I heard that's your new idea for ours."

Turner nodded. "We are going to test it first. Eva ordered some supplies, and once she gets them, she's going to apply prosthetics to a couple of people and snap their pictures. William is going to run the photos through his program, and we will see if we can fool the computers."

"What about the eyes?"

"She said she has a few ideas about that as well."

"It would be interesting to see." Roni picked up the ready steaks and transferred them to a platter. "With everything you have to do, I don't think my grandma is a priority at this point. If it were easy, then why not. But it doesn't make sense to devote too much time to her."

Roni's mouth was saying one thing, but his expression was saying another. The kid was disappointed.

Turner clapped Roni on his back. "If the quilting is the

only thread we have, that's true. But if I get one more thread or two, then the fun begins."

Roni's slim face brightened with a smile. "We can cross-reference them. Did you find anything else?"

"Not yet."

"What are you looking for?"

"Anything. Favorite vacation spots. A boyfriend from college. Another hobby. Do you remember your mom mentioning anything?"

Roni rubbed a hand over his jaw. "The only thing I remember vividly is her talking about how everyone was shocked by the drowning since her mom was an excellent swimmer. Maybe she also won some swimming competitions?"

"If she did, it didn't come up."

"That's all I have."

"I'll look into that. Now, how about those steaks?"

6

ANANDUR

"*A*re you comfortable, lass?" Anandur asked with a smirk.

Wonder was checking out the fully reclining seat even though the airplane was still on the ground. "Very. I think I can sleep here."

"That's the idea. It's a sixteen-hour flight. I wanted you to be comfortable and get us first class seats, but I found out they are separated by a divider." He lifted her hand to his lips for a kiss. "Business class seats are only separated by the armrest. It's cozier."

"Do you usually fly business class? Or did you splurge on me?"

"I hardly ever use commercial flights, but when I do, I need to fly business because of the legroom. I can't fit back there." He turned and looked at the poor schmucks sitting in coach.

As frugal as Anandur was, and as painful as it was for him to pay triple the price for business class, Anandur couldn't spend hours sitting in those torture chairs, fighting for elbow room with whoever sat next to him.

Only skinny kids could sit comfortably in coach, if that. Anyone over five and a half feet tall or weighing more than a hundred pounds was squeezed like a sardine.

Wonder pulled her chair up and buckled up. "How safe is it to fly on an airplane?"

"Supposedly, safer than driving a car."

She narrowed her eyes. "Why supposedly?"

Anandur glanced at the couple sitting across the aisle, and then at the passengers sitting in front of them. The row behind them was still unoccupied.

He leaned closer to whisper in Wonder's ear. "We can survive most car accidents, but if a plane explodes or crashes and catches fire, chances are that we wouldn't make it."

Wonder lost some of her color. "How often does that happen?"

Evidently, it had been the wrong thing to say to someone who'd never flown before. "Rarely. You have nothing to worry about."

She wasn't happy with his answer. "Define rarely. Is it once a year? Once a decade?"

Anandur scratched his beard. "I don't know. But we can find out." He pulled out his phone and typed the inquiry. "There are several crashes a year, but only about two hundred fatalities on average. That's a very low number considering that annually about six billion people take to the sky."

Wonder's eyes widened. "Wow, that's a huge number. I would've never guessed that so many people travel by plane." She leaned back in her chair and put her feet up on the footrest in front of her. "I guess I have nothing to fear."

He squeezed her hand. "I love it that you're a rational girl. For a moment there I was afraid you'd panic the instant the plane took off."

Her brows dipped as a look of irritation crossed her face. "I don't like it when you call me a girl."

Anandur chuckled. "What about my sweet girl? You don't like that either?"

Her lips twitched with a stifled smile. "I don't hate it."

"And how about my beautiful, gorgeous, sumptuous girl?"

She still fought the smile. "I guess it's not so bad."

"What would you like me to call you?"

Turning to look at him, Wonder narrowed her eyes that started blazing with inner light. "Call me a woman." Her voice deepened on the last word.

Damn.

With her dark, long lashes descending over her jade eyes, her hooded gaze had sex written all over it.

Wonder had been beautiful when he'd first seen her in a pair of simple jeans and a bouncer's T-shirt, now she was stunning.

Not only that, she was growing comfortable inside her new, more polished and sophisticated skin. She'd either gotten another makeover from Amanda or had learned how to do her own hair and makeup.

It wasn't much, but even that little had made a big difference. The truth was that right now Wonder didn't look like a girl.

She was all woman.

Her hair was down, cascading in soft waves around her

shoulders and fanning over her crisp white shirt, and even though her luscious lips were covered in lipstick, and he hated the taste of it, Anandur wanted to kiss the living daylights out of her.

The problem was that getting excited in public was a really bad idea for an immortal male.

Running a hand over his face, Anandur tried to get his immortal tells under control. "Please don't do that. Not in public."

"Do what?" Wonder pretended innocence, batting her long eyelashes.

Except, she was a lousy actress. The girl was flexing her feminine muscles. What she didn't know, though, was that the game had consequences, and whoever dared to play with fire got their fingers singed.

He leaned closer. "You act all sexy when you can't back it up?"

"Who said I can't?"

"Right here? Because I can put a shroud around us and take you up on your offer." He couldn't, but it was a good way to call her bluff.

As he'd expected, Wonder backed off, casting a nervous glance around. "You wouldn't."

"Why not?" He waggled his brows. "I like a little adventure, and you need to learn that implying something you don't mean has consequences. But I'll wait until we are in the air."

"Why?"

Damn, he adored her endless why questions. "Have you ever heard about the mile-high club?"

The guy sitting across the aisle stifled a chuckle.

Wonder shook her head.

"I'll tell you after take-off."

"Why?"

"Once it gets noisy in here, our nosy neighbors won't be able to eavesdrop."

Wonder leaned her head on his shoulder. "You can whisper it in my ear. No one will hear a thing."

His girl wasn't the patient type, which was good, since he loved having her so close, but he should've waited with the explanation, because the moment he was done, Wonder turned to him with a scowl.

"In the bathroom?"

"Shh, keep it down."

"Sorry," she whispered. "But that's really gross."

"Come back here." Anandur patted his shoulder. When she did, he put his hand on her other cheek. He wasn't done taunting her yet. "As I said before, I can shroud us. We are not limited to what humans are willing to resort to."

"You know," she said, her low tone sounding flirtatious again. "As someone who a moment ago was asking me to tame down my sexy, you're not following your own advice. Your naughty thoughts have consequences." She pointed a discreet finger at his bulge.

Anandur laughed, loving that she was so quick to recover and didn't shy away from a challenge. "Two points awarded to Wonder. You win again."

With a contented sigh, she put her arm across his middle and shifted her cheek to rest against his bicep. "I always win. Get used to that, big guy."

7

LOSHAM

"I have chartered a plane just as you requested, sir," Rami said as he put down the plate in front of Losham.

The meal had been delivered from a local steakhouse—a decent enough establishment but far from gourmet. The days of lavish spending were, unfortunately, in the past but, hopefully, would return in the near future.

"What about the patsies? Do you have a plan for that?"

Rami sat at the other end of the table and unfolded his napkin. "I'm still working on the details, sir. Every time I think I have it all figured out, I find another flaw in the plan."

"Give me an example. Maybe I can help."

"Twenty-two humans disappearing at the same time is going to make the news, which is bad since Lord Navuh might have someone monitoring the headlines from our area. You know how suspicious he is."

"What if you get the patsies from somewhere else?"

Rami shook his head. "I don't know why we need them

at all. If we blow the plane up over the ocean, I doubt anyone is going to search for body parts floating around, especially if the thing goes up in flames and burns."

"You might have a point."

Staging a convincing "accident" for his twenty-two defectors was not easy to accomplish. On the one hand, the more supporting evidence they had, the more believable the staged accident would appear. But on the other hand, providing that evidence might do more harm than good, especially if it got public attention.

"Is there a way we can load the plane with corpses?"

Rami arched a brow. "And where do you suppose we can get a fresh supply of those? They can't be too rotten."

"Humans die all the time. It shouldn't be difficult."

"It's true that there is no shortage of dead humans, but their bodies are not dumped in the trash. They have burial services and cremation services and the like."

Losham lifted a finger. "There you have it. You can get fresh bodies from the cremation places. You thrall whoever operates the place to substitute dummies for the bodies."

"I don't think they get that many in one day, and time is of the essence."

That was indeed a problem. Rami was the only one Losham could entrust with the task, and there was a limit to what his assistant could do.

Regrettably, Losham would have to get his hands dirty and help.

"I assume that they keep several in the freezer until the ceremony. Make a list of crematoriums and tomorrow we will each take half. We will also need two large vans to stash the bodies in. Whatever we get will have to do. Some body parts are better than none, right?"

8

WONDER

*a*fter the abject poverty Wonder had seen through the cab's windows, the opulence of the Four Seasons hotel stood out in stark relief.

The reception clerk smiled a big fake smile. "Here are your keys. The bellboy will bring your luggage up shortly."

"Thank you." Anandur snatched the packet and took her elbow. "Let's see what a thousand bucks a night buys in this joint."

Wonder swallowed. A thousand dollars a night? That was way too much to pay for a hotel room. Even the view of the pyramids wasn't worth that much. They were going to see them up close anyway. Unless Anandur hadn't reserved a room and that was the price for a two-bedroom suite.

That would be disappointing.

She waited until they were alone in the elevator. "Why did you pick such a pricey place? I'm sure there were more affordable options."

With a face-splitting grin, Anandur pulled her into his arms. "I wanted the best for my girl."

That was sweet, but it didn't answer her implied question about sleeping arrangements. Besides, a simple girl like her didn't need luxurious accommodation. In fact, the fancy hotel with its snooty personnel was somewhat intimidating. "I would've preferred something more plebeian."

"Ooh, a fancy word. Where did you hear that one?"

Wonder chuckled. "Amanda, who else?"

"Was she referring to me?"

"No, silly, she loves you, same as everyone else. You're the clan's darling. She was referring to shoes, or rather boots. I wanted those short, comfortable ones that are so popular. I thought they would be perfect for traveling, but she killed the idea with her 'plebeian' remark."

"Twelfth floor," the electronic voice announced, and a moment later the doors slid open.

"That's us." Anandur snatched a quick kiss before letting go, then took her elbow and led her down the corridor to the last door.

Holding her breath, Wonder waited for Anandur to open the door. Two-bedroom suite or one? She crossed her fingers behind her back. *One, make it one.*

When the door opened, Anandur blocked the view of the interior with his broad chest, and instead of moving aside and letting her through swung her into his arms.

"What are you doing?"

"Carrying my princess over the threshold." He strode into the fanciest living room Wonder had ever seen, and that included the luxury homes she'd seen in magazines.

It was indeed a room fit for a princess. Which she wasn't.

For some reason, being called that bothered her. The title didn't belong to her, it belonged to someone else.

A whiff of a memory skittered through Wonder's brain of a tiny young woman with a huge mass of red hair and beauty that was almost too painful to look at. Unfortunately, the memory was gone before she could grab hold of it.

"Why are you frowning, lass?"

Wonder shook her head. "I thought I remembered someone. It was like waking up from a dream. The moment you open your eyes, it's gone."

"I hope it wasn't another guy."

Anandur had said that with a smile, but his arms tightened around her almost painfully.

"It was a girl. I'm sure of that. The impression I was left with was of unnatural beauty."

"What triggered it?"

"The word princess." She waved a dismissive hand. "It was probably an image of one of the Disney princesses. They are all so unnaturally beautiful because they are not real."

"Disney, eh?" He strode toward an interior door. "And here is the bedroom. Fit for royalty." He pushed it open with his foot.

"Oh, wow. This room is so big we can play basketball in here."

Despite the room's size, there was only one big bed.

Hallelujah.

"I don't know about basketball." Anandur laid her gently on the bed. "But we can certainly play some other games in here." He leaned over her, the heat coming off his big body enveloping her like a blanket.

Was he referring to sex?

Suddenly, Wonder didn't feel all that brave. "Are we going to see the pyramids today?" She scooted back against the stack of pillows.

When Anandur didn't respond right away, Wonder's heart started beating faster. Did he mean now?

She wasn't ready yet. She needed more time, not because she had any second thoughts, but because intimacy took time to build up, time they hadn't had together yet.

Things were moving too fast.

Except, maybe it was better that way? Just yank the Band-Aid off and be done with it?

But then Anandur smiled and pulled back. "The pyramids, yes. We should get going if we don't want to miss the tour."

Wonder puffed out a relieved breath. "We are going on a tour?"

"I hired a tour guide and a couple of his musclemen just so we don't get bothered by the local peddlers. I was told that they get quite aggressive and I don't want to beat up people on my vacation."

"I doubt anyone would dare to bother a guy your size. And if they do, I can beat them up for you," Wonder teased as she slid off the bed.

"Right, as if I'm going to let any of those fuckers get near you. I'd rather have a couple of local goons ensure that no one touches you. Because if I have to do it, the offenders would go home with broken limbs or end up in the morgue."

It was startling to watch Anandur transform from an easy-going charmer into the killing machine he could so easily become. And yet, it didn't detract from his attractiveness even one bit. On the contrary, Wonder liked that darker side of him no less than she liked the sunny one. The combination of the two polar opposites was what made Anandur who he was. Being a Guardian was more than a job or a title for him, it defined him. He was a fierce protector through and through.

Not that she needed him to provide protection, but she craved it.

With Anandur, Wonder didn't have to be strong, she didn't have to be alert, she could let go and know with absolute certainty that she was safe.

9

WONDER

"*J*ames Brock at your service." The guide offered his hand first to Wonder and then to Anandur. "And those are my two assistants." He waved at the two burly men flanking him. "Muhammad Sharif and Ahmed Beladi."

"*Ahlan wa sahlan*," Ahmed said with a slight bow.

Muhammad nodded in agreement.

"*Ahlan bik*," Wonder replied.

James grinned. "The lady speaks Arabic."

"Only a little."

"Well, let us be on our way. There is plenty to see." James opened the back door to the SUV. "Madam?"

"Thank you."

Ahmed and Muhammad sat up front, with Ahmed taking the driver seat, while James climbed in the back with Wonder and Anandur.

"Is it your first visit to Egypt?" James asked Anandur.

"For me it is. Wonder visited before but only Alexandria, not Cairo."

"Well, then you're in for a treat. There is much to see. The pyramids and the Sphinx are, of course, the main attraction, but the Egyptian museum is a must as well. Highly recommended. You might also want to visit the Khan el-Khalili market and the mosque of Muhammad Ali."

"I would like to see the market," Wonder said.

"It's a tourist favorite." James smiled and leaned back as Ahmed pulled into traffic. "Shopping for the ladies and belly dancers for the gentlemen."

Wonder wasn't interested in either. The market was probably the central hub of the city the way it was in Alexandria. If her goal was retrieving her memories, and if she had ever been to Cairo before, then the market was the most likely place to hold clues.

Visiting the pyramids was probably not going to do that, but it didn't make sense to visit Cairo and skip one of the Seven Wonders of the World. Besides, she wasn't that keen on getting her memory back. It scared the hell out of her.

"Let me give you a little bit of background about what you're about to see." James took off his sunglasses, revealing a pair of pale blue eyes with laugh lines feathering their outer corners. "The great pyramid is the largest stone building in the world. It's made from about two and a half million slabs of limestone and granite, and its total mass is estimated at ninety-three million cubic feet weighing seven million tons."

That sounded like a lot, but the numbers were meaningless to her without something to compare them with.

When his description didn't elicit the appropriate awe, James added. "Just for comparison, the Great Pyramid of

Giza contains more stone than all the cathedrals and churches and chapels of England put together."

Since she'd never been to England, that still didn't tell her much, but if he used it as a comparison, it must've been impressive. "Wow. That's incredible."

A satisfied expression on his tanned face, James continued. "It's an unparalleled marvel of engineering, and not only because of the incredible size and weight. The pyramid is perfectly aligned with the cardinal points of the compass, the sides incline at a perfect angle of about fifty-two degrees, which means that the ratio of its height to its circumference is the same as the radius of a circle to its circumference."

"Impressive," Anandur said.

James had lost Wonder as soon as he started talking math because her knowledge was restricted to basic arithmetic. To cover her ignorance, she pretended to look interested, which encouraged the guide to continue.

"It's also perfectly level. The shift in its horizontal alignment is less than a tenth of an inch over the seven hundred and fifty-eight feet of each side. That level of accuracy far exceeds modern standards for high rises. It's extraordinary given the millennia of the pyramid's existence. Just think about it. The platform upon which the Great Pyramid stands is only twenty-two inches thick, and yet it has withstood continental shifts, earthquakes, and Earth's wobble around its own axis, not to mention the weight of the pyramid itself."

Wonder chuckled. "That's why it's called one of the Seven Wonders of the World. That Pharaoh sure had an inflated ego to build something like that as his tomb."

James shook his head. "It wasn't a tomb. There was no mummy in the king's chamber."

"Grave robbers?" Wonder asked. The brochure in the hotel's lobby said the pyramid was built as a tomb of some Pharaoh whose name she'd forgotten.

"No, the chamber was sealed when it was first discovered and what was inside was documented. There was nothing except what looked like a granite sarcophagus that was empty. There were no decorations and no writing on the walls. It was empty and bare."

That was strange. "What was it built for, then?"

James shrugged. "There are many theories, but since none of them can be proven one way or another, I won't bother going into them. Once we are done, you can go on the internet and find out for yourself. There are many books on the subject as well."

Wonder glanced at Anandur, who'd remained mostly silent throughout the ride. Did he know something about it?

Probably, but it wasn't as if she could ask him with James present.

Regrettably, though, and especially after all of the guide's hyping of the pyramids, the reality was a big letdown.

It started with the crowded parking lot, full of peddlers who were pushing and shoving their goods into the arms of reluctant tourists, and continued with the camel drivers shouting and hassling for rides and pictures. The Egyptian security did nothing to protect the tourists, standing idly on the sidelines and watching the big mess with bored expressions on their faces.

Fortunately, the two bodyguards proved incredibly useful as a deterrent. If not for them, Wonder had no doubt the visit would have ended in one hell of a brawl. Anandur would've sent those touts to the hospital or the morgue, and she would've helped him. The local police would have surely intervened at that point and arrested them, or tried to.

"I wish we'd stayed in the car," Wonder told James when they returned from their tour. "The pyramids sounded much more exciting when you described them."

The guide held the car door open for her and smiled. "I've learned to tune the crowds out and focus on the magnificence of the structures built in a bygone era of excellence. There were giants upon the earth in those days."

ANANDUR

"*D*o you want to see the market today?" Anandur asked.

Since the pyramids failed to stir up any new memories, he hoped the market would.

She shook her head. "I'd rather go back to the hotel and take a shower."

"Same here. And after we freshen up, I vote for dinner in one of the classy restaurants on the premises." The Four Seasons was like an island of luxury and opulence on the backdrop of the largely dilapidated, overcrowded metropolis that according to James was currently home to over twenty million people.

Wonder sighed. "Sounds perfect." She closed her eyes.

He would've wrapped his arm around her and brought her head to rest on his shoulder, but they were both sweaty and dusty, the clothes clinging to their bodies. The most contact Wonder had accepted throughout the tour was holding hands.

Anandur blamed James for her disappointment with

the pyramids. He'd paid a premium price to get the highly recommended guide, and to be frank the guy had been very knowledgeable. But if he hadn't sung the pyramids' praises before they got there, she might have enjoyed visiting the site more.

Or maybe not.

He certainly hadn't. Between the pushy, loud touts, the heat, and the smells of unwashed bodies, he'd been inclined to cut the tour short even though it had been his first visit.

Probably his last, too.

And to think this was just the first day of their vacation. He'd planned a long trip to cover all the major attractions, thinking it would be a romantic getaway that would bring Wonder and him closer.

Except, there was nothing romantic about the abject poverty they'd witnessed, and the sad remains of a once great civilization.

Expectations, as was often the case, exceeded reality by a large margin.

Hopefully, that wouldn't be the case for Wonder and him.

Anandur rubbed the back of his neck that had mercifully cooled down thanks to the car's air conditioning. As someone who'd shagged thousands of women, he shouldn't be so anxious about his ability to meet or exceed the expectations of one virgin. And yet he was.

Was tonight a good time? Or should he wait a couple of days and let the tension build?

The problem was that, right timing or not, he was running out of rope to hold himself back. And yet he would summon the strength if Wonder wasn't ready. But how would he know if she was or not?

Did she know it herself?

Damn. Maybe he should call Amanda for advice, or Carol?

Right. He wasn't a prideful guy, but still.

"We made it back," James said as Ahmed stopped in front of the hotel. "It was a pleasure serving as your guide. I hope you'll recommend my services to friends and family." He pulled a bunch of business cards out of his shirt pocket. "There is a twenty-five percent discount for anyone presenting one of these."

"Thanks." Anandur took the cards. "I'll pass them around."

"Much appreciated."

As Muhammad opened the passenger door, Anandur handed him a folded twenty-dollar bill. "Thanks for the service, man."

"*Shukran.*" Cracking his first smile of the day, the bodyguard shook Anandur's hand.

After helping Wonder out, Anandur went over to the driver, handed him another twenty, and shook his hand. "Good job."

"It was nice of you to tip the guys," Wonder said as they entered the elevator.

"I meant it when I said they did a good job. Imagine how much worse the experience would've been without them scaring away the pushy peddlers and rude camel drivers."

"I don't want to think about it. All I want is to get into the shower and wash the day off, then eat something good and get in bed. The jet lag is catching up with me."

It seemed that his plans of seduction would have to wait. Wonder's first time should not happen when she was exhausted after a long flight and a tiring day in the heat. On the other hand, she probably didn't require more than four hours of sleep. Maybe after the nap she would be refreshed enough?

Hope springs eternal.

"We can order room service instead of going out to eat," he offered.

She looked up at him with grateful eyes. "That sounds great. I was dreading getting dressed after the shower."

"Does that mean what I think it means?" Anandur waggled his brows as he waved the keycard over the lock and pushed the door open.

She blushed. "It means that I want to put on my comfy sleep shirt. What did you think it meant?"

"Isn't it obvious?"

"You want me to parade naked around the suite? What about room service?"

"After."

Wonder blushed again and looked away.

He hooked a finger under her chin. "I was just joking, lass." He planted a soft kiss on her lips. "Go get into the shower, and I'll call room service. What do you want me to order for you?"

"Whatever you're ordering for yourself. I'm not finicky."

That was true. Wonder was the opposite of high maintenance. She demanded nothing and asked for very little.

An easy to please girl.

Hopefully.

11

WONDER

onder rested her forehead against the marble shower wall, letting the powerful spray pelt her back.

Gods, she was such a dummy. What the hell had possessed her to mention the stupid sleep shirt? Why had she brought it on this trip at all?

That old, faded thing had no place in a luxury hotel, and certainly not in bed with Anandur. She was supposed to look pretty and sexy, not like a homebody.

It was all Amanda's fault. When Wonder had asked her about what she should wear to bed, the answer had been nothing. After that, they all had a good giggle, and Wonder hadn't given it another thought.

Big mistake.

Did she have the guts to step out of the shower with only a towel wrapped around her body, and then drop it dramatically on the floor?

Was she brave enough to issue an invitation like that?

Not really. It was good as a fantasy but way too scary in reality.

The truth was that she had no idea what to do and how to act. Perhaps the best thing was to leave it all to Anandur. He was the one with lots of experience.

Ugh, she hated thinking about him with other women, even if it was irrational. He'd lived for almost a thousand years. What did she expect? For him to remain celibate and wait for her, even though he hadn't known she existed?

Stupid.

But what if he expected her to initiate? Gods knew he hadn't done anything until she pushed him. Maybe that was his mode of operation?

An attractive man like him didn't need to work hard on seduction. She'd seen it time and again at the club. All an attractive guy had to do was show up, and the women took it from there. Less attractive men had to work for it and deal with a lot of rejection.

She often wondered how it affected them.

Did it make them tougher and more successful because they had to be more resourceful to get girls?

Did they grow to hate women? Or maybe they appreciated them more because they had to work for it?

Easy come, easy go was a popular saying. Effortless wins were not as appreciated as those achieved by investing a lot of hard work.

After all, having to fight for it made the victory that much sweeter.

Was that why some women played hard to get? Maybe she should too?

Ugh, it was all so complicated. Amanda and Carol had lots of experience luring guys, and their advice was good for women like them, but not for a newbie virgin with zero seduction skills.

Except, maybe showing up was good enough.

She was attractive, maybe not gorgeous, and perhaps not as feminine as Carol or as impressive as Amanda, but Wonder had noticed guys looking at her with lust in their eyes.

Sometimes, she caught the same kind of expression on Anandur's face. Even to her inexperienced eyes, it was quite apparent that he wanted her.

Except, he wasn't acting on it. Maybe he needed a little push, and then he'd take it from there. It had worked with their first kiss, and it should work just as well now.

Encouraged, Wonder turned off the spray and stepped out of the shower. Reaching for one of the big fluffy towels that were stacked on the bottom shelf of the vanity, she noticed two folded bathrobes on the one next to it.

That was a good solution to her sleep attire dilemma. She could put one on instead of the old oversized shirt.

First, though, she needed to blow dry her hair and style it as best she could. Anandur seemed to prefer it loose around her shoulders.

It had been so damn hot on the tour that Wonder had had to braid her hair to keep it away from her face and neck. Now that she wanted to look her best, a more sophisticated style was needed.

A round brush in one hand and a blow dryer in the other, she felt confident she could do a decent job. It had looked so easy when Gertrude had done it, but Wonder found out it was anything but. The stupid brush kept either getting tangled in her hair or falling out of her hands.

"Are you okay in there?" Anandur knocked after the thing hit the floor for the second time.

"I'm fine. The brush fell." Great, now he'd think she was clumsy.

"Take your time. The food is not here yet."

That was a relief. She would've hated to keep Anandur waiting. If he was as hungry as she was, he was probably getting antsy. Not a good mood for a romantic evening.

In the end, Wonder had managed to curl the bottom a bit and to smooth out most of the frizzy parts, but it was a far cry from Gertrude's professional results.

Oh well, she'd done her best.

Next, she eyed the three bottles of lotion the hotel had supplied. Sniffing each one in turn, Wonder chose the one she liked best and applied it liberally. Amanda had said that moisturizing was part of a daily routine every woman should adopt, even an immortal. There were many more items on that list, most of which Wonder had forgotten.

Where did women find the time to do all that? Or the patience?

When the small bottle was empty, Wonder donned the robe, double knotted the belt, and took one last glance at the mirror.

Well, it was as good as it was going to get, so there was no reason to keep on fussing.

Heart racing, Wonder sashayed into the suite's living room. "Is the food here?" she asked, affecting the most nonchalant tone she could muster, hoping that the strong smell of the lotion she'd smeared all over was masking the scent of her nervousness.

"Nope, not yet." Anandur's eyes blazed with inner light, but he kept his voice neutral as if seeing her in a robe did nothing for him. "Fancy hotel restaurants take their sweet time." He put down the television remote and got up. "I'm going to hit the shower. If they come while I'm in there, just sign the bill. They will charge it to the room."

"Okay."

Relieved to have a few minutes to get her racing heart-beat under control, Wonder released a puff of air and plopped down on the couch.

12

ANANDUR

*W*ithout looking back, Anandur strode into the bathroom, hoping that his quick exit prevented Wonder from noticing the wood he'd sprouted in his jeans.

Damn, that robe had almost done him in. The white terry fabric accentuated Wonder's creamy, dark skin, and her wavy dark brown hair, while the length was just right for showing off her long legs. Then there was the deep valley between her generous breasts that was pushing the robe's lapels apart.

If he'd stayed a second longer, he would have done things he would've regretted later. Wonder needed patience and a gentle touch, none of which he could've summoned at the moment if his life depended on it.

A cold shower was in order. An ice bucket would've been even better.

Unfortunately, even on the lowest setting, the water wasn't cold enough to cool his arousal. His shaft still throbbed painfully, demanding his attention.

Planting one hand on the marble wall, he reached for it.

A groan escaped his throat as his fingers closed around the hot length and squeezed. Damn, ever since he'd met Wonder, he'd been masturbating as frequently as he had as a teenager, which had been a very long time ago.

As a young man, Anandur had mastered the art of quick seduction, and ever since there had never been a shortage of willing partners, even in the days when promiscuity had not been the norm.

The thing was, for an immortal male masturbation never really solved the problem. Without biting, he could achieve only partial release. Still, it was better to relieve some of the pressure than descend on Wonder like a wild beast.

Would she fight him off?

A primitive part of him reared its head, excited at the prospect of subduing a powerful female. The girl was strong enough to offer quite some resistance, but the question was whether she would.

Anandur suspected that Wonder was a pleaser, and pleasers derived the most pleasure from submitting. Still, she might feel the corresponding primitive urge and resist him so he could prove worthy of her submission.

Fuck, the image of her powerful body going soft under his tightened the tension in Anandur's balls, and as the images of her surrender kept flashing through his head, the pressure built until it hit critical velocity.

On a silent roar, Anandur threw his head back and ejaculated all over the glass enclosure.

When it was finally over, the shower looked like a giant vat of pudding had exploded inside of it.

Messy, but he felt much better.

His venom glands were another story. The only way to release that pressure was to bite, and he wasn't one of those guys who could do that with a pillow or a blanket. The venom would not release into anything other than living flesh.

The best he could do was control his fangs. Taking several long calming breaths, Anandur had them retract almost completely. The bad news was that it wasn't going to get better than that. The good news was that even in their slightly elongated state, they could pass as larger than normal canines.

He'd better hurry, clean up the mess he'd made, and finish showering. The food had probably already arrived and was getting cold. Normally, Anandur would've heard the knock on the door and then Wonder making small talk with the waiter, but he'd been somewhat preoccupied.

Damn, he was such an irresponsible moron.

They were in a Third World country, and he'd left her alone to answer the door in that sexy robe.

One hell of a shitty Guardian he was for not thinking it through before making a mad dash to the bathroom to hide his boner.

What if something had happened to her while he was busy jerking off? He should've never left Wonder alone to wait for the room service.

Not bothering to turn the water off, Anandur grabbed a towel and wrapped it around his hips while rushing out of the bathroom.

The sight of Wonder sprawled on the sofa had him panic for a moment, but then the sound of her soft, even breaths registered.

She had fallen asleep, that's all.

And the bloody room service hadn't arrived yet. Or maybe it had, and Wonder didn't hear the knock?

Now he was stuck waiting for it. Wonder was sleeping, so he couldn't leave her alone until the food arrived, but the mess he'd left in the shower wasn't going to clean itself, and he hadn't washed properly either.

What to do?

First thing first, he went to the bedroom and grabbed the comforter to cover his girl. The air conditioning was blasting cold air just over her head.

Next, he went back and grabbed the phone off the nightstand.

"This is Mr. Wilson. We've been waiting for our food order for over an hour. What's going on?"

"My apologies. Let me check on it. Can I put you on hold for a moment?"

"Sure," he barked through gritted teeth.

Fancy hotel my ass.

After several long moments, the guy came back. "I'm so sorry, sir. Your order got misplaced. I put a rush on a new one, and it should arrive in twenty minutes or less. No charge, of course."

They'd better. "How the hell did you misplace my order?"

"My apologies. It was delivered to the wrong room and the guest signed for it."

Fuckers. "You should charge it to that room." That would teach them to steal other people's dinner.

"We will take care of everything, sir."

"Twenty minutes or less."

"Yes, sir. And I will add complementary dessert. Anything in particular you would like?"

"All of it. Two of each item on your menu."

"Yes, sir."

"And a bottle of wine. House is fine."

He was taking advantage of the situation, but there was a limit to how far he could push them. Then again, it was the Four Seasons, and they were charging an obscene amount for the suite. The least they could do was provide outstanding customer service.

"Yes, sir."

Somewhat mollified, Anandur sat on one of the armchairs facing the door and let out a breath. At least the concierge had taken responsibility for the blunder and was trying to make amends. Besides, there was no hurry now. Wonder had fallen asleep, and he wasn't going to wake her up until she got the rest she needed. Not even for food. The girl was exhausted.

Maybe in a few hours, when she woke up all refreshed, he would feed her and then continue his seduction plan.

With a sigh, Wonder turned on her side, burying her face in the sofa's back cushions and sticking her cute bottom out the other way.

Anandur was tempted to come closer and snake his hands under the robe that had ridden up her thighs. But then, as she started snoring softly, he shook his head at his own stupidity.

He'd been thinking with his dick instead of his head. If he cared for the girl, the most he would do tonight was hold her while she slept. That was what Wonder needed after a fourteen-hour flight and a pyramid tour in the smoldering heat of Cairo, not his amorous advances.

Perhaps he was going to text Amanda after all.

Only another woman would know what a virgin dreamt of for her first time. It would be humiliating for a man of his advanced years and vast experience to ask for advice, but Anandur was willing to pay the price if it meant making Wonder's dreams come true.

13

NICK

*N*ick took his earphones off and turned to Eva. "I need to go home early today."

As she leaned back and folded her arms over her enormous belly, the executive chair groaned in protest. "You are home."

Only officially.

His stuff was still in the upstairs bedroom of the house he worked and lived in, but Nick was spending every free moment with Ruth, including nights. Not mornings, though, which was regrettable.

He would've loved to have breakfast with her.

Except, Ruth woke up hours before him. Under her management, the café opened at six in the morning, which meant that she had to get out of bed at the ungodly hour of five. Since Nick didn't start his workday until much later in the day, Ruth usually tiptoed out, careful not to wake him up.

Sundays, though, the café was closed, and they stayed in

bed, snuggling until mid-morning, and then had breakfast out in her garden.

Nick loved those Sundays. It would've been great if every day of the week started like that.

It was about time he moved in with Ruth, but he hadn't been invited, and until she suggested it he wasn't going to broach the subject.

In the meantime, Nick was going to prove that he was helpful around the house, handy when something needed fixing, and generally a great guy to have around. One of these days Ruth was going to realize what an asset he was and ask him to move in with her.

He waved a dismissive hand. "You know what I mean. I need to go early so I can help out with dinner. Ruth invited her sister and her boyfriend, and also another couple—a cousin of hers with his wife."

Eva arched a brow. "Did Ruth ask for your help?"

"No, but so what? I know she needs it. The girl thinks she is a superwoman, working fourteen-hour shifts at the café and then coming home and preparing dinner for a bunch of guests. The least I can do is help with the prep and the cleanup. That's what a good boyfriend should do, right?"

Eva's big belly heaved as she laughed. "You must be in love. The old Nick did everything he could to wiggle out of chores and never volunteered to help."

"Not true. Who ran to the supermarket every time you needed something?"

"That's because it was a good excuse not to do the other stuff you were supposed to do."

She'd got him there. Eva always saw right through him.

"I need to go," he said as he closed his laptop. "Is it okay if I finish tomorrow?"

"It's fine. Go help out your girlfriend." Eva waved him off. "And best of luck tonight."

That was a strange thing to say. It wasn't as if he was the one cooking. "Good luck with what?"

"Dinner, of course." Eva picked up the partial report he'd prepared for her and pretended to get busy reading.

"I'm not the cook."

"Whatever, you know what I mean. Now off with you."

"Thanks. I'll see you tomorrow morning."

"Say hello to Ruth for me."

"I will."

Something about Eva's good luck comment still bothered him. Nick routinely blurted nonsense that had nothing to do with whatever was being said, but his boss didn't.

It must've been the pregnancy's fault. The bigger Eva got, the odder her behavior was becoming. He'd even caught her wiping tears from her eyes while watching a Hallmark movie. Totally out of character for his tough as nails boss lady.

Come to think of it, Ruth was acting strange too. What was the deal with her inviting guests to dinner twice in one week?

It wasn't like her.

From a recluse, his girlfriend was suddenly turning into a social animal. Well, that was a bit of an exaggeration. Inviting a few close friends and family hardly warranted the title, but still.

Was it possible that she was pregnant too?

Nah, she couldn't be. Ruth had told him that she was on birth control, and he had no reason to doubt her.

Maybe that was her way of getting him more involved with her family, which was awesome because it showed that she was serious about him and was committed to their relationship.

Slinging the strap of his duffle bag over his shoulder, Nick leaped over the three steps leading from the house's front door to the walkway and aimed the clicker at his car.

This latest effort on Ruth's part was a very good sign. He'd decided a while ago that she was the one for him, and that he was all in, like in proposing at the first opportunity. But until this encouraging development, Ruth had seemed a bit distant, as if she was still afraid of making a commitment.

Would she say yes if he popped the question now? Or would she freak out and tell him that he was rushing things?

It was better to wait. But how long?

Maybe he should start dropping hints?

Unlike guys, women were supposed to be good at catching those. If Ruth were receptive to the idea, she would prompt him to continue, and if she wasn't, he could turn it into a joke.

In the meantime, he should do his best to impress her family and friends, or at least get them to like him. That would no doubt score him some points.

Making a quick stop at the supermarket, Nick got two pricey bottles of wine and a small bouquet of flowers for the table. That would impress the ladies.

What about the guys, though?

Roni was not a problem, the two of them got along fine,

especially since they were close in age and worked in related fields, but the cousin was an enigma.

He found it strange that Ruth had never mentioned her cousin Brundar before, and suddenly she was inviting him and his wife for dinner.

Supposedly, Nick had met the dude at Eva and Bhathian's wedding, but he'd gotten so drunk that evening that the party was one big blur in his head. If Ruth had introduced him to her cousin or any other family member, Nick had no recollection of it.

The only clue he had about Cousin Brundar was Ruth mentioning having family in Scotland. Brundar sounded Scottish, right?

Maybe. Nick knew next to nothing about Scots except that they liked to drink whiskey and that they called it Scotch when it was made in Scotland. Perhaps in addition to the wine, he should get some Macallan. That should impress Cousin Brundar from Scotland.

14

RUTH

"*B*eautiful." Ruth took the bouquet from Nick. "They will make the table look so festive."

He pulled her in for a quick one-armed hug and planted a kiss on her lips. "I'm glad you like them." Letting go of her, he lifted his shopping bag from the floor and followed her to the table. "You still didn't tell me what the occasion is. Is it your cousin's birthday or something?"

Avoiding Nick's smart eyes, Ruth put the bouquet in the center of the dining table. "No, it's not." Searching her brain for a good excuse, she came away with nothing. "I'm trying to be more social, that's all." As if he were going to believe that.

Nick's smile turned forced. "I see." He put the shopping bag on the table and pulled out a bottle of Scotch. "Just in case, I got him a good whiskey. Macallan is a top brand. He is Scottish, right?"

"He was born in Scotland, yes. That's very thoughtful of you. I'm sure Brundar is going to love it."

"Good." Reaching into the bag, Nick pulled out two

bottles of wine. "Anything need cleaning?" he asked as he put them on the table.

"Only a few dishes in the sink."

"I'm on it. Anything else?"

"No, I'm done. Everything is ready."

"Then I suggest you take a break and get some rest. I'll finish up here."

"Thanks." She kissed his cheek. "I'll grab a quick shower."

Actually, Ruth was planning on taking a long one and not coming out until the doorbell rang.

Keeping herself in check and hiding her anxiety from Nick was draining, she wasn't that good of an actress. And then there was the guilt. Reminding herself that there was no other choice wasn't helping much.

The game plan was simple. Roni and Brundar were going to goad Nick into drinking excessively, then at some point slip a sleeping potion into one of his drinks. When he was out, Brundar was going to bite him.

Even though it was necessary, Ruth hated the deception.

Except, she preferred to live with the guilt of lying to Nick than the guilt of ruining his life and taking away his freedom.

The lie was a lesser evil.

Repeating that sentence throughout her shower and while doing her hair and getting dressed helped a little, so she kept the mantra going as she stood at the window and waited for her guests to arrive. She didn't dare leave the bedroom until Sylvia's car was parked in the driveway.

"Hi, Ruth." Roni was the first at the door. "I got tequila

and whiskey and vodka." He lifted a liquor store shopping bag. "I didn't know what Nick likes."

"I'm not sure either." When they were together, Nick mostly drank beer and usually no more than one. "I think he is a lightweight."

"I'll say." Sylvia leaned in and kissed Ruth's cheek. "Do you remember how drunk he was at Eva's wedding?"

"How can I forget?" She'd kissed him for the first time that night.

"I, on the other hand, can't remember a thing," Nick said as he walked into the living room. "Except for the kiss, that is." He wrapped his arm around Ruth's shoulders. "That's when Ruth and I finally started dating seriously." He chuckled. "That sounds corny."

She snuggled closer and lifted her face to plant a quick kiss on his jaw. "It sounds sweet."

"I agree." Sylvia followed Roni inside.

Ruth was about to close the door when Brundar's car pulled up to the curb.

"My cousin is here." She wrapped her arm around Nick's trim waist. "He is a little odd, so don't think it's because of you. He's like that with everyone."

"Odd in what way?"

"You'll see. Just don't offer him your hand for a handshake."

"Got it."

As always, Nick was easy. No long explanations were needed, and no rebuttals were voiced. He just accepted things the way they were. Hopefully, this attitude would carry over to his post transition reaction.

"I must've been really drunk," Nick said as Brundar got out of the car and walked to the other side to open the door for Callie. "The dude is not someone easily forgotten. What's with the ponytail? Is he a rocker?"

Ruth chuckled. "Not as far as I know. I'd be surprised if he can carry a tune."

"Good evening," Brundar said as he and Callie approached. "I'm Brundar, and this is my mate Callie."

"Hi," Callie said with a small wave of her hand. "Nice to meet you, Nick."

"The pleasure is all mine." Nick bowed his head instead of offering either one his hand. "Please, come in."

He was being overly formal, which was a good bet when meeting new people. Apparently, Nick wasn't as socially inept as he pretended to be. It seemed that his goofy, oddball character came out to play only with people he considered friends.

"I hear that you're an awesome cook," Callie said as they sat at the dining table.

"I've heard the same about you."

The girl blushed. "It's a hobby. I like trying new recipes. I was even thinking about opening a restaurant in the village."

"In New York?" Nick asked.

"No, in Woodland Hills," Callie said without batting an eyelash. "But the rent is too steep."

The girl was quick on her toes.

"Running a commercial kitchen is not the same as cooking for fun. Did you ever work in a restaurant?" Ruth asked.

"I was a waitress, so I know exactly how crazy it can get in the kitchen."

"Speaking of a kitchen, I'd better check on my beef cake. It should be just about ready."

"I'll help." Sylvia jumped up before Nick could open his mouth.

"Do you mind if I join?" Callie asked. "I want to check out your cookware."

"I'll gladly show off my culinary toolkit."

As the three of them ducked into the kitchen, Roni took charge. "I'm dying to taste this tequila. The guy at the liquor store said that this one is the best. You guys want to join me?"

In the kitchen, Ruth leaned against the counter, inhaled deeply, and then exhaled slowly through her mouth.

"It's going to be okay, Mom." Sylvia pulled her into her arms.

"Brundar is very gentle," Callie whispered. "He only looks brutal."

"I'm not worried about that. I just hate deceiving Nick, and I'm scared that it's not going to work."

Sylvia squeezed her tighter. "It's going to be fine. You'll see. Nick is going to transition, and you guys are going to live happily ever after. But just so we are clear, I'm never calling him Daddy."

15

NICK

"Fuck, my head." Nick managed to crack one eye open.

It was completely dark, but he smelled Ruth's perfume, the one he'd gotten her for their three-month anniversary. She was right there next to him, sitting on the bed.

He reached for her with his hand. "What's going on?"

The last thing he remembered was toasting Sylvia's graduation, one of many toasts the six of them had made throughout dinner to celebrate this or that. If it had been only him against the Scot, Nick would've quit after the third tequila shot, but with the three girls keeping pace with Brundar and Roni, Nick could not have shamed himself by being the only guy with an alcohol tolerance lower than the girls'.

"I'm sorry," she whispered.

"About what? I'm the one who should apologize for getting plastered like that."

"For your poor head. Do you want Advil? After your last headache, I bought some in case you got another one."

That was so thoughtful of her. "Sure. Can you get me three?"

"I have the bottle here."

He heard her twisting the cap off the bottle and shaking out some pills.

"Here you go." Taking his hand and turning it palm up, she placed the three pills in the middle and closed his fingers around them, then she took his other hand and put the water glass in it.

The woman must possess not only bat ears but also a bat's sonar vision. "Can you switch on the light? Just a little? I can't see shit."

"Sure."

Ruth got up and walked over to the bathroom. Turning on the small light over the mirror, she left the door open a crack.

"Thanks."

As Nick popped the pills into his mouth and washed them down with the water, Ruth sat down next to him.

"How do you feel? Are you queasy?"

"Now that you mention it, I am. Shit, I hate barfing."

"If you need to, I have a bucket ready."

Pills, water, and a barf bucket. Ruth was well prepared for handling her drunk boyfriend.

"Did I embarrass you in front of your family?"

"What? No, of course not. Why would you think that?"

"I can't compete with your tolerance for alcohol. They must think I'm a wuss."

"No one thinks that."

Right. As if she was going to tell him if they did. "Are they still here?"

"No, they went home."

Great. While they had been okay to drive, he had passed out. Unless they hadn't been and had acted irresponsibly. "Wasn't it dangerous for them to drive after all the alcohol they consumed?"

Ruth waved a hand. "They weren't even drunk. After you passed out, we had plenty of coffee. They were fine."

Great. Talk about humiliating.

Except, Nick had a feeling that this was just the tip of the iceberg because he didn't remember making it to bed. "How did I get here?"

"Brundar carried you."

Nick grabbed a pillow and put it over his eyes. "Great. Just kill me now. I must've left one hell of an impression on your cousin and his wife."

"You did. They both think you're awesome."

"And you're a terrible liar."

"I am not lying! Callie said that you're a lot of fun and a really nice guy, and Brundar nodded in agreement, which is the most that can be expected from him."

That sounded more probable.

Brundar had hardly talked at all during dinner. Callie had done all the talking for both of them, with her mate or husband, or whatever they called their union, only nodding in agreement or answering in monosyllables when asked something.

Strange dude, although not completely unpleasant. No one who loved his wife as much as Brundar loved Callie could be a bad guy. Nick hadn't seen him smile even once, but the guy's pale blue eyes softened every time he looked at her.

"Your cousin loves his wife a lot. Are they newlywed? And why does he call her his mate? Is it a Scottish thing?"

Ruth looked away, pushing the glass closer to the pill container on the nightstand. "They are not officially married." She cleared her throat. "They said their vows to each other in private."

"Sounds awesome. Is that why he calls her his mate instead of his wife?"

Ruth shrugged. "I guess."

Despite the pounding headache, it was clear to him that Ruth was uncomfortable talking about her cousin. Still, he wasn't going to let this deter him from testing the waters and dropping some hints about marriage. The topic of Brundar and Callie's nuptials or lack thereof was just too good of an opportunity for sending out feelers.

"It sounds like you don't approve."

She shrugged again. "They can always get married, there is no rush."

Crap, that wasn't what he wanted to hear. "There is no reason to wait either. It's obvious that they are in love. So why not celebrate it with a nice ceremony, and have their friends and family share in their happiness?"

With a sigh, Ruth lay down and cuddled close to him. "You're such a romantic, Nicki."

He wrapped his arm around her and kissed the top of her head. "And you're not?"

"To be a romantic you need to also be an optimist and believe in happy endings. I have a hard time doing that. Anxiety and optimism don't go hand in hand. I tend to focus on all the possible negative outcomes."

That wasn't a fun way to live. Poor Ruth. Living with anxiety was a drag.

"That's why you have me. I have enough optimism for the two of us."

WONDER

*T*he road stretching ahead of them was in surprisingly good condition—a true highway with four lanes going in each direction. The distance between Cairo and Alexandria was about two and a half hours by car. With the traffic flowing smoothly, they should be arriving at the city shortly.

"Do you have Mrs. Rashid's address?" Anandur asked.

"Yes. She is so excited to see me. And you too."

He arched a brow. "Oh, yeah? What did you tell her about me?"

"That you're my boyfriend and that you're helping me find out about my past. She said that it's very admirable and that she can't wait to meet you."

"I feel like I'm about to meet your parents."

"Up until your clan adopted me, she was the closest to a family I had. I just wish she could've stayed in the States so we could keep in touch. But in addition to her daughter Serena and her family, Mrs. Rashid has six more children and fifteen grandchildren who all live in Alexandria. She can't leave. Besides, her husband suffers from advanced Alzheimer's, and their children take turns taking care of him. That's a lot of help she wouldn't have in the States."

"True. Humans have it tough."

Indeed. On the other hand, though, having seven children was something immortals could only dream of. Wonder would be lucky to have one.

With Anandur.

When they finally got around to having sex.

Unbelievable. After stressing so much about seducing Anandur that she'd thought her heart was going to leap out of her chest, she'd fallen asleep on the sofa and couldn't even remember him carrying her to bed.

He was so good to her.

This morning he'd even brought her breakfast in bed and had insisted on feeding her. Wonder should've felt awkward about being babied like that, but the truth was that she'd loved every moment.

It was nice to have someone taking care of her for a change, and it was even nicer knowing that Anandur loved doing it.

The man was a giver, and he was spoiling her as if she were a real princess. Wonder was quite sure Anandur would've never booked such fancy hotels or rented a luxury sedan for the drive if he were traveling by himself.

He was too frugal for that. And yet, he was throwing money at her as if he had an endless supply of it.

"Where are we staying in Alexandria?"

"The Four Seasons, of course."

"Why did you book such pricey hotels? I'm sure there were more affordable alternatives."

"I've told you, only the best for my girl." He took one

hand off the steering wheel and reached for hers. "I love pampering you."

"Are you sure you can afford it? I would feel really bad if you spent your life savings on spoiling me. I would've been very happy with much less."

He chuckled and squeezed her hand. "We could live permanently in the Four Seasons suite just from the interest I'm earning on my investments. Guardians are paid well, and I've been one for a very long time. And as I'm sure you've noticed, I don't spend much either."

"Wow, I'm impressed."

Who would've thought that modest Anandur, who wore plain Levis and T-shirts, was loaded?

Lifting her hand, he kissed the back of it. "I'm a good catch, Wonder. You should stick with me."

"I know, silly, and not because of your investments. You're an amazing guy. I would've chosen you even if you were as broke as me."

"What about Esag?"

She shrugged. "Forget about Esag, I don't even want to regain my memories. This trip was your idea, not mine."

Her gut clenched uncomfortably at the half-truth. On the one hand, Wonder wanted to know who she was and where she came from, and Esag's name still caused a little twitch in her heart, but on the other hand, she was falling in love with Anandur.

Heck, who was she kidding?

She was already in love with him, and the feeling intensified the more time she spent with him. From the moment he'd stopped resisting the pull between them, Anandur hadn't done a single thing wrong.

"Oh, lass, you have no idea how happy it makes me to

hear you say you've chosen me. But we both know that regaining your memories is important. I just hope that once you do, your feelings for me won't change."

It was her turn to lift their joined hands and kiss Anandur's fingers. Was it too soon to tell him that she loved him? He hadn't said it yet either, not the exact words, but he'd implied it plenty of times.

Maybe it was good that she'd fallen asleep last night and they hadn't had sex yet. Shouldn't they say the words first? Wasn't love a prerequisite for lovemaking?

It was confusing.

Wonder had seen complete strangers hook up in the club and go somewhere to have sex. But that didn't mean she would've been able to do that. Having sex wasn't just about fulfilling a physical need, it was about intimacy, a connection between two people.

Still, feelings of friendship and appreciation were probably enough. But then the distance between those and love wasn't big. What was love if not friendship and appreciation combined with sexual attraction?

"What are you thinking about that is making you frown like that? Are you worried about going back to Alexandria?"

"A little." Wonder hadn't thought about that at all, not until Anandur had mentioned it. She'd killed a man in that city and had run for her life. "What if the police are looking for me?"

"We will buy you a pair of big sunglasses to hide your amazing eyes. And with the nice new clothes you have on and the haircut Amanda gave you, no one will make the connection to the ragged urchin you were."

ANANDUR

"*W*onder!" The small round woman pulled Wonder into her arms, kissed her on both cheeks, and then pushed her back. "You look so different."

"I hope in a good way."

Mrs. Rashid put her hands on her hips and cranked her neck to regard Anandur with the intensity of a mother checking out her daughter's new boyfriend. "Is that your doing, young man?"

Anandur pulled out his most charming smile. "I can't take credit for Wonder's beauty. It's all her."

A wide grin spread over the woman's weathered face. "It takes the care of a good man to make a woman look like that."

"If you say so." He didn't think Wonder would appreciate the remark.

Modern women didn't like to hear comments that implied their wellbeing was dependent on a man in any way. He found it silly. A partner, whether male or female, was immensely influential and had the power to either enhance or diminish one's wellbeing.

"Just look at those sparkling eyes." Mrs. Rashid waved a hand over Wonder. "And that glowing skin. This is what love does to a woman."

Wonder blushed and lowered her eyes, neither agreeing nor disagreeing. Did it mean that she was in love with him? Or did it mean that she knew he was in love with her?

He was, but he'd never told Wonder that he loved her. Not because he was scared of revealing his feelings, but because he didn't think she was ready to hear it.

Except, if he was planning to take her virginity tonight, which he was, shouldn't he declare his love for her first?

Damn. He should've asked Amanda. Out of all the questions he'd texted her last night, this one would have been the most important and the least embarrassing. Maybe he would sneak another text while Wonder was busy with Mrs. Rashid.

After all the careful preparations he'd done for tonight, it would be a shame if he ended up making a careless blunder.

Being in love wasn't something he had experience with. In that regard, he was as much of a newbie as Wonder.

"Hasina," the old man sitting on a tattered armchair called out. "*Min hum duyufk?*"

"This is my friend Wonder and her fiancé Andre," Mrs. Rashid answered in English.

"*Ahlaan wasahlaan bik fi manzili.*"

"He says welcome to my home." Mrs. Rashid shook her head. "I should invite guests more often. This is the first

85

time he has talked in days." She sighed. "Come, sit down on the couch and I'll get the coffee going."

"Thank you." Anandur followed Wonder to the sofa.

The living room was tiny, and the furniture was old and tattered, but everything was spotless. Framed pictures of the Rashid children and grandchildren adorned the weathered walls, and handmade cushions and throws were scattered over the furniture to hide the worst spots.

The thing was, Mrs. Rashid and her husband weren't poor. Their modest dwelling was in a good neighborhood, and the ten-story building even had an elevator that was still functioning. This was probably considered luxury for an average middle-class Egyptian family.

"Are you familiar with Turkish coffee, Andre?" Mrs. Rashid put down a tray with four tiny porcelain cups and a steaming copper pot filled with black, aromatic coffee.

"I had some in the past."

"Would you like extra sugar in it? I cooked it with one teaspoon per cup, but it might not be enough for you. It's very strong coffee."

"I'm sure you made it perfectly."

A grin spread over the woman's face. "You're a charmer, aren't you?" She poured Anandur a cup and handed it to him.

"I approve of this one," she told Wonder. "You've chosen well this time." She poured her a cup as well.

"I don't know what happened before the coma, Mrs. Rashid. I don't think I was abused. I think it was an accident."

"Did you regain any of your memories?"

"Just one. I had a boyfriend, but I know I wasn't married."

Mrs. Rashid sighed. "Husband, boyfriend, it doesn't matter. Abuse can happen to anyone in any situation. I'm just glad you got out alive and found happiness. Not everyone's story ends as well." She smiled at Anandur. "When you kids start planning your wedding, take into account that I'll need a lot of advance notice. Sea voyages take time and finding an affordable cabin on a freighter is not easy."

Wonder put down her coffee cup. "We are not anywhere near talking about marriage, Mrs. Rashid. We've only known each other for a few weeks."

The old woman smiled sheepishly, the twin dimples in her cheeks making her look years younger. "And yet here you are, traveling together across the globe. I know what I see, child. This is love. Don't let it get away. We are lucky if we get one chance like that in a lifetime." She glanced at her husband and sighed. "Enjoy it while it lasts."

They stayed for another half an hour or so, with Mrs. Rashid demanding to hear everything about Wonder's life, and Wonder answering as truthfully as she could.

"As lovely as it is to sit here and chat, we need to get moving if we want to visit the market today." Anandur pushed to his feet.

After several hugs, kisses, and quite a few tears, they finally said their goodbyes and left.

"She is a nice lady. I like her," Anandur said as he opened the passenger door for Wonder.

She wiped the few remaining tears with the back of her hand and got inside. "The feeling is mutual. She likes you too, but then, everyone does. You're a charmer."

Anandur pulled into the street. "I'm sure not everyone shares your opinion. Especially not the enemies I fought."

Wonder chuckled. "I don't think the dead and the

living-dead Doomers in stasis care one way or another. And I doubt any of your enemies are still around."

"You know me well, love."

WONDER

*A*s they strolled hand in hand through the narrow passageways between the market stalls, everything looked different to Wonder, smaller, dirtier.

Was it just this country, or did everything pale in comparison to the United States? Not that she'd seen much of it. San Francisco and Los Angeles might have been anomalies. Except, she'd watched enough television shows to get exposed to the rest of the country. Even neighborhoods that had been depicted as poor and crime-riddled looked affluent compared to this.

It was like coming from a different world.

"Anything?" Anandur asked.

"The only memories I have of this place are the ones after waking up. Though to tell you the truth, I remembered the place as much bigger and less dirty."

"You're not in Kansas anymore, Dorothy."

"Is that a saying?"

"It's from a famous movie. You should see it sometime. *The Wizard of Oz.*"

"We could watch it together." She leaned into him despite their stickiness level.

The outdoor market was hot and humid and brought unpleasant memories. She'd been all alone, confused, frightened, and without prospects. Anandur was her pillar of strength, a solid reminder that this was well behind her and that she would never be alone again.

"I don't know if I can stream Netflix here. I'll ask the concierge about it."

"Maybe we should head back to the hotel? I don't think this is working." It was on the tip of her tongue to tell him that she'd rather wait for the movie until they were back at the village. Tonight, she had different plans, and they didn't involve watching anything other than Anandur's magnificent body with no clothes to conceal any of it.

"Let's walk around some more. We've just got here. Maybe you'll see something familiar that will push another buried memory to the surface."

That was what she was afraid of. One of the thugs she'd overpowered might recognize her despite the big sunglasses and Amanda's fancy designer clothing that made Wonder look like a wealthy American tourist.

She clung even closer to Anandur. The big redhead courted even more attention than her. She was a tall woman, but at least her coloring didn't stand out, and the sunglasses covered the unusual color of her eyes.

"What's the matter, lass? You seem jumpy."

"What if one of those thugs is here and recognizes me?"

A growl started deep in Anandur's throat. "You have nothing to worry about. I'm looking forward to it. Finishing that job for you would be my pleasure."

Wonder shook her head. "I'm not afraid of them." She leaned closer and whispered in his ear. "I'm afraid of the police. I might get arrested for murder."

"That's not a problem either. I can thrall whoever they tell about you and make them forget the accusation."

"I can do that too. But it's still too risky. How many people can you thrall at once?"

He scratched his beard. "One."

"So can I. What if there is more than one police officer?"

"I'll take one, and you'll take the other. How is your thralling ability?"

"Decent, I guess. I don't know what's considered good."

"Show me. Can you cast an illusion? Make yourself look like someone else?"

The most she'd done was to conceal her bruises and her torn clothing. She'd never tried to look like someone else.

"What do you have in mind?"

"Make yourself look like a man. I can't see the illusion, but we can check people's reaction to you, whether they address you as a man or a woman."

That should be interesting. "I'll give it a try."

It took a lot of concentration, but she managed to fool people for about five minutes before having to drop the shroud. The energy needed to maintain it while talking to the various vendors was draining out fast.

"Not bad," Anandur said. "Quite impressive for a woman."

That was a sexist remark. Worse, it was another reminder of her being a freak. It wasn't enough that she was strong like a man and could detect other immortal males in the same way they detected one another, she could also thrall like a male.

"Ugh. I hate those comparisons. I thought all immortals could thrall."

"Easy, tiger. Generally, women are not as good at this because they don't have enough practice. Guys have to become good out of necessity."

"True. I guess my circumstances made it a necessity as well."

"They did."

"Can we go now? We've circled the market twice already, and I'm sweating. I want to go back to the hotel." And practice being feminine. She was going to take a shower and put on the sexy lingerie Amanda had bought for her.

"Just two more stops. I want you to show me where you were attacked and the building site where you woke up. If possible, I would like to see the caverns."

"Fine." She took his hand and led him out of the market.

"Are you in a hurry?" Anandur asked as she lengthened her strides.

"I want to get it over with."

If she could, she would've jogged there. But that was sure to attract attention. And she was still wary of encountering one of the thugs who'd attacked her. First, because she didn't want to deal with the local police. Secondly, because she didn't want to kill anyone ever again.

Anandur was right that the scum didn't deserve to live, and that killing them would save numerous future victims. But Wonder didn't want to be the one to do it.

It was a cowardly approach, but she just didn't have the stomach for it.

"It happened here," Wonder said as they reached the end of the alley. "They came at me from both directions." She swallowed the bile rising in her throat.

Pulling her into his arms, Anandur kissed the top of her head. "It's okay, lass. You're a strong fighter. They couldn't get you then, and they can't take you now. And it has nothing to do with me being here with you."

His words didn't help because fear wasn't the problem, but his arms around her did the trick. He cared for her despite what she'd done.

"I know. I just wish this memory would vanish together with the other ones."

"Show me your moves." Anandur took a step back and assumed a threatening pose.

She shook her head. "I don't want to."

"I'm coming at you, lass, whether you're ready or not." He started toward her.

Except, he didn't move as fast as she'd expected. Big mistake on his part.

As Anandur's hand reached for her shirt lapel, Wonder caught his wrist and pulled hard. Extending her leg to trip him at the same time, she sent him flying over her shoulder.

The ground shook as Anandur's big body hit the pavement, and if he weren't an immortal she would've worried about him getting hurt. Instead, she followed him down, straddled his torso, and sat on him. Not that her weight would keep him down, but she also pinned his arms over his head.

"Do you concede defeat, big guy?"

He grinned at her, happy as could be. "Fates, you're

beautiful. I could gaze into those jade eyes of yours forever."

A sense of déjà vu swept through Wonder.

Another face had smiled at her from the same position, and he had said something similar.

Letting go of Anandur's arms, she lifted a knee and got off him. "Esag," she whispered. "I did the exact same thing with him. He was the one who trained me." Dizzy, she sat on the ground and cradled her head in her hands.

Anandur sat up and reached for her, pulling her onto his lap. "Then I'm grateful to him. His training saved you."

She nodded. "I remember his face now."

"Was he handsome?"

"Yes."

"More handsome than me?"

She shook her head. "You're more handsome, and you're also older than he was."

"You have no idea how glad I am to hear that." Anandur pretended to release a relieved breath. "Do you remember anything else? What did he wear? What did you wear?"

Wonder frowned. All she had was a face and a distant memory of a feeling. She'd been attracted to Esag, but they hadn't been a couple. Had it been only an infatuation? A sexual attraction?

Another memory surfaced. Her legs had been bare because her skirt had ridden up. She remembered the feel of Esag's hands on her skin. His touch had burned because she'd wanted him so much.

"I had a skirt or a dress on. It rode up my thighs. That's all I remember." It was just a little lie, a half-truth, but she didn't want Anandur to know that she'd been attracted to Esag.

"You trained in a dress? That doesn't make sense."

"I know." She shrugged. "Maybe it's a false memory. Maybe I dreamt it."

ANANDUR

*A*s they drove slowly through Alexandria's afternoon rush hour traffic, Wonder looked out the car's passenger window. Not a big talker on any given day, she seemed even less inclined than usual to engage in conversation.

Normally, her silence wouldn't have bothered Anandur, but after the eventful experience in the alley, it worried him. The crease between her brows hadn't eased since they'd left the place. On the one hand, it was good that another memory had surfaced, but, on the other hand, it had further confused Wonder.

"Let it all out, lass. Tell me what troubles you. Don't be afraid to hurt my feelings. I can take it."

It was a lie. He would be crushed if Wonder told him that she still felt love for the guy. Except, that was why they were in Egypt digging for memories. The issue had to be settled one way or another. Hopefully, in Anandur's favor.

"I don't think I really loved Esag," she said, still looking out the window.

Anandur felt like a heavy weight was lifted off his chest.

"I think I was attracted to him," she said quietly, refusing to meet his eyes. "And he was attracted to me."

He hated to say it, but it needed to be said. "Mutual attraction is the first step. Love could've come later."

Finally, Wonder turned to look at him. "That's the thing. I don't think there was a later. Something happened. Maybe I got injured and fell into a coma before there was a chance for Esag and me to take it any further. Now I'll never know."

That was bad.

Now he had to fight not only a ghost but a what if. Those were the worst. An unfulfilled potential that would be like a nagging itch always casting doubts on his and Wonder's relationship. More than ever, Anandur needed to find the guy and prove to Wonder that what she felt, or could've felt, for the guy was not as powerful as what she felt for him.

But what if he was deluding himself?

What if he was overconfident, and the other guy won?

Damn. Him and his overinflated ego.

Anandur had been so sure of himself and of Wonder's feelings for him that he'd had a big production seduction plan for tonight. After a long texting session with Amanda, he'd thought he had a fail-proof action plan to give Wonder the best first time possible. And after giving it some more thought, he'd decided that he would lead into it with a romantic dinner and telling her that he loved her.

Should he even continue with the plan?

What if she'd changed her mind about wanting him to be her first?

After all, she hadn't told him she loved him yet. Maybe she didn't?

Perhaps the best thing for him to do would be to wait for Wonder to initiate. Or at least throw a big fat hint or two that she was still interested.

One of Amanda's ideas was to surprise Wonder with a pampering session at the hotel's spa. He'd modified it to something more private, but now that the whole plan was in danger of going up in smoke, maybe he should ask her if she was interested in a massage. As the saying went, presumption was the mother of all fuckups.

"I prepared a surprise for you when we get back to the hotel."

"A surprise?" She looked more concerned than excited.

"I ordered a masseuse to come give you a massage in our room. But if you prefer to do it in the hotel's spa, I can call and request a different appointment."

Wonder grimaced. "Thank you, but I don't know how I feel about a stranger putting his hands on me."

As if Anandur would have ever allowed a guy's hands anywhere near her. Unless it was a medical emergency and there were no female doctors available, no male other than him was going to touch Wonder.

He'd specifically requested a female masseuse. "Her hands, not his. I would never allow another male to touch you unless it was to save your life. But since you're an immortal with miraculous healing abilities, that's a remote possibility I don't need to worry about."

"Oh, okay. I don't mind as much if it's a woman."

Wonder still didn't sound enthusiastic about the idea.

"If you don't like massages, I can cancel the appointment. It's supposed to be a treat, not a chore."

Chewing on her lower lip, Wonder wrapped a lock of hair around her finger. "I've never gotten a massage before. Is it pleasurable?"

"It feels good. The masseuse usually puts soothing music on, then rubs oil or lotion all over your body while kneading your muscles. It can be very relaxing." According to Amanda, it was the perfect way to put a girl in the right mood. Especially a virgin who might be a little apprehensive.

Wonder let the lock spring free, then coiled it again around her finger. "It sounds intimate."

Had he imagined it, or had she sounded a bit breathy? Did Wonder have fantasies about being with another woman?

Some men might have found the idea exciting, but not him. Well, watching mud-wrestling females was fun—he'd had no problem fantasizing about Lana with another woman—but not Wonder. To his surprise, Anandur found out that he was the possessive type. No one other than him, male or female, was going to touch his girl that intimately.

But what if that was what she wanted? Wonder was so inexperienced and naive that she might not have realized that she was attracted to other females.

Nah, it was a stupid notion. She'd just told him that she'd had the hots for that Esag dude. Besides, she hadn't faked her arousal when they'd had their little snogging session. Hell, the girl orgasmed like a firecracker.

There was no way Wonder was into women.

"It can be very intimate, even arousing." Unintentionally, his voice dropped by a whole octave.

"Do you know how to give a massage?" She glanced at him from beneath lowered lashes.

Anandur's venom glands began swelling up in tandem with the other part of his anatomy. "I do."

"I think I'll enjoy the massage much more if you do it. I like your hands on me."

The scent of her arousal flared, filling the car's interior. It took all of Anandur's willpower to keep his hands on the steering wheel and not to pulverize the thing.

"I'll cancel the appointment." He cleared his throat. "I made dinner reservations for later tonight. Should I cancel them as well?" He hazarded a quick glance at Wonder's flushed face.

"I'd rather dine in the room if you don't mind."

Brave girl. Wonder's cheeks were so red they must've felt on fire, but that hadn't stopped her from telling him what she wanted.

It seemed he'd just gotten his answer, and not as a subtle hint, but as a big-ass billboard painted with bold, neon colors.

20

WONDER

"*I* want to check out the shops," Wonder said as they got back to the hotel.

She was going to fix the sleepwear situation and buy herself something sexy.

"I'll come with you."

That was the last thing she wanted. "Don't you want to hit the shower? It will only take me a few minutes. I don't need an escort."

Anandur eyed her suspiciously, then sighed and relented. "As long as you stay inside the hotel, I guess it's okay."

"I'll be fine. I won't take long." She kissed his cheek.

Reluctantly, Anandur got into the elevator, looking at her like it pained him to be separated from her even for a few minutes.

She waited for the doors to close before bolting for the shops. Hopefully, she could get what she wanted quickly enough to make it to the room while he was still in the shower. It would be quite embarrassing to show up with her newly purchased sexy nightgown.

The price she ended up paying for the gown was outrageous, but she hadn't batted an eyelash as the clerk had run her debit card. It was worth it. She'd even added a T-shirt in case Anandur wanted to see what she'd bought.

It was all worth it to make her first time special.

No guts no glory, as Natasha used to say.

Well, Wonder had proved that she had the first. Now it remained to be seen if her guts would earn her glory.

Everyone cautioned that the first time was never particularly good. Amanda had said that Wonder should keep her expectations low, and Syssi had agreed, not in so many words, but it had been clear from her grimace. Carol's opinion differed, but Amanda had dismissed it, saying that she just didn't remember her first time right and had romanticized it.

It was supposed to start out painful and awkward. The good news for her was that the venom bite was going to fix everything and guarantee a mind-shattering orgasm.

Since her new girlfriends had all done it with humans, they hadn't been as fortunate. There had been no healing bite for them, and no euphoric orgasms. At least Amanda and Carol had the benefit of their own rapid healing ability, so their pain hadn't lasted long, but Syssi had been a human at the time, which explained the grimace.

Poor girl.

Wonder was lucky to have an immortal male as her first.

Yeah, she was one lucky girl, and not just because of Anandur's fangs and venom. She'd snagged herself the perfect guy. He was charming but not false, dominant and possessive but also sweet and considerate. She knew he would do everything to ensure her pleasure.

Despite what Amanda and the others had said, Wonder's first time was going to be glorious.

There was no way it could have been good with the smiling guy in her elusive memories, because it wasn't likely that Esag was an immortal, which meant that he could have never given her the pleasure Anandur was going to.

Even if she'd had feelings for Esag, it was good that she'd forgotten them.

She had to believe that everything had happened for a reason. Fate had saved her from a doomed union with a human so she could be with her perfect guy.

As Wonder returned to their suite, the sound of running water was a huge relief. She had a few moments before Anandur got out to get rid of the evidence. Quickly removing the price tag of her new nightgown, she bundled it together with the sexy lingerie Amanda had gotten her and wrapped it all in her old T-shirt.

Waiting for Anandur to be done, she closed her eyes and imagined him in the shower. His big powerful body glistening, his biceps bulging as he lifted his arms to wash his hair...

Stifling a moan, Wonder forced her eyes open. It was too early to get all worked up. She needed to wash first. Maybe in the future, after they had been together intimately, she would join Anandur in the shower. For this first time, though, she needed to prepare alone.

The bathroom door opened and Anandur stepped out. "That was some quick shopping." He glanced at the plastic bag on the bed.

With only a towel wrapped around his hips, Wonder got an eyeful worth salivating over. Broad chest, bulging biceps, and an eight-pack, the reality was better than her fantasy. Shortly, she was going to have her hands all over that magnificence.

Yum.

Wonder couldn't wait. "My turn," she chimed as she rushed by him into the bathroom.

"What did you get?" he called after her.

"A T-shirt. I'll show you later."

Wonder had left it in the shopping bag on purpose, so if he took a peek, it would look as if the shirt was the only thing she'd bought.

Keeping secrets wasn't a good start to a committed relationship, but a girl was entitled to some privacy, and she only needed to keep it a secret for tonight. Tomorrow, or maybe in a few days it wouldn't matter if she told him about her seduction plan. They would probably have a good laugh about it.

Standing under the pulsating spray of hot water, Wonder felt quite satisfied with herself. Getting the night-gown had been a last moment impulse, and she was so glad she'd done it. The thing was beautiful and sexy, and it made her look feminine, like a princess.

More to the point, the sheer gown would send a clear message, leaving no more doubts in Anandur's mind as to Wonder's readiness and eagerness. It was an invitation even the most obtuse male couldn't misinterpret.

According to Amanda and Syssi, men didn't get subtle cues. If she wanted Anandur to do this or that, she had to be clear and decisive in her words and actions.

There was an art to that, Carol had advised. Acting too

bold might seem pushy, and acting too coy might get lost in translation. A smart woman knew how to navigate between the two extremes.

Wonder thought she was doing it just right.

Taking her time, she washed her hair and then let the conditioner do its thing for several moments. Slowly but surely she was learning the intricacies of feminine grooming. She was never going to achieve Amanda's level of perfection, but she could approach Syssi's.

Hair that wasn't messy or frizzy, a tiny bit of makeup, and flattering clothes were enough for her. Wonder didn't need to look like she'd just stepped out of the cover of a fashion magazine.

Done with the shower, she blow-dried her hair but skipped the moisturizing. After all, Anandur was going to take care of that.

A shiver ran down her spine as she imagined his hands caressing every inch of her exposed skin, which hopefully would be all of it.

Stop it!

If she kept on fantasizing, she was going to end up running out naked and attacking Anandur.

Wonder chuckled.

She had a feeling he would've loved it. Perhaps even more than seeing her in the sheer nightgown with the sexy set of bra and panties under it.

Except, she wasn't doing it only for him. She was also doing it for herself. The luxurious lingerie made her feel beautiful and desirable, and the semi-sheer long nightgown made her feel more mature and sophisticated.

Looking at her reflection in the mirror, Wonder was happy with what she saw. Anandur might take everything off in a matter of minutes, but she would have her grand entry.

Taking a deep breath, Wonder took one last glance at the full-length mirror, and then put her hand on the door handle.

Courage, girl, you can do it.

21

ANANDUR

*A*ll of Anandur's careful planning had been a waste of time and effort. No professional massage to put Wonder in a relaxed mood, and no declarations of love over a romantic dinner in the Four Season's fanciest restaurant.

He needed to come up with a new plan and fast. Any moment now Wonder would get out of the bathroom and ask him for a massage.

There was only one way that could end.

Not a bad prelude to sex, but Anandur was adamant about telling Wonder how he felt about her before taking her to bed.

Perhaps a romantic dinner on the suite's balcony would do?

Nah, it was too hot and humid. He would have to settle for the suite's living room. Hopefully, room service in this hotel would function better than the one in Cairo. Should he offer a bribe? Or would a threat work better?

Anandur picked up the phone and dialed the restaurant

extension. "This is Mister Wilson from room five hundred and five. I would like dinner delivered to my suite. What can we do to ensure that it is delivered as quickly as possible?"

After choosing items from the menus and several promises of guaranteed satisfaction, Anandur put the phone down and headed to the bedroom to get dressed.

Lucky for him, Wonder wasn't a fancy dresser and liked him in jeans. Besides, it was all he had. Pairing them with a button-down dress shirt should do it.

The knock on the door came much sooner than he'd expected. "Room service," the waiter announced as Anandur opened the door.

"Come in." He took a step back to let the guy wheel the table inside.

"Would you like me to set the table for you, sir?"

"Please do."

Anandur had requested the whole romantic dinner package, including candles and flowers and a bottle of fine wine. Naturally, he'd also added fresh orange juice for Wonder. But setting it up nicely was above his skill level, especially if he wanted it ready before Wonder stepped out of the shower. A professional would do it much faster.

When the guy was done, the small table looked perfect. "Would you like me to stay and serve dinner, sir?"

"That won't be necessary."

"Very well. Could you sign here, sir?"

Anandur scribbled the fake name the room was reserved under and handed the guy his tip in cash. "Thank you."

The waiter's eyes widened at the generous amount of US dollars. "Thank you, sir," he said with a bow.

"You're welcome." Anandur opened the door and hastened the guy out.

The hairdryer's motor had been whining for a while now, which meant Wonder was almost done.

A minute or two after the waiter had left, he heard the bathroom door open, and a couple of seconds later Wonder sauntered into the living room.

It was most fortunate that the waiter was gone. For him.

Wonder's flimsy white nightgown was so sheer, Anandur could see every detail of the lacy pattern on the sexy bra and panties set she had underneath.

Beautiful didn't begin to describe her. His girl outshone every Victoria's Secret model he'd ever seen, and Anandur had seen them all, and not only in the catalogs Amanda had been saving for him. He'd been following the tall and busty beauties on the internet for years and knew each one by name.

But no more. He was done with that.

Uncharacteristically rendered mute, Anandur resorted to waving one hand over Wonder's perfectly proportioned statuesque body, while putting the other over his racing heart.

Wonder smiled. "Does that mean that you like what you see?"

He nodded like an idiot.

"I guess it means you do." She glanced at the table. "Are we having dinner first?"

No one could accuse Wonder of not being direct.

He pulled out a chair for her. "Yes, we are." Could he eat with his eyes closed?

Wonder glanced down at her nightgown, shook her head, then padded to the table and sat down.

As he pushed her chair in, Anandur wondered what that head shaking had been all about. Did she doubt the effect her sexy lingerie had on him?

"You look good enough to eat, lass, but I need to feed you first." He sat across from her and waggled his brows. "After I fatten you up, there will be more of you for me to devour."

With a wink, he uncorked the wine and poured it into their goblets. "Are you ready to try wine, or would you like me to pour you some orange juice?"

"I'll try the wine." She lifted the goblet and sniffed it. "It smells good."

"Cheers, love."

"Cheers." She took a tiny sip.

"Let's drink to old memories and new ones. May all of them be joyful." He winked again. "I plan on making a lot of new memories with you."

"I'll drink to that." Wonder clinked her glass to his.

As long moments passed with them cutting and chewing, Anandur tried to decide on the perfect time to tell Wonder that he loved her.

It would be a first for him, and probably the last.

Not the words themselves, he planned on repeating them many times over, but only to Wonder. It had taken him almost a millennium to fall in love, chances were it wouldn't happen again. Wonder was the one for him.

Except, he still hadn't figured out what was the right moment to do it. Who would've thought it would be so difficult.

Telling the woman he loved while chewing a steak was

as romantic as texting her the declaration. Should he wait until they were done?

Maybe over coffee?

"Would you like coffee after dinner?"

Wonder put her knife down. "Sure."

"How about dessert?"

She cast him a questioning glance. "If I didn't know better, I would've thought that you're trying to stall."

Anandur sighed and pushed his plate away. "I'm not stalling. I'm looking for the perfect moment."

"What is a perfect moment?" Her question wasn't mocking, it was sincere. But she hadn't asked him the more important one: a perfect moment for what?

Rubbing the back of his neck, he looked into her intense eyes and got lost for a moment. "I don't know. That's why I'm still searching."

Wonder wiped her mouth with the napkin and pushed to her feet. "I'm going to brush my teeth. Maybe you'll figure it out while I'm gone."

He nodded, watching the enticing sway of her perfect hips as she walked toward the bedroom.

Sexy tigress. That was his new nickname for her. It was sure better than virgin child.

The thing was, Wonder was both. The seductive walk was natural, it was a part of her innate femininity, not something she did consciously. The girl was too innocent for that, and it hadn't escaped his notice that her lingerie and nightgown were all white.

A bridal white. A virginal white.

He doubted she'd done it on purpose either. The white just looked great against her dark coloring.

Fates, he didn't know how to make it right for her.

Everything would've been so much simpler if Wonder weren't a virgin. He would've taken her to his bed after their first kiss.

Maybe he was just overthinking it.

Yeah, he definitely was.

Anandur put his fork and knife down, wiped his mouth, and pushed away from the table. The simplest way was the best. He was going to walk into that bathroom, pull Wonder into his arms and tell her he loved her.

Then he was going to lift her up and carry her to bed.

22

WONDER

*B*rushing her teeth had been a good excuse to run off before the stupid tears started running. Wonder had been so sure she looked sexy and desirable, but apparently it wasn't enough.

Or maybe it wasn't about that at all. Maybe it was about not wanting a woman who was still thinking about another guy.

What was the perfect moment Anandur was waiting for?

And what did he want to do at that moment? Tell her that he changed his mind? That he didn't want to be with her until she'd gotten Esag out of her head for good?

She should've never admitted to remembering more. That must've been what had caused Anandur's change of heart, and her comment about not being sure she'd loved Esag had apparently done nothing to mitigate the previous one about remembering having been attracted to him.

It had started so promisingly. After Anandur had made

that comment about eating her up after dinner, she'd gotten so excited imagining all the things he was going to do to her.

Had he changed his mind after that comment? Had he regretted making it?

That was what he must've been thinking during those long awkward moments of silence that had stretched between them over dinner. She'd convinced herself that it was nothing, and that Anandur was too hungry to carry on a conversation, but apparently his mind had been churning over Esag.

Sometimes, honesty wasn't the best option. She should've kept her mouth shut.

Damn it, she'd been so close. Now she would be going home the same as she'd left.

A virgin.

Ugh.

Grabbing a towel, she wiped her mouth. It was all minty fresh, except, much good that was going to do for her. It wasn't as if kisses were on her horizon tonight. The only question was who got to sleep in the big bed and who got the couch.

When the bathroom door opened, she expected Anandur to tell her that coffee had been delivered; she hadn't expected him to grab her elbow and turn her around.

"Come here, lass," he said as he crushed her against him and planted a hard, closed-mouth kiss on her lips. "I was looking for a perfect moment to say this, but I realized that any moment is a good one for what I have to say. I love you." He looked into her wide open eyes. "That's it. I said it. Now I'm taking you to bed." Anandur lifted her up and swung her around, so she was cradled in his arms.

For several seconds, Wonder was too stunned for words. Anandur loved her? That was what he'd been trying to say throughout the evening?

How had she misjudged his intentions so completely?

Wrapping her arms around his neck, she whispered, "I love you too."

He grinned down at her. "Good."

"That's it? Good?"

"Aye. I love you, and you love me, and we are going to make love. That's good, true?" He laid her down on the bed and sat next to her. "I know it's a pathetic declaration of love. I wanted it to be special, but it didn't work out. I planned a romantic candlelight dinner at the hotel's restaurant, and a relaxing massage, but you wanted none of that."

Gods, it was all her fault. In her rush, she'd spoiled Anandur's plans.

She lifted her hand to his cheek. "I'm sorry. Do you want to do all of that tomorrow? We can wait another day."

He chuckled. "Who's stalling now, lass?"

She lowered her eyelids and smiled. "I don't want to wait."

"Good, then take off this nightgown and lie on your tummy. I promised you a massage."

Oh, gods. It was finally happening.

"Okay." She pulled the nightgown over her head, tossed it on the floor, and flipped around to lie on her belly.

Anandur's big hand rested on the small of her back. "I'm going to unclasp your bra."

"Okay," she whispered.

He popped the clasp open and slid the shoulder straps down her arms. "Can you take it off for me?" He moved her hair to the side and kissed the back of her neck.

Without lifting up, Wonder pulled the bra out from under her, and then let it flutter down to the floor. All that remained were her panties, and that wasn't much coverage at all. Although not a true thong, the strip of lace in the back still left most of her butt cheeks bare.

"And now these." Anandur hooked his thumbs inside the elastic on both sides. "Lift up your beautiful bottom for me."

She did as she was told, feeling both incredibly exposed and aroused. It was good that her face was buried in a pillow. If she had to look at Anandur, she would've lost her nerve.

As he pulled the panties all the way down her legs, caressing every inch on the way, his strong hands were gentle. For such a big man, his touch was incredibly tender.

"Fates, just look at you," Anandur rasped as he cupped one butt cheek. "Perfection. I have never seen such a gorgeous ass." He cupped the other one and kneaded it lightly. "Guess which part I'm going to massage the longest?" Now both of his hands were cupping and kneading her cheeks. "There is a lot of tension here that needs my attention."

Regrettably, he had to abandon her bottom to squirt lotion into his palms. "I'm going to warm it up a bit." Bending down, he kissed each cheek, at the same time rubbing his hands together.

As she waited for them to return, Wonder bit on her lower lip.

She should've felt embarrassed about lying naked with her lady bits on full display for Anandur's eyes, especially since he was still fully dressed, but she didn't.

Wonder felt sexy, desired, loved, and more than ready to take this all the way to completion.

23

ANANDUR

*T*alk about restraint.

As Anandur rubbed the lotion between his palms, looking at the magnificence sprawled before him, the thoughts swirling in his head had nothing to do with massage. Not even a sensual one.

If Wonder weren't a virgin, he would've lifted her hips up, so that gorgeous heart-shaped ass was up in his face, and had gone for some feasting. And when she was ready to explode, he would've ridden her fast and hard until they both climaxed.

But that wasn't lovemaking.

Even though the scent of Wonder's arousal permeated the bedroom, and the hint of moisture between her legs beckoned him to taste her, she wasn't ready for that. Not for the feasting and not for the rough ride.

But it wasn't only about Wonder needing tenderness her first time, it was also about Anandur wanting to take his time with her and learn what she liked and what kind of touches she responded to and how.

He had a feeling Wonder would like it slow and easy, but he'd been wrong before.

Females were complicated creatures.

Looking at Callie, Anandur would've never guessed that she was into the kinky games his brother liked to play. And yet, the two seemed to live in perfect harmony, or as perfect as it ever got between two individuals sharing each other's lives.

The other possibility was that Brundar had made a complete one-eighty with Callie, but Anandur doubted that.

Bottom line, making assumptions based on superficial impressions was a mistake Anandur wasn't going to make. An exceptional lover was attuned to his partner's needs and made sure to fulfill them.

Wonder was his future, his one and only, and making things perfect between them was crucially important. Fate might have brought them together, but that didn't mean they had it made and no effort was required on their part.

Life just didn't work like that.

He wanted to know what excited her, which moves elicited the loudest moans, and which parts of her body were the most sensitive to touch.

Hopefully, she was responsive all over, because every inch of her was delectable. As if per his exact specifications, the girl was built on a generous scale, so there was no shortage of beautiful skin to caress and kiss and lick. He could spend hours learning every curve and dimple.

"All warmed up," Anandur said before putting his hands on her glorious ass. "Good?"

At the contact, she sucked in a breath. "Yeah, it feels good."

He was tempted to reach with his finger and touch her moist center, but it was too early for that. Instead, he slid his palms up her long torso, kneading muscles all the way to her tensed shoulders.

"Relax, sweetling," he murmured.

"I'm trying."

Poor lass, the anticipation was stressful, he got that. But it was part of the fun. "It's okay. I'll massage the tension away."

He slid his palms down her arms, massaging and kneading his way to her hands and then her fingertips.

Encouraged by her soft sighs and quiet moans, he spent a few minutes on her fingers. When he was done with that, he squirted another dollop of lotion into his palms and went to work on her legs.

As he slipped his hands dangerously close to her center and then continued downward, Wonder released a frustrated groan.

"Patience, love." He leaned and nipped one plump buttock.

Squirming a little as if wanting to get away, Wonder made a small sound of protest, and yet the scent of her arousal intensified.

He nipped the other one.

"Ouch." Her complaint didn't sound convincing.

"It was just a little nip. I can't help myself. This gorgeous butt is good enough to eat." He soothed and kneaded for a few moments.

"There is no way I'm going to relax like this," she murmured into the pillow.

"Then just enjoy. Concentrate on the feel of my hands

on you. I love exploring your magnificent body." He went back to massaging his way down to her calves.

She sighed. "I love your hands on me too. A lot. But the anticipation is killing me."

He grabbed one foot and started massaging her arch.

"Oh, that feels heavenly."

He leaned and kissed each cute little toe. "How about this?"

"Almost orgasmic, with emphasis on the almost."

He loved that she wasn't shy with him and was giving him some lip. Playfully, he slapped one butt cheek. "Watch it, young lady."

"Or what?" She wiggled her bottom at him.

"Or there'll be more of this," he slapped the other cheek. "Then this," he massaged the small sting away.

"Hmm, I kind of like the combination."

Fates, give me strength.

Wonder was a perfect blend of innocence and sass, and moment by moment she was losing the last of her inhibitions, which meant that he was doing something right. She felt safe to let go with him and be herself.

Her true self.

At this rate, he'd be ready to blow in no time, and that was despite taking care of business in the shower. Twice. But that was not what he had planned. The idea was for him to hold back for as long as he could and focus on his girl's pleasure.

Suddenly, he was gripped by the need to see her beautiful face. Would she be as bold when looking into his eyes?

What would her expression be? Coy? Teasing? Shy?

"Turn around, love."

Anandur held his breath as he waited for Wonder to do as he'd asked.

She took her time, hesitating for a long moment before slowly turning to lie on her back. He almost expected her to try and cover up her breasts, or her bare mound, but she did neither.

Her arms resting at her sides, Wonder gazed up at him, captivating him with the intensity of feeling in her mesmerizing jade eyes. Like twin green flashlights, they bathed his chest in soft illumination.

With an effort, Anandur tore his eyes away from that hypnotizing gaze to admire the rest of her.

His breath caught in his throat at the sight of long, smooth limbs, broad and yet delicate shoulders, and generous breasts that were tipped with dark, stiff nipples.

As if in a daze, his hands reached for them with no conscious thought on his part.

With a moan that sounded more like a whimper of relief leaving her parted lips, Wonder arched up, pushing her breasts into his palms.

Impatient girl.

As she looked up at him, her eyes sultry with desire, he fought hard to resist the need to give her everything she wanted. But he knew that the more he prolonged her anticipation, and the more aroused he got her, the easier it would be for Wonder to take him.

She was a big girl, which was very fortunate for both of them, but he was an exceptionally big male, and she was a virgin.

Patience and caution were the name of the game.

His restraint had to be strong enough for both of them.

24

WONDER

*E*very touch brought Wonder pleasure. Even the ones that had stung a bit. Was it because she was so aroused?

Or was it because it was Anandur who was touching her?

Everything she'd imagined about their coming together had been a little off. She hadn't anticipated that it would feel so right. There was supposed to be some awkwardness, or shyness on her part, but surprisingly there was none.

This was where she belonged, in Anandur's big muscular arms that were treating her with such tender care.

She felt safe with him. She felt at home with him, and it had nothing to do with location. Wherever he was, that was where home was.

Putting her hands over his on her breasts, she murmured, "I love you, Anandur. This is real."

"Oh, lass," he said as he dipped his head to kiss her. "I love you too."

Lowering himself on top of her, he took her mouth in a gentle kiss, careful so his fully extended fangs didn't injure her.

As if she cared about a little nick.

"Kiss me hard." She wrapped one arm around his neck and cradled the back of his head with the other, holding him to her as she deepened the kiss.

As he allowed her to take over where their mouths were fused, and their tongues were dueling, his hands on her breasts squeezed and teased and his fingers pinched her nipples.

There was no question who was in charge, and it was exactly the way Wonder wanted it. Except, she would've preferred him naked on top of her, so she could feel the hard press of his manhood on her skin and not through his jeans.

"Why are you still dressed?" Wonder whispered as she let go of his mouth.

His hands slid down her sides, skimming her hips and sliding around her inner thighs. "I'm keeping my pants on until I wrest the first orgasm out of you." His palm moved over her heated center and cupped her there.

Closing her eyes, she bit her lip to stifle a moan. "How many orgasms are you planning on wresting out of me?" Her question was supposed to sound teasing and confident, but it came out sounding needy and throaty.

His middle finger tapped over the most sensitive spot on her body. "As many as I can."

He wouldn't have to work hard for that. A few more taps, and she was going to explode like a firecracker.

Was it okay, though?

Would he think she was wanton? She'd heard guys at the club refer to women as sluts. But what did it mean? What was the definition of a slut?

Was it a woman who loved sex? And if yes, what was wrong with that? Didn't they all come to the club with that in mind?

Wonder didn't know much about men or how they thought, but according to Carol their brains functioned differently. It was hard to tell what went through guys' heads.

Except, Anandur had told her that he loved her, and she was pretty sure he'd been sincere. Didn't it mean that he accepted her the way she was?

Perhaps he would be happy that she was easy to please.

Sliding down her body, he kissed her nipple, and then the other one. "Perfect." He planted one more kiss on each before sliding further down.

Wonder tensed. What was he planning?

Pushing up on his knees, he put his hands under her knees and pulled her legs up, exposing her feminine center.

Suddenly self-conscious, Wonder tried to bring them back together.

"No, sweetling, you don't hide from me." With a hand on each knee, Anandur pushed her legs apart. Lowering his face to the underside of one, he nipped the soft skin there.

Was he punishing her for initially resisting?

If that had been his intention, then he was missing the mark because the little sting only heightened her arousal.

After licking the sting away, he kissed the spot and continued his trek up the inside of her thigh, nipping and licking and kissing on his way to her center.

Again, Wonder tried to close her thighs, the impulse to do so more instinctive than deliberate. She had a vague idea of where Anandur was going with that, she wasn't completely ignorant, but for some reason, her subconscious was resisting.

It seemed like too much, too close, too soon.

He nipped her inner thigh in warning. "Don't. This is mine."

She shivered as he blew on her wet folds. "You're just as beautiful down here as everywhere else." He planted an open-mouthed kiss on her lower lips. "You should see yourself. Your petals are blooming for me, opening in invitation. It's a wonderful sight to behold." He lifted his face and smiled. "Like all of my Wonder."

Well, if he thought she looked pretty there, Wonder wasn't going to argue.

Relaxing, she released the tightness that had gripped her bottom, letting it rest on the mattress.

"That's better." Anandur dipped his head back down.

When the first lick over the side of her wet folds wrestled an uncontrollable jerk from her, Anandur's hands clamped on both sides of her inner thighs, holding her in place. "Easy, sweetling, just relax and enjoy the ride. I promise it's going to be good."

Something in his soothing richly dark tone did the trick, allowing her to ease back and surrender to the pleasure.

After all, Anandur always kept his promises. Besides, this man was her future. He was her mate. There was no need to feel shy around him, or apprehensive. He could see all of her and touch whatever he wanted in any way he pleased.

In turn, when the time came and she gained some experience, she was going to do the same to him.

Parting her folds with several tender strokes, Anandur used just the tip of his tongue to flick at that sensitive bundle of nerves at the top of her slit.

When he flattened it over her entire entrance, Wonder's eyes rolled back in her head, and she let her knees fall apart, no longer caring if it made her seem lewd.

Anandur's deep-throated groan was the only warning she got before his tongue speared into her. Caught off guard, she arched against him, her fingers threading into his curly hair.

Low in her belly, the coil was tightening at a breakneck speed, ready to spring free at any moment.

"Anandur," she whispered in a desperate plea for that elusive touch that would set it free, catapulting her over the edge.

25

ANANDUR

*D*espite Anandur's gripping hold on Wonder's thighs, her hips were gyrating uncontrollably. She was such a strong lass. Her release was going to be magnificent.

Anandur would've liked to prolong the build-up some more, but the truth was that he was at the end of his rope as well. Once Wonder reached her climax, she would be ready for him.

Teasing her entrance with his fingers, he worked one inside. When she moaned and arched her back, asking for more, he withdrew and returned with two.

If she weren't a virgin, he was sure Wonder would've climaxed the moment he penetrated her with his fingers, but she was so tight that even the two digits were a stretch for her untried sheath.

How the hell was she going to take his shaft?

Gently pumping, he flicked his tongue over her clit, once, twice, and as more moisture coated his fingers, he curled them, pressing the tips against that special rough-ened spot on the wall of her channel.

"Anandur," she groaned. "I'm so close."

Thank the merciful Fates.

As he thrust his fingers deeper inside her, he closed his lips over her clit and sucked it in gently.

Her channel tightening hungrily around his digits, Wonder threw her head back and uttered a soft cry as an outpour of wetness coated them with her essence.

His cock twitched painfully, desperate to be where his fingers were.

But he had to take this slow. He had to make Wonder's first time so memorable that she would get hot and both-ered every time she thought about it even a hundred years from now.

A thousand.

He had to make this blissful expression on her beautiful face last throughout her virgin voyage. No grimace was going to mar it. Not if he could prevent it.

Helping Wonder ride out her climax, he gently pumped in and out of her until her shudders subsided.

When she opened her eyes and smiled contentedly, he knew she was ready for him. "Anandur," she whispered his name with awe in her voice.

And wasn't that enough to make him grow a few inches taller? And longer?

"My Wonder." Awash with feelings, he planted a soft kiss to her quivering flesh before pushing back to his knees.

With a hard yank he pulled his shirt over his head and sent it flying to the floor, then he pushed down his jeans and kicked them off. With a soft thud, they landed some-where behind him.

Her eyes widened as he fisted his cock.

"Don't be afraid, sweetling, I'll go slow."

"I'm not afraid," she whispered. "I want you."

After rubbing the crown up and down her drenched folds until it was covered in her juices, he placed it against her entrance and applied the slightest of pressures.

She tensed, her hands fisting the bed sheet beneath her.

Leaning over her, he rested his elbow beside her head and kissed her gently, tenderly, while running the swollen head of his shaft up and down her slit some more. When she relaxed under him, he pushed a fraction of an inch inside her, looking into her eyes for any signs of distress.

"Good?" he rasped.

She nodded.

With a Herculean effort, Anandur forced himself to inch into her slowly, excruciatingly so, until he reached the barrier and stopped. Before surging past it, he needed to let Wonder get accustomed to the invasion. The more patient he was, the less pain she was going to experience when he broke through.

A long moment passed with Wonder's harsh breaths the only sounds disturbing the silence.

As he fought to hold still, muscles quivering from the effort and sweat pouring out of him as if he was running a double marathon in the Egyptian desert, Anandur gritted his teeth. "Are you okay, lass? Am I hurting you?"

She shook her head, but Anandur wasn't sure which part of his question she was answering. Did the shaking mean that she wasn't okay, or did it mean that he wasn't hurting her?

When her hips stirred beneath him, he got his answer.

Pushing one hand under her bottom, he angled her up before surging inside her with one powerful thrust.

As the barrier broke, Wonder cried out, and there was no mistaking the anguish in that cry. She was in pain.

With tears pooling at the corners of her eyes, Wonder put her hands on his chest and pushed. "Get off me!"

She was strong, stronger than many of the guys he'd subdued on the training mat, but Anandur held on, his hand under her buttocks preventing her from bucking him off.

Fates, how he hated causing her pain even for a moment. He had to remind himself that Wonder was an immortal and that her pain would not last long.

"I'm so sorry, lass." He dipped his head and kissed her eyes, then licked the salty tears away. "It's going to get better in a moment. I promise."

That was the beauty of her immortal body. It would adjust, and her discomfort would ebb in a matter of seconds.

Breathing in and out through clenched teeth, she nodded.

He waited until the tension in her body started to ease. "Better?"

"Yeah." She let out a long breath.

"Thank the merciful Fates." He kissed her again but didn't start moving. When he felt her buttocks unclench in his hand, he asked, "Ready for more?"

"Go slow."

"I will, love." He pulled out just a bit, rocking himself gently inside her.

After a few moments of that, she whispered, "More."

Rising on straightened arms, Anandur pulled almost all the way out, but instead of surging inside her, he inched back. Sweat dripped from his forehead, and his arms shook from the effort to hold back, but he was adamant about giving her the time she needed to adjust. It was well worth the struggle if he managed to make Wonder climax on her virgin voyage.

She moaned when he withdrew again, and then cried out when he drove deep inside her, but this time it wasn't a cry of pain, but one of pleasure.

Once more he withdrew and drove back inside her, elation sweeping through him as Wonder lifted up to meet him halfway.

"Yes, love, just like this." Gradually increasing the tempo, he gazed into her eyes, making sure she was right there with him for the ride.

26

WONDER

*W*onder had been mentally prepared for pain and lots of it, but the reality was so much better than what she'd braced for.

After her climax, she'd been so aroused and so ready for Anandur to join them, that the initial stretch had felt only slightly uncomfortable, and she'd even mused that the hardships of a girl's first time were greatly exaggerated.

But when he'd pushed through her virgin barrier, the pain was so sharp it brought tears to her eyes. Her prior conviction that she could brace through the experience evaporated together with what was left of her post orgasmic bliss.

The penetration burned. There was nothing pleasant about it, not even the feel of Anandur's chest on top of hers. Despite her resolve to bear through it, her hands instinctively rose to push him away and her hips lifted in an attempt to buck him off.

His huge shaft felt like an iron rod that had been heated

up and was now scorching the delicate tissue of her channel. She needed him to pull out right away.

"Get off me!"

But he was ready for her, holding on tight with a hand under her bottom. "I'm so sorry, lass." There was real regret in his eyes, and his fangs had retracted to half of their fully extended size. He dipped his head and kissed her tears away. "It's going to get better in a moment. I promise."

She believed him. Anandur always kept his promises.

With every muscle in her body coiled tight, Wonder breathed through the pain. One breath, two, three…

Long moments passed with Anandur holding himself still, his powerful arms shaking and sweat pouring out of him from the exertion.

At those moments, she hated and loved him at the same time.

Just as he'd promised, though, with each consecutive breath the pain diminished a little more, until there was nothing left of it but a feeling of incredible fullness.

Slowly, her muscles loosened and her bottom started unclenching in Anandur's grip.

It had taken mere seconds for the pain of losing her virginity to subside to a tolerable level, and throughout all that time she was quite sure Anandur hadn't breathed at all.

Now that she was no longer suffering, he sucked in a breath and then let it out in a whoosh. "Better?" he asked.

"Yeah." She let out a long breath.

"Thank the merciful Fates." He kissed her. "Ready for more?"

She wasn't sure but nodded anyway. "Go slow."

"I will, love."

His big body on top of hers, he braced most of his weight on his forearms, letting her feel only a fraction of it as he pulled out a little, and then pushed back. More rocking than thrusting, he was letting her get used to the sensation.

Slowly, the pleasure started building up again. "More," she breathed.

Lifting up on straightened arms, he gazed into her eyes as he pulled out, and then slowly pushed back into her.

With his fangs once more fully elongated, and his eyes blazing, he looked magnificent, a powerful immortal male who was fighting his natural instincts to ensure her pleasure.

She cried out when he surged inside her on his next thrust, but not in pain. It felt good.

As always, Anandur had kept his promise. With the discomfort gone, her pleasure mounted despite the tight fit.

Heart swelling with love and gratitude, Wonder lifted up to meet Anandur's increasingly hard thrusts.

"Yes, love, just like this."

Wrapping her arms around him, she brought his chest down to hers. It was slick with perspiration, but she didn't mind. The feeling of closeness was incredible.

For a few moments, they rocked together like that, but then Anandur lifted his head and the expression on his face scared and excited her at the same time. The tenderness from before was gone, replaced by savage need.

She wanted it, was ready for the wild ride that he was about to give her. Anandur had been holding back for her, but the time for restraint was over.

Wonder was about to experience his full power unleashed.

Guiding her arms over her head, he threaded his fingers through hers. She could've gotten free if she wanted to, but why would she? This was good.

"I love you," she murmured into his neck.

With a groan, he pinned their entwined hands to the mattress as the tempo and power of his thrusts increased.

Wonder was powerless to do more than receive the pounding. Even lifting up to meet him halfway was impossible because he was driving into her with such incredible force.

Unexpectedly, the coil deep in her belly started winding up again, another explosive climax building up momentum.

"Anandur," she groaned as the tightness became unbearable. "I need…" She didn't know what to ask for.

He hissed against her neck, his tongue flicking over the spot he was going to sink his fangs into. Locking her head between their joined hands, he immobilized it for his bite.

A split moment later, she felt the sharp burn of twin incisors piercing her neck, followed by Anandur's seed exploding into her. The coil sprang free, and an orgasm crashed over her before the first drop of venom had a chance to enter her system.

When it did, she climaxed again, and again.

27

NICK

S hoving the vacuum cleaner into the closet, Nick glanced at Ruth, then walked up to her and dipped his head to take a sniff of the sauce she was stirring in a large pot.

Spaghetti Bolognese, one of his favorite dishes.

"Not that I mind, but why did you invite guests for dinner again? The other one was only the day before yesterday."

Ruth paused the stirring and shifted to her other foot. "I'm doing it for Brundar. He needs to make friends."

That was a worthy goal, and an ambitious one. It was hard to make friends without talking. The dude was weird.

"Why is he like that? And what's his deal with shaking hands? Is he a germophobe?"

Ruth shrugged. "No one knows. I guess it's the result of some childhood trauma. Brundar doesn't talk about it. Or maybe it's PTSD."

That made more sense. The guy was pretty like a store mannequin, and just as animated, but he had a deadly vibe about him that was hard not to notice. A commando, no doubt.

"Where did he serve?"

She waved with the wooden spoon. "No one knows that either."

"He must be Special Forces."

"Yeah, I think so. Anyway, I thought it would do him good to spend time with friendly, outgoing people. That's why I invited Roni the other time, and today I invited Jackson and Tessa."

Calling Roni friendly was a stretch. Nick liked the dude, but Roni was sarcastic and offensive and probably pushed most people away and not the other way around.

But whatever. If Ruth wanted to help out her cousin, that was cool with him. Maybe he could get Brundar to talk about his missions, provided some of them weren't classified.

Brundar and Callie arrived right on time, the knock on the door sounding on the dot of seven with a military precision.

Jackson and Tessa showed up ten minutes late.

"Let's get right to it," Ruth said, herding everyone to the table. "Before the spaghetti gets mushy."

"Delicious," Tessa said after wiping her mouth with the napkin. "I'm not a pasta lover, but you might have made a convert out of me."

"My pleasure," Ruth said.

"Scotch?" Brundar said his first word of the evening.

"Not for me." Nick wasn't going to fall for that again.

"Jackson?" Brundar asked.

"I don't like scotch. What else is there to drink?"

"I can make you vodka cranberry," Ruth offered.

"Sounds good."

"I'd like one too," Tessa said.

That was a surprise. As far as Nick knew, Tessa only drank wine and not much of it. "Since when do you drink vodka?"

"Since I discovered it tastes great when mixed with something else. I love screwdrivers. Do you have orange juice, Ruth?"

"I do." Ruth started to push to her feet.

Nick put a hand on her shoulder. "I'll get it."

"No, that's okay, I'll do it." She practically flicked his hand off and made a dash for the kitchen.

What was going on with her?

She'd been acting strange lately, jumpy as hell and avoiding looking into his eyes, but Nick couldn't figure out why. Add to the mix the frequent dinner get-togethers she was arranging, and he was certain something was up.

But what?

They hadn't had a fight, the café was doing well, and she wasn't on her period. In fact, Ruth didn't get them at all. She'd told him that her contraceptive eliminated them entirely.

Which was great. Nick still remembered how everyone had to tiptoe around Sharon when she'd been getting hers. Thankfully, she'd found something that fixed it for her, so they didn't have to deal with her crankiness every month. Tessa had never made a fuss, and Eva, well, Eva was an alien from another planet.

A very pregnant alien.

A moment later Ruth returned with the two juice bottles. "Here is the orange juice, and the cranberry juice. Which one do you prefer, Tessa?"

"The orange juice."

"I'd like the cranberry," Jackson said. "But let me mix the drinks. You've worked hard enough making dinner."

For some reason, Ruth didn't object to Jackson's offer.

"Let me mix you one too, Nick. You can't be the only one not drinking. What's the fun in that?"

Talk about peer pressure. "Fine, but make it light. I don't want a repeat of what happened at the other dinner."

Mixing the drink for Tessa, Jackson lifted a brow. "What happened?"

"They got me drunk, that's what happened. I blacked out."

"Who are they?" Jackson handed Tessa her drink and started with the next.

"Brundar." Nick pointed at the blond. "And Roni. They kept toasting to everything under the sun. And let me tell you, Ruth and Sylvia must have some Irish blood in them because they kept up no problem."

"Scottish," Ruth said. "We have quite a tolerance."

"Roni is not a Scot." Nick was quite sure of that.

"Maybe he has some Irish in him," Tessa suggested.

"Germans drink a lot too." Jackson finished making the two cranberry cocktails and handed one to Nick.

"The British. More than the Germans." Brundar surprised everyone by offering his opinion. "Also the Brazilians and the Dutch."

Nick took a small sip from his drink, adamant about going slow and not getting goaded into having more than one. "I see that you've researched the issue."

Brundar shrugged. "I co-own a club. I see all kinds."

That was the biggest surprise of the evening. Brundar

the Special Forces dude, or even Brundar the undercover spy, Nick could believe. But a club owner?

"What kind of a club is that?"

"A nightclub," Callie said. "I serve drinks at the club, and I have to agree with Brundar. Germans are light-weights compared to the Brits."

"I wonder why that is," Ruth said while sipping on her own cocktail. "It must be something genetic."

As the discussion about alcohol tolerance continued, Nick absentmindedly finished his drink and was immediately handed another by Jackson.

"I made it light for you," the guy said, making it impossible to refuse.

With an inward groan, Nick took the glass.

He ended up having three, which should've been okay, but by the end of the evening, his eyes started to droop. It felt more like being tired than drunk, and sleepy.

Maybe it was the food. He'd had two heaping helpings of the spaghetti and then two big slices of the tiramisu. Was it possible that he was a diabetic?

"I don't feel so good," he said. "I think I ate way too much."

"Do you need to barf?" Jackson pushed away from the table and walked around to where Nick was sitting. "Let me help you to the bathroom."

"No, that's okay. I'm not nauseous, just tired." He was feeling faint, but to admit that would've been too embarrassing.

A young guy like him should be able to tolerate a couple of diluted cocktails and a big meal.

"Let me help you to the bedroom, then." Jackson moved to wrap his arm around Nick's torso.

Pushing his arm away, Nick stood up on shaky legs. "I can make it to the bedroom on my own."

"As you wish, dude."

"I'll turn the bed down." Ruth jumped to his side.

Nick wanted to tell her to stay, but the truth was that he wasn't sure he'd make it. The dizziness was intensifying by the minute.

When they got to the bedroom, he dropped on the bed before Ruth had the chance to remove the coverlet. "Just let me sleep a little."

"It's okay, Nicki. Good night." She kissed his cheek.

He was still semi-conscious when Ruth turned off the light and closed the bedroom door. It crossed his mind that it was strange that she hadn't seemed worried by what was happening to him.

Maybe she didn't know what symptoms diabetics exhibited. Not everyone spent hours a day watching random YouTube videos.

ANANDUR

*W*onder took a long gulp from the water bottle, then handed it to Anandur. "I think we should go straight to the hotel and save the sightseeing for tomorrow. It's getting dark."

"It was a long day, but we can still squeeze in the *Colossi of Memnon*." Steering with one hand, he drank his fill before returning the bottle to her. "We'll have a quick look, take a few pictures with the statues, and then continue to the hotel."

"Okay." She screwed the lid back on the bottle and put it inside the cooler bag.

Anandur waited patiently until she was done, then took her hand, brought it to his lips for a kiss, put it on his thigh, and covered it with his.

Unless he was touching her in some way, a feeling of irrational unease started churning in his stomach, intensifying until he made contact with her again.

It had been like that since they'd left the hotel in the morning, and all during the long hours of driving south from Alexandria to Luxor, including the stop at Abydos to visit the monuments there.

Fourteen hours in total, during which Anandur had trouble thinking of anything other than getting Wonder naked as soon as possible.

So yeah, he was an old lecher, but it wasn't as if Wonder was going to object. The lass seemed just as impatient for him as he was for her.

The ruins in Abydos had provided plenty of nooks and crannies for the two of them to kiss and neck away from prying eyes. In a backward country like Egypt, such behavior would not have been tolerated, and Anandur didn't want to get his hands dirty beating up opinionated humans during his vacation.

Heck, it was much more than a vacation. It felt like a honeymoon.

Except for the wedding, all the ingredients were there. A couple in love, first lovemaking, luxury hotels, and fascinating sights.

Anandur was spending more on this vacation than he'd spent in his entire long life on everything he'd ever bought, and it was worth every penny. Pampering Wonder was his prerogative, it was his duty and his pleasure. The amount of satisfaction he was deriving from that rivaled that of his Guardian job, which until now had been the primary source of his self-esteem, and what had defined him as a person.

Now, he was Wonder's mate first and a Guardian second.

Did Brundar feel the same about Callie? Probably.

Why the hell hadn't the tight-lipped bastard said anything?

Most likely because Anandur wouldn't have understood and would've made fun of him for being a lovesick sap.

Casting a sidelong glance at Wonder, he caught her smiling again. She'd been doing it a lot since last night, which meant that she had loved their lovemaking.

It was quite an accomplishment, if he said so himself.

Tonight, he was going to show her that this was just the beginning, and that she still had a lot to learn about all the ways he could pleasure her.

Damn, he shouldn't have gone there. Now his stiff shaft was wedged uncomfortably, and he had to release Wonder's hand to rearrange himself.

She glanced down at his crotch. "What were you thinking about just now?"

"I'll give you one guess."

Her eyes widened in mock innocence. "Me?"

"No, the Queen of England. Of course, you."

She pouted. "That's why I wanted to head straight to the hotel. You were the one who wanted to stop for sightseeing."

He retook her hand and kissed the back of it. "All in good time, lass. The anticipation is half the fun."

An evil smirk lifting the corners of her mouth, she breathed, "Oh, yeah? Tell me all the wicked things you're going to do to me so I'll know what to anticipate." She enunciated the last word.

"Minx. Your delectable ass is in danger of getting spanked for mercilessly teasing an old man."

The smirk turned into a full-on grin. "I'm counting on it."

With a groan, he shifted in his seat. "Ugh, lass. You're killing me."

A satisfied expression on her beautiful face, Wonder got comfortable in the passenger chair. "You'll live. How far to those statues you just have to see?"

"We are almost there." He pointed with his chin at the road sign. "It's the next exit."

Due to the late hour, there were only a few cars in the parking lot when they arrived. His tiny pocket camera in hand, Anandur got out of the car and circled around to open the door for Wonder. As usual, she didn't wait for him to do the honors.

"Can you let me be a gentleman and wait for me to open the door for you?"

"It's silly. I don't need help getting out of the car."

"True." He took her hand. "You don't need help with most things, but it's my pleasure to offer it."

"So what are you saying, that I need to do it for you?"

She was right. It was silly and old-fashioned. Except, it made him uncomfortable every time she did that. Maybe he was the one who needed to adjust, not her.

"No, lass, I don't want you doing anything you're uncomfortable with. I'm the old fart who still lives by outdated rules of conduct."

She stopped and turned to him, then wrapped her arm around his neck and brought him down to her for a kiss. "Stop saying that you're old. And if it makes you happy to open the door for me, I can wait for you to do that." She lifted a finger. "On one condition."

"Name it."

"You kiss me every time you give me a hand up."

Like that was a tough bargain. "Done."

Strolling hand in hand, they approached the nearly sixty-foot-tall mammoth statues. In the past, the two depictions of King Amenhotep III had guarded the king's temple. But very little remained of the once impressive structure, and the statues' faces had suffered significant damage.

Regrettably, the destruction had happened long before Anandur's birth, so even if he'd had a chance to visit, he would not have seen much more than he saw now.

"Let me take a picture of you. Stand over there," he directed Wonder in front of one of the statues.

"Is here good?"

"Perfect." He started snapping photos when a prickling sensation in the back of his neck had him look over his shoulder.

Several tourists were milling around, taking pictures and conversing in a number of languages. None looked threatening or acted strange, and yet that slight prickling wasn't going away.

Just to be safe, he strode over to Wonder and wrapped his arm around her waist.

"What happened? You look worried."

"I felt something." He rubbed the back of his neck. "Do you feel anything?"

She looked up at him. "What should I pay attention to?"

He leaned to whisper in her ear. "Remember what you told me about sensing immortals? That."

Wonder glanced around. "I don't feel anything," she whispered back. "But that doesn't mean there are none. I need to be really close to sense their otherness. Besides, I think it got numbed after spending time in the village and being exposed to so many."

"Let's go back to the car. If you feel anything on the way, let me know."

"Okay."

Taking a meandering route to the parking lot, Anandur made sure to pass by as many of the groups of tourists as he could without it looking suspicious, but the tingling sensation didn't intensify next to any of them, and eventually it subsided completely.

"Anything?" Wonder asked as he turned on the engine.

"Nope. Must've been something else that caused it. My neck is so sweaty and dusty that it might have been a reaction to that."

29

WONDER

"Wow, Anandur, this hotel is even fancier than the Four Seasons," Wonder said as they entered the lobby.

Once again she was grateful for Amanda's generous donation of designer outfits and accessories. Wearing her own clothes, even the new ones she'd bought for the trip, Wonder would've felt like one of the maids instead of a guest.

Anandur, on the other hand, acted as if he owned the place, even though he was wearing his usual attire of jeans and T-shirt. Not that he didn't look awesome. The teal color of the shirt worked well with his reddish skin tone and fiery hair.

He was such a handsome man, and so impressive, that fancy clothing was unnecessary to make him stand out. Add to that his charm, and everyone at reception was bending over backwards to please him.

Then again, they could've thought he was some eccentric billionaire or a famous actor on vacation.

"Right this way, sir, madam." The guy from reception escorted them to their room, pointing out the various hotel amenities on the way.

He even opened the door for them but didn't come in. "Your luggage will be delivered momentarily. May I order anything for you from the bar or one of our restaurants?"

"No, thank you." Anandur's body language made it clear that he wanted the guy gone as soon as possible.

"Very well, enjoy your stay at the Sofitel."

"Talkative fellow," Anandur said as he closed the door. "I think he just wanted to look at you some more. The dude couldn't take his eyes off you. Lucky for him, he focused on your face. If I'd caught him looking at your cleavage, I would have provided him with a new face free of charge."

Wonder hadn't noticed the guy looking at her. Anandur must've been imagining it. Still, she liked that he was jealous and protective of her.

"It's quite a room." She glanced around.

The ceilings were at least eighteen feet high, and it was generously sized, with enough space for a large bed and a sitting area. It wasn't a suite like in the Four Seasons, but the furniture was fit for a king. Or a queen.

Crossing the room in three long strides, Anandur opened the door to the bathroom. "Come and take a look at this."

"It's very nice." The bathroom, although featuring modern facilities, was made to look old-fashioned like the bedroom, with gold-plated faucets and gold-trimmed mirrors and vanities with curling legs.

It seemed, though, that Anandur hadn't been referring to the decorative elements, but to the large, glass-enclosed shower. "Big enough for two." He waggled his brows.

A knock on the door prevented her from picking up the banter.

Their luggage had arrived.

Anandur tipped the guy and promptly kicked him out.

"Now, where were we?"

She arched a brow. "Shower?"

"Oh, yeah," he said as if he'd forgotten. "I made dinner reservations for nine, which gives us roughly an hour to get ready." He shook his head. "I'm afraid we will have to share the shower if we want to make it on time."

An hour was plenty of time for both of them to shower separately and to get dressed. Wonder was inexperienced, but not so utterly naive as to not get his meaning.

Except, she liked messing with the big guy. Pranking the prankster was fun, even if she wasn't all that good at it yet. Practice would take care of that.

"Maybe you can call the restaurant and change the reservation to ten? That would give us plenty of time to get ready without having to share the shower."

He looked almost comical as his face fell. Like a little boy who was denied his favorite toy. "I can try. But they might be closing the kitchen at ten."

She cracked up. "Just kidding. I would love to share a shower with you. Come here, big guy." She wrapped her arms around his neck and lifted her chin. "Kiss me."

"We might never make it to the shower."

"It's a chance I'm willing to take."

The kiss quickly turned into a mad scramble to get naked without tearing their clothes off each other.

Anandur almost fell on his ass as he tried to pull off his

pants while unbuttoning her blouse, and her hair got tangled in the straps of her bra.

"Sorry, lass." Anandur gently untangled the strand from the strap and dropped the garment on top of the pile of clothes on the floor.

Mission accomplished, they stood bare in each other's arms, skin touching skin. It felt incredible to keep on kissing while caressing the hard contours of Anandur's muscular body.

Lifting her up, he carried her inside the shower and turned the water on. "Are we washing your hair, love?"

"Yes."

He grinned as if she'd given him a precious gift. "I've never done that before." Sitting on the bench, he pulled her down onto his lap and reached for the shampoo.

Was that what he wanted to do? Wash her hair?

It was a nice gesture, but Wonder had been hoping for something else and felt a little disappointed.

Unless it was payback for before and he was teasing her. In that case, she was going to play along. "First, you need to wet my hair thoroughly, and only when it's sopping wet, gently massage in the shampoo."

Careful not to spray water in her eyes, he pulled her head back against his chest. Using the handle, he wetted her hair.

Surrendering to Anandur's gentle ministrations, Wonder closed her eyes. Having him wash her hair felt amazing, much better than she'd expected. She felt taken care of, cherished, and loved.

"Am I doing this right?" he whispered in her ear, the hot air from his mouth tickling the sensitive skin.

"Perfect."

As he rinsed out the shampoo and then repeated the process, Wonder concentrated on the feel of his strong fingers massaging her scalp, thinking that all he was going to do was just wash her. She almost dozed off when he rinsed her hair again and smoothed conditioner onto her long strands.

He pressed a gentle kiss to her neck. "Now I'm going to soap you all over, sweetling. Are you ready for that?"

"Yes, please."

"So polite." He hooked a finger under her chin and turned her face to him for a kiss.

By the glow in his eyes and the size of his fangs, Anandur had more than soaping on his mind.

Which was fine with her.

Rubbing the body wash between his palms, he kissed her neck and then palmed the undersides of her breasts.

Slowly, he circled her soapy mounds but avoided her stiff nipples.

Wonder let out a frustrated groan.

Breathing into her ear, he nipped at her earlobe and then licked the spot to soothe the sting. "Tell me what you need, love."

In response, she reached for his palms and pushed them up to cover her achy peaks, a relieved sigh leaving her throat at finally having the contact she needed.

But then the annoying man did nothing, just cupping her breasts and nuzzling her neck.

Ugh, he wasn't going to give her what she wanted unless she asked for it. Why was he playing games with her?

Giving him another moment to see if he'd do what she wanted him to, Wonder couldn't decide if she hated this game or loved it. On the one hand, she didn't want to have to ask, but on the other hand, being coerced into doing so was kind of exciting.

Why?

No clue.

Except, Anandur probably knew exactly what he was doing, and she trusted him. He wouldn't do anything just to annoy her, he had a game plan in mind, and Wonder had no doubt that his end goal was maximizing her pleasure.

Squeezing her eyes closed, she blurted, "I need you to touch my nipples."

He rewarded her with a soft kiss on her neck. "That's my girl." He thumbed her stiff peaks and then pinched them lightly. "Like this?" His hot breath fanned over her ear.

"Yes, more."

Chuckling, he lifted her and turned her sideways on his lap, then dipped his head to pull one nub into his mouth. Sucking on it gently, he alternated with hard flicks of his tongue.

"Yes, just like that."

As he switched to take care of the other one, his hand cupped her sex, just resting there and not applying the pressure she needed.

Wonder moaned, grinding her hips over his hard, pulsating shaft. Anandur was just as aroused as she was, so maybe the added friction would prompt him to stop playing games. She was losing patience. Besides, they had dinner reservations so he couldn't drag it out indefinitely.

Maybe she should take the lead and straddle him?

He wouldn't mind, right?

The idea seemed good only until Anandur's fingers

started circling her wet folds, and as they got closer and closer to where she needed them most, Wonder couldn't concentrate on anything else. Between the suction on her breast and the delicious things he was doing down below, her climax was imminent.

When he pushed two fingers inside her channel and then pressed the heel of his palm to that most sensitive spot, there was no more holding back the intense wave of pleasure washing over her.

She bucked up, throwing her head back against his shoulder on a silent scream.

"Oh, lass." Anandur sounded as if he was grateful that she'd orgasmed for him, then took her mouth in the most tender of kisses.

Was he the best, or what?

The affirmation came a moment later.

Lifting her up with one strong arm, he then lowered her onto his shaft, filling her so completely and so deliciously that her ebbing pleasure shot up, and she nearly orgasmed again just from that.

"Anandur," she groaned.

Sitting on his lap, impaled on his manhood, there was little she could do except gyrate her bottom in invitation. Anandur didn't need much prompting, though. Holding her in his strong arms, he lifted and lowered her in an ever increasing, untiring tempo, hitting the end of her channel with each powerful thrust.

She was hovering over the edge, her sheath grabbing onto the hot length swelling inside her and stretching her further than she thought possible.

They were both so close.

This was when he was going to bite her, and that thought alone was enough to trigger her second orgasm.

Through her blissed-out haze, Wonder heard Anandur hiss a moment before his seed shot into her and his fangs locked on the spot where her neck met her shoulder.

As another climax hit her hard and fast, she shouted his name, her body convulsing uncontrollably until the venom's euphoric effect loosened her limbs, turning them into goo.

30

ANANDUR

a towel perching precariously over her breasts, Wonder brushed out her wet hair. "How about you cancel the reservation and order dinner delivered here? We can eat on the balcony."

They had barely ten minutes to get ready, and the damn towel was just begging for him to grab it and yank it off, but Anandur was adamant about having the romantic dinner he had planned for the day before.

As much as he would have loved having another round with Wonder, in bed this time, he wasn't a randy teenager. He could wait for after dinner.

Then, he was going to treat himself to some dessert and Anandur wasn't thinking of cake or ice cream. Although on second thought, there were some naughty things he could do to Wonder with that.

Stop it. If he didn't banish these thoughts from his brain, they weren't going to make it to the restaurant tonight.

"You're not wiggling out of it again, love." He waved a hand. "Put on something nice, and let's go."

She grimaced. "I didn't bring a dress."

So that was her problem. Tomorrow he was going to take Wonder shopping for one. "There is no rule that says you have to wear a dress to a fancy restaurant. Pants are fine."

Sighing dramatically, she lifted the hairdryer and turned it on. Then turned it off again. "Do you have anything other than jeans? I may not know much, but I'm sure jeans are not appropriate for a restaurant in a place like this."

"Nope, but don't worry. They are not going to turn us away."

He had a pair of black jeans that weren't faded yet. That and one of Dalhu's designer button-down shirts would do just fine.

Waiting for Wonder to get ready, Anandur checked his emails, texted Brundar to ask for updates, and sent a few of the pictures he'd taken of the attractions they'd visited to Callie and to his mother.

Helena had been overjoyed to hear that he too had found someone, but she hadn't offered to come for a visit. Wasn't she curious about Callie and Wonder?

Perhaps she was waiting for an invitation. Or what was more likely, it hadn't crossed his mother's mind. It wasn't as if there was a protocol in place for this like there was for humans. It wasn't a common occurrence for clan members to find mates. This was all new.

But didn't that make it all the more exciting?

If Anandur had a child, and that child found his or her mate, he would've wanted to meet him or her. Hell, if one of his friends, or any clan member for that matter, found a mate, Anandur wanted to meet that person. Happy news wasn't so frequent as to get trivialized.

But then Helena was different. The woman wasn't the motherly type. Whether it was because she was self-absorbed or just scatterbrained, he wasn't sure. But since she was his mother, and he loved her, Anandur had to believe it was the latter and not the former.

"I'm ready." Wonder walked out of the bathroom with her hair cascading in soft waves around her shoulders, wearing a white silk blouse over tight black pants. Gold-colored, flat-soled sandals adorned her pretty feet.

He got up. "You look beautiful."

She gave him an appreciative once-over. "You look very handsome yourself." She waved a hand between them. "We color-match."

Wrapping his arm around her shoulder, he led her out the door. "We match, period. A perfect fit." He kissed the top of her head.

Down in the restaurant, the host didn't bat an eyelash at their attire, but he did sneak furtive glances at Wonder.

As usual, she didn't notice a thing.

"What do you suggest I order?" Wonder asked after examining the menu. "I don't even know what most of those things are. There should be a translation in plain English for ordinary people like me."

Her lack of education was a sore point with Wonder, and yet she preferred working to studying. They were going to address that when they returned home. As his mate, she would become a clan member, and as such she would qualify for the education stipend the clan offered.

Not to embarrass her, he pretended to be as baffled as her by the French terms on the menu. "I know what filet mignon is. It's a fancy French name for a steak. Should we get two?"

She arched a brow. "Two? Are you kidding me? One steak for you is an appetizer."

That was true, but with the prices these highway robbers were charging, he wasn't going to order more than one for himself. He had the money, but that didn't mean it was okay to throw it around like it grew on trees. That was only okay where Wonder was concerned. He had no problem spending it all on her. But not on himself.

Thankfully, and for all the wrong reasons, the host had handed Wonder a menu without prices. She would've paled.

Anandur closed the leather-bound folder. "I'll ask if they have larger cuts."

"For me too. I'm hungry." She unfurled the napkin and put it over her knees.

With a grin spreading over his face, Anandur reached for her hand. "You have no idea how pleased I am that you have a healthy appetite."

She arched a brow. "Why shouldn't I? It's not like I get sick."

"No reason whatsoever."

It was adorable that the girl didn't even know what the comment was all about. The thought of eating like a bird to impress a guy had never crossed her mind.

"Where to tomorrow?" she asked after they placed their order.

"There are still plenty of attractions to see in Luxor. There is the Valley of the Kings, where many pharaohs are buried, like the famous Tutankhamen and Ramses VI. Then there is the temple of Luxor with its avenue of sphinxes that connects it to the *Karnak* temple complex. After we are done with those, we'll drive to Aswan and stay the night there."

"How long is the drive?"

"About five hours."

She picked up a piece of bread from the basket. "You've planned a nice trip for us, and I enjoy visiting the sites, but it is pretty useless as far as my memories are concerned. What made you decide to go to all these places?"

He shrugged. "Just points of interest that were highly recommended. Other than Alexandria, everywhere else was like throwing darts at the map. Wherever they hit was as good a place to visit as another. You don't know where you're from."

"I wasn't born in Egypt, that's for sure. I had to learn the language from scratch. Only a few words sounded familiar to me."

"Can you say something in your language?"

Wonder frowned. "The memory of it faded as well. I think and dream in English now."

That was strange. He could understand memory loss due to trauma, but Wonder had retained her native language for a while, up until it was replaced by English.

Leaning forward, he reached for her other hand and clasped both as he searched his brain for the right words that wouldn't hurt her feelings. "I'm not a psychologist, but is it possible that you didn't want to remember anything about your old life?"

"Maybe. The thought crossed my mind." She leaned toward him and continued in a whisper. "Maybe I had a shitty life. Maybe something bad had happened to me, and I wanted to forget it. I love my new life. Whatever was before couldn't be better than this. So why bother remembering it?"

Why indeed?

Anandur no longer feared Esag's ghost hovering over his and Wonder's relationship and casting shadows on it. What they had was too powerful and all-consuming for anything to threaten it, real or imagined. But he couldn't conceive of living a life without knowing how it had started. It would've driven him crazy.

Anandur would've done everything he could to find out who his mother was, and whether he had siblings, and who his people were.

Immortals, same as humans, needed context for defining who they were.

"I'm glad that you love your new life, and I hope I can take credit for some of it, but I think it's important for you to find out who you are and where you're from."

"You can take credit for most of it." She dipped her head and kissed his knuckles. "The love I found with you is the main reason for my happiness. Not that I don't love the village and being part of a wonderful community, I do, but it's mainly you, Anandur. I love you, and I want a future with you. That's way more important than my past. I know who I am and I know what I want. That's good enough for me."

31

NICK

*N*ick opened his eyes and squinted against the glaring sunlight coming through the open window.

What time was it?

Damn, he'd overslept and was late for work. Eva had never been the easiest of bosses, but since she'd gotten pregnant, she'd become a tyrant. He would have to listen to a long-winded lecture about how punctuality reflected on one's work ethic, yadda, yadda, yadda.

But wait a minute, if yesterday was a Saturday, then today was Sunday, not Monday.

Sinking back against the pillows, Nick brought his hands to his temples and squeezed. He wasn't feeling good. His head hurt, and his whole body ached. In fact, he was pretty sure he had a fever, which would explain why he'd collapsed last night.

He'd been coming down with a cold or the flu.

Where was that bottle of Advil Ruth had gotten him? And where was Ruth? Sunday was her one day off, and she usually slept in, cuddling in bed with him. It was his favorite day of the week.

"Ruthie?" he croaked.

His throat hurt. Definitely the flu.

There was no response.

Weird. With her bat ears, she should've heard him no matter where she was in the house, even if he'd whispered. Unless she'd left to run some errand.

Oh, right, it was Sunday, which meant that she was probably outside, working on her garden, weeding or planting or whatever. Nick didn't pay much attention to her boring hobby.

She enjoyed it, though, claiming that gardening was very relaxing and satisfying.

Right. Like sweating in the sun and getting dirty was fun. But whatever. Being a couple didn't mean he had to love everything she did, and vice versa. Ruth wasn't into technology, except for how it could serve her, while Nick had to know how everything worked and liked to talk about it.

When he did, Ruth's eyes would glaze over in two minutes flat.

Crap, his head hurt, and his bladder was full. He needed to get out of bed. Maybe the bottle of Advil was in the bathroom?

The world spun as Nick got up, and padding to the bathroom took longer than usual because he had to use the walls to brace against.

It seemed he'd caught a particularly nasty bug. Eva would be upset when he didn't show up for work on Monday. They had a big corporate surveillance project going on, and she needed him. The equipment was in, but someone needed to monitor it, and they had no one else to do that.

Maybe he'd feel better by tomorrow morning, but he doubted it. Nick didn't get sick often—in fact hardly ever —but when he did, it usually hit him hard and lasted for days.

A quick glance out the bathroom window confirmed that Ruth was in the garden. He spent a long moment watching her work, admiring her legs in the old cutoff shorts she wore when gardening. As far as he was concerned, those shorts were the best part about her hobby.

When nature could no longer be denied, and his bladder was about to explode, he had to tear his gaze away.

Finished with taking care of business and brushing his teeth, Nick stepped into the shower and cranked up the hot water.

Too hot. He felt faint as he got out, nearly collapsing on the shaggy bath mat. Somehow, he managed to drag himself back to bed.

Sometime later, Ruth poked her head round the door. "Good morning," she chimed as she saw him awake. "Or rather, good afternoon."

"Hi," he rasped.

She walked in and sat on the bed next to him. "How are you feeling? You don't look so good." Frowning, she put her hand on his forehead. "I think you have a fever."

"I feel like shit. Can you bring me Advil and water? And then maybe some tea?"

Smiling happily, she jumped to her feet. "Of course. I'll be right back."

He loved her to pieces, but the girl was really odd. Why

the hell was she acting so cheerful when he was feeling so crappy? Was it her way of cheering him up?

"Here you go." Ruth hurried back with a glass of water in her hand. "Three Advils." She dropped the pills into his hand and then sat on the bed.

Popping them into his mouth, he washed them down with the water. "Thanks."

"Besides the fever, what else bothers you?"

"The usual flu stuff. Achy muscles, sore throat, chills."

"My poor baby." She put her palm on his forehead again. "I think I should call a doctor."

"For the stupid flu? It's a virus. There is nothing a doctor can do except to tell me to rest and drink lots of liquids. I already know that."

"Maybe it's something more serious? I'm going to call Bridget, my cousin who is a doctor. You might have met her at Eva's wedding. She is short and has fiery red hair."

"As if I remember anyone I met there. I should stay away from alcohol. I'm starting to think that I'm allergic to it."

"Maybe you are." Ruth pushed to her feet. "I'm going to call Bridget." Bending down, she planted a quick kiss on his forehead. "Try to rest a little before she gets here."

"Okay." Nick would've argued more if he had the energy, but his eyes were refusing to stay open. He could nap until Ruth's cousin got there.

As he drifted away, the image of Ruth's smiling face was at odds with the circumstances. Was she happy about him getting sick? Maybe she needed an excuse to invite her cousin the doctor?

When he opened his eyes again, it was to stare at a pair of impressive boobies hovering over his face.

Those didn't belong to Ruth. She wasn't that well-endowed.

"Hello, Nick." The boobies retreated, and a face with a halo of red hair slowly came into focus. "I'm Doctor Bridget. How are you feeling?"

"Like crap."

"It's understandable. You're running a fever of a hundred and two."

"I took Advil."

The redhead chuckled. "That was a long time ago." She turned to a tall dude Nick hadn't noticed before. "Julian, can you hand me the tape measure?"

Nick remembered Ruth telling him about her cousin Bridget, the doctor. She hadn't mentioned any Julian. "Who is he?"

"My assistant. Julian is also a doctor. He is here to observe."

An intern. He didn't know they made house calls.

The doctor took the tape measure from her assistant and started taking Nick's measurements.

"Am I dying? Are you measuring me for my funeral tux?"

The doctor chuckled. "No, Nick. You're not dying. There is a new bug that attacks the joints. One of the first signs is shrinkage."

The doctor's assistant snorted out a laugh. "Sorry. The word shrinkage reminded me of a joke."

Yeah, shrinkage had disturbing connotations. "I don't want to shrink."

"It's a rare bug. I'm just being cautious."

After she was done with the tape measure, Julian the assistant handed her a syringe and a long rubber tube.

"I need to take a blood sample."

"Go ahead."

She was a pro. He hardly felt the pinprick of the needle.

"All done," she said after filling up several ampules. "You can go back to sleep."

WONDER

*I*t was close to midnight when they arrived at their hotel in Aswan. Another Sofitel that was just as luxurious as the one in Luxor, except the old-world decor was not as old.

Wonder liked this one better, and not only because of the beautiful furniture. From their room's balcony, they had unobstructed views of several of the small islands dotting the Nile river.

"I'm going to call room service before they close the kitchen." Anandur picked up the phone and dialed the extension. "What would you like to eat?"

"If they have the same menu as the other Sofitel, order me what we had last night. It was delicious." As had been the sex after that.

Their third, if she wasn't counting multiple orgasms.

Not only was it getting better and better, but it also seemed that her appetite for sex was growing stronger as well. She'd been salivating over Anandur the entire day and imagining what they were going to do once they got to the hotel. It didn't matter that it was late, and that she was tired. Wonder wasn't about to give up on making love with her guy because of trivial things like that.

Unlike the other places, which they'd stayed in for only one night, they were going to stay in Aswan for several and rest. She'd have plenty of time to catch up on sleep.

Shower first, though. She was sticky and grimy from a long day of sightseeing. Pulling out her toiletries from the suitcase, Wonder headed for the bathroom.

"Double serving like yesterday?" Anandur asked.

"Naturally." She winked at him before closing the door to the bathroom.

He'd asked about the portion size, which the two of them had ordered supersized last evening, but it could have also applied to the sex they had twice. Once before dinner and once after.

Well, technically the second was more like the third and the fourth as well, but who was counting?

Apparently, she was.

Anandur threw open the bathroom door and strode in. "The kitchen is open until one in the morning." He started removing his clothes. "I already put in the order, so we should hurry up with the shower."

Bummer. She could think of a better way to spend their time. Wonder had fond memories of the shower at the other Sofitel.

Well, there was always tomorrow morning. This was going to be the lazy part of their trip. No more getting up early and rushing to see the sights. Frankly, as fun and as intriguing as the trip had been, she was getting tired of running from place to place.

Down at the restaurant, Wonder was surprised to see

that they weren't the only late diners. The place was as full as if it were five in the afternoon and not after midnight, including families with small children.

It must have been the time zone difference. Travelers were arriving from all over the world, though some of them were obviously from the region given that the women were covered from head to toe. The poor things looked like walking tents, with only a narrow slit allowing them to see.

Eating was not a picnic for them either. It involved lifting the face-covering a bit and pushing the fork under it for each bite. Room service would've been a much better option for them, unless the women were required to wear the tent garment at all times.

She hadn't researched that custom, so she couldn't say, but it made sense that they would at least be allowed to breathe easily in the confines of their own homes. Or hotel rooms.

A shiver ran through Wonder as she was reminded of wearing that exact type of garment. After waking up from her coma, she'd stolen it from a clothesline to cover her skeletal appearance. As such, it had been very useful, but she still remembered the stifling heat and lack of breathable air.

She couldn't comprehend the purpose of such a custom. Maybe she was just an ignorant young woman who knew very little about the world, but she knew that she'd suffered when wearing that garment. Why would women agree to it? And why would their men want to torment them like that? The men didn't wear layers of clothing in the heat, or cover their heads, or their faces.

Talk about discrimination.

But apparently, one could get used to anything because the women didn't look like they were suffering. Talking loudly, laughing, and checking this and that on their smartphones, they behaved like women everywhere did.

"Follow me, please," the host said after checking off their names on his list. "Your dinner will be served momentarily."

Anandur rubbed his stomach. "I'm so glad I ordered ahead of time. I'm starving."

"Me too." She glanced up as the host led a family to the table across from them; a man, three women covered from head to toe, and several small children.

This was another thing Wonder couldn't understand. How could the women tolerate sharing a husband?

She could've never been able to share Anandur. Just the thought of such a preposterous idea enraged her. Not a violent person by nature, Wonder nonetheless felt her hands fisting involuntarily. She would've fought any female who tried to take him away from her. To the death if it came to it.

"Easy, tigress." Anandur leaned forward and took her hand. "Your eyes are glowing," he said in a whisper. "What has gotten you so angry?"

"I could never share you with another woman. You're mine." She cast a sidelong glance at the family sitting across from them. "I don't know how they can tolerate it."

"They have no choice, and they know nothing else."

Wonder humphed. "Apparently, the concept of liberty and justice for all didn't reach these parts yet."

A sad smile tugged at the corner of Anandur's lips. "That's not entirely accurate. The concept was born not far from here thousands of years ago, but then humanity regressed. It has taken a lot of work to bring it back, and we only started seeing progress about a hundred years ago. Did you know that liberty and justice for all didn't apply to American women until the 1920s?"

That couldn't have been right, but then Anandur had no reason to lie to her. "That's horrible." She leaned closer and whispered, "Humans are no better than apes."

At that moment Wonder felt nothing but contempt for humanity at large. Why did the clan even bother helping them?

They were not worthy.

He chuckled sadly. "Immortals are no better. Remember what I told you about the Doomers and how they treat their females?"

Right, she'd forgotten about that. This trip with Anandur was about joy and love. It was easy to forget the troubled world outside their happy bubble.

"I don't want to talk about this stuff anymore. I've been having so much fun with you. The injustice of this terrible discrimination against women just ruined it."

Anandur puffed up his chest. "Don't fret, my dear. Sir Anandur to the rescue. With his weapon of choice, a bow made of humor and a quiver of silly jokes, he is ready to fight off the dark dragons of gloom."

33

ANANDUR

*B*y the time they finished their dinner, Anandur had made Wonder laugh so hard she couldn't breathe.

He was damn proud of himself.

"That was one hell of a performance. You should do stand-up comedy," she said as they exited the elevator on their floor.

"I perform only for people I know. But..." he opened the door to their room, "I'm not opposed to getting rewarded for my entertainment services."

"What do you have in mind?" Given her smirk, Wonder knew exactly where he was going with that.

He lifted her into his arms and carried her to bed. "I'm partial to choosing my own rewards."

"Are you now?" She leaned back on her forearms and smiled at him. "And I have no say in it?"

"You can say yay or nay. That's all." He removed her sandals one at a time, kissing the arch of her foot before lowering it to the bed. Next were her stretchy pants.

Pulling from the bottom, he yanked them off her together with her skimpy panties.

As soon as her soft, bare mound was exposed, his fangs punched out over his lower lip. Then she parted her legs a little, and the sight of glistening moisture coating her petals put up a rush order to his venom glands, demanding they fill and get ready for action.

Fates, they hadn't even started, and she was already aroused and ready for him.

He was one lucky bastard.

Between one eye blink and the next, Anandur kicked off his shoes, pulled down his jeans, and yanked his button-down off.

There was something he'd wanted to do since the first time he'd seen Wonder's glorious ass but had refrained because of her virginity. Now that they had several love-making sessions under their belts, Wonder could handle some rough handling.

Anandur couldn't wait to release his inner beast and have wild, unrestrained sex for the first time in his life.

There would be no more fragile humans for him to be extra careful not to hurt. With her virginity taken care of, his powerful immortal female could take everything he dished out. Not only that, she'd given him plenty of indications that she would love it.

"I'm going to teach you something new tonight," he said as he bent down and gripped her hips.

"Oh, yeah?"

"Do you know what doggy style is?" He flipped her around to lie on her belly.

"No, but I can imagine."

Pulling on her hips, he arranged her so she was on her

knees with her beautiful ass sticking out, and then climbed on the bed behind her.

Wonder lifted on her forearms and looked at him over her shoulder. "Like this?"

Leaning, he put his hand on the back of her neck and applied a little pressure. "You'll be more comfortable resting your head on the pillow."

"Okay." She sighed and let him rearrange her as he pleased.

Her willing submission flipped the switch on a part of him he didn't know existed, filling him with a strange mixture of tenderness and possessiveness.

He loved that she entrusted herself to him.

His hold on her nape was loose, he wasn't applying any pressure, its purpose was to guide and remind Wonder to stay in position, not restrain her.

Fisting his shaft, he rubbed it against her wet folds, up and down, coating it with her copious juices and hitting her sensitive bud on every upstroke.

"Are you ready for me, love?"

Instead of answering, Wonder undulated her hips to increase the friction.

"I take that as a yes." He positioned the tip at her entrance and slowly fed his shaft into her.

"Gods," she moaned into the mattress.

When he was as far as he could go, he let go of her nape and gripped both sides of her glorious ass, working his hips to grind against her soft flesh and get even deeper.

The fit was still tight, but Wonder didn't seem uncomfortable. Pushing back against him, she rocked her hips in encouragement.

He started moving, slowly at first, letting her grow

accustomed to the fullness, then faster and harder until the entire bed was rattling from the force of his thrusts.

He was close, his fangs dripping with venom and demanding that he sink them into his female and pump her full of his venom, making her his and ensuring her addiction to him.

Even in the midst of the frenzy, he realized how crazy that sounded.

Fates, where did that come from?

Was letting go of his beast turning him into a Neanderthal?

And yet, even though his mind was trying to fight the foreign thoughts assailing him, the need to bite and possess was undeniable.

Wonder's bowed back was damp with perspiration as he leaned over her. Blanketing her with his body, he reached under her to gently rub a finger over the center of her pleasure, while using his other hand to immobilize her head in preparation for his bite.

For some reason, this time around the need to sink his fangs into her was overpowering, stronger even than his need to climax. Dipping his head, he forced himself to stop and lick the spot before releasing a loud hiss and biting down.

On a scream, Wonder's sheath squeezed around his shaft. She arched beneath him, spreading her knees even wider to get him to go deeper.

With his fangs still embedded in her neck, he kept pumping into her until his seed jetted out in a searing eruption of seemingly endless streams. When he was finally spent, he sealed the puncture wounds with a few flicks of his tongue and then collapsed sideways, pulling Wonder with him.

He must've fallen asleep.

When Anandur woke up sometime later, he was still buried deep inside Wonder, and he was still hard as if he hadn't come like a fucking geyser.

Wonder was out, her even breaths slow and deep.

He would've gladly gone another round, but his girl was clearly exhausted. She needed the rest.

Carefully, he pulled out, grimacing at the messy puddle he'd just added to. There wasn't much he could do about it, though. Padding to the bathroom, he wetted several washcloths and grabbed a clean towel to cover the mess.

Wonder didn't stir as he cleaned her. He did what he could with a couple of wet washcloths, and then used the towel to pat her dry. She slept throughout his ministrations, even when he lifted her up to put the towel under her.

Pressing a gentle kiss to her nape, Anandur spooned her and covered them both with the blanket.

Heart overflowing with feeling, he thought about Brundar.

He understood his brother better now. When Brundar had thought Callie was a human, he had been willing to break clan law and leave everything and everyone behind to be with her.

That was the power of love, or maybe it was the power of love for an immortal mate, which Callie had turned out to be.

As much as Anandur loved being a Guardian and cared deeply about his people, he knew without a doubt that he would've left them behind for Wonder. Fortunately, he wouldn't have to, so all was good. It was just shocking to realize how much she'd come to mean to him in such a short time.

Wonder had become his everything.

Was he addicted to her?

It wasn't supposed to work so fast on males. Not even on females. He'd only bitten her a few times. Months were needed for an addiction to set in.

Except, he'd heard that for some it happened faster than for others. Maybe love was the secret ingredient that hastened the addiction.

If it was indeed so, he was already an addict.

Thank the merciful Fates.

34

RUTH

*T*wenty-four hours had passed since Bridget made the call to transfer Nick to the village clinic.

Supposedly he was transitioning, but there was no definite proof. He hadn't grown even a fraction of an inch, and Bridget had said it was too early to perform the skin test to see how fast a cut healed.

Ruth wasn't too happy about Julian taking over Nick's care either. He was a nice kid, and maybe one day he would be a great doctor, but until then she would have preferred Bridget taking care of Nick.

"Where am I?" Nick asked.

It wasn't the first time he'd asked that. He'd been slipping in and out of consciousness and not remembering her answers. Sometimes it was only a deep sleep, and sometimes it was more. She'd stopped looking at the monitors because it was driving her crazy.

Ruth smoothed his damp hair away from his forehead and then kissed it. "You're in Bridget's clinic, Nicki. She wants to keep an eye on you. Do you want a drink of water?"

Already back asleep, he didn't answer.

The IV drip he was hooked up to provided the fluids he needed, so drinking was optional, but he'd sounded like his throat was dry.

"I heard him waking up again." Julian strode into the room.

"Just for a moment, then he fell asleep again."

"You should go home, Ruth. Or at least take Sylvia up on her offer and crash in her guest room or on her couch. You haven't had any sleep."

"I'm fine. I dozed off a few times."

"Sitting in a chair."

She shrugged. "I'm not going anywhere. I get a panic attack when I'm taking a bathroom break."

"Nick is in good hands." Julian put a hand on her shoulder. "I am here, and my mother is thirty seconds away. You have nothing to worry about."

"I know that in here." She pointed to her head, then put her hand over her heart. "But in here it's a different story. Logic doesn't apply."

"How about I get you a cot?"

"Could you? That would be great."

"Give me a couple of minutes."

It took him a little longer, but when Julian returned, it was with a cot and a pillow and a blanket.

"Thank you." She helped him set things up. "I don't know if I'll be able to sleep, but at least I can lie down and stretch."

"You're welcome."

When he left, Ruth lay on the cot and closed her eyes,

listening to the steady beat of the monitoring equipment. The technology baffled and unnerved her, perhaps because she didn't understand it, but she could imagine Nick checking it out. He would be like a kid in a candy store, his eyes sparkling with interest as he figured out what each was doing and how. He was such a wiz with technology, while to her it all sounded like a foreign language.

"Hi, Mom," Sylvia whispered as she entered the darkened room. "I brought you lunch." She put a brown shopping bag on the rolling tray table. "I'll just leave it here. You can go back to sleep."

"I'm not sleeping." Ruth sat up. "Did you bring coffee?"

"Of course." Sylvia pulled a thermos out. "I'll pour you a cup."

"Thanks." Ruth palmed the paper cup, took a few sips, and then put it down on the table. "You shouldn't call me Mom in here," she whispered. "Nick wakes up from time to time."

Sylvia waved a hand. "He's too out of it to pay attention."

"That's what you think. Nick is a very sharp guy."

"I know." Sylvia sat on the chair. "Isn't it funny that we both chose guys who are into tech?"

"And who are younger than us, me especially." Ruth grimaced. "Yeah, I noticed the similarities."

"I wonder why. Is Grandma into tech?"

Ruth snorted. "No, she isn't. And if you ever call her Grandma, she'll disown you." Her mother could be vicious at times, especially when her vanity was offended. It was good that they lived on different continents.

Sylvia was a strong and confident young woman. Her

mother would've found a way to undermine all the good work Ruth had done.

"Where is Julian?" Sylvia poured coffee from the thermos into another paper cup.

"Hanging around. Why?"

"I wanted to ask him about the psychic convention. I didn't have a chance to talk to him since he returned. Did he tell you anything about it?"

Ruth reached for the container with her lunch and flipped the lid open. "It completely slipped my mind. I'm too anxious to think about anything other than Nick."

"I get it. It took Roni three days to transition, and although Bridget kept reassuring me that he was doing fine, I was so damn worried. It's not fun. I hope it doesn't take Nick that long."

Ruth sighed. "If he's transitioning. I'm not sure what's going on. His measurements are still the same, and it's too early for the healing speed test."

"He's transitioning. Nick is a healthy guy, and his blood tests came back clean. There could be only one reason for his symptoms."

"Not true. I've done some reading online. You have no idea how many things can happen to a human. All kinds of crazy viruses attacking the brain and causing loss of consciousness, bacterial infections that are difficult to detect at first, and other scary stuff."

Shaking her head, Sylvia moved to sit next to Ruth on the cot and wrapped her arm around her shoulders. "You're just feeding your anxiety, Mom. Bridget and Julian know what they are doing, and if they are not worried, neither should you be. Don't search for scary shit on the Internet and try to make amateur diagnoses."

With a sigh, Ruth put her head on Sylvia's shoulder. "You're right. I need to believe he is going to be okay."

"That's the spirit. How about I stay and watch Nick, and you go get a shower at my place? You can borrow some of my clothes."

"Why? Do I stink?" Ruth hadn't showered since the day before, and she'd been gardening before finding out that Nick was running a fever.

Sylvia chuckled. "No, you don't stink, but you'll feel better after a hot shower and a change of clothes." She glanced at Ruth's cutoff shorts. "Imagine Kian stopping by to check up on Nick. You'll be embarrassed about him seeing you in these." Next, she lifted Ruth's hand. "And you have dirt under your fingernails."

That was the clincher. "Do I need a key?"

"The door is unlocked. Just go in. You know where everything is."

"Thanks." Ruth kissed her cheek. "I'll be back in fifteen minutes or less."

"Take your time. Nick isn't going anywhere, and I'll call you if there is any change."

35

NICK

*E*ven though Nick had been slipping in and out of consciousness, he was aware of his surroundings —a hospital room full of monitoring equipment, or rather a clinic. He remembered Ruth telling him that he was in her cousin's clinic. The IV and the wires connected with sticky pads to his body meant that he was really sick. But he still hadn't figured out what was wrong with him.

Ruth was there every time he opened his eyes, looking worried and asking how he felt. He even remembered the redheaded doctor with the big boobies checking on him once, or was it twice?

Her tall assistant had taken measurements at least a couple of times, maybe more if he'd done it while Nick was out. Sometimes he could hear the guy and Ruth talking in hushed voices.

But every time Nick asked what was happening to him, the answer he got was that they were still running tests.

He wasn't sure, but he thought he'd also heard Eva's voice. Had it been a dream, or had she come to visit him?

She'd probably come.

His boss was like a mother to him, so naturally she would visit him in a hospital when he was so sick. Maybe even dying.

But mostly it was just him and Ruth in the room. Her presence was reassuring. Sometimes, he would know she was there only from hearing her heartbeat or smelling her unique fragrance. Not the perfume, but what her skin smelled like under it.

Nah, that didn't make sense. He must've been imagining it, or had dreamt it. The few times he'd actually opened his eyes, she was either sitting on a chair or lying on a cot. Neither the chair nor the cot was close enough for him to hear her heartbeat or smell her skin. It must've been just a comforting memory from the many times they'd slept together entwined in each other's arms.

"Nicki? Are you awake?" He could feel her hovering over him, her warm breath caressing the cold skin of his face.

Hey, did it mean that his fever was gone?

"I think so," he croaked.

"Let me get you some water."

Water sounded heavenly. His throat was so dry.

"Here you go." She stuck a straw in his mouth. "Just don't drink too much at once. You might get nauseous."

He couldn't even if he wanted to. His throat was so tight that it could only handle a few drops at a time. Slowly, though, he finished everything in the cup.

"Can you get me more?"

"I'll ask Julian. I'm not sure it's okay." She made a move to walk away.

Feebly, he reached for her wrist. "Don't go. I don't want

to be alone."

"Oh, Nicki." Ruth bent and kissed his cheek. "I'll just poke my head out the door and call him. He must be in one of the other patient rooms. A Guar... I mean a guy broke his leg, and Julian is resetting the bone."

"Then leave him to it. I can wait."

"He's probably done." She pulled her wrist out of his weak grasp and rushed to the door. "Julian, Nick is awake. Can I give him a second cup of water?"

"I'll be right there. And yes, you can give him another cup. Just have him sip on it slowly."

Nick heard the guy's answer as if he were in the room with him. The doctor must've been standing right there in the corridor.

Ruth refilled the cup, brought it over, and held the straw to his mouth.

"I can hold it." He took it from her. He was weak, but not completely enfeebled.

His hand shook a little from the effort, and a few drops of water spilled on the sheet.

Nevertheless, it made Ruth grin from ear to ear as if he'd just finished a marathon. "I'm so glad you're feeling better. Your fever is down, and your blood pressure has stabilized."

"Good. Now would someone tell me what's wrong with me?"

She lifted a finger. "Wait just a little longer. Julian needs to run one last test."

Tests usually meant waiting for results, not an immediate answer. "Can you tell me what they suspect? They must have some idea of what's going on with me."

As Ruth opened her mouth to answer, the young doctor

entered the room holding a small metal tray. "I'll take care of this, Ruth."

Looking relieved, she stepped away from the bed to make room for the doctor.

After wetting a gauze square with a strong-smelling disinfectant, the doctor took hold of Nick's hand. "I'm going to clean your palm and then make a tiny cut."

"Why?"

"I can learn a lot from how fast the bleeding stops. Don't worry. You're barely going to feel it, and the discomfort is going to last only a moment."

Which in doctors' lingo meant excruciating pain. But whatever, he needed answers, and if he needed to suffer through some "discomfort" so be it.

"Go for it, doc. But after that, I want some answers. You must at least suspect something." Either that or the doctors in this clinic were incompetent and didn't know what they were doing.

If he didn't get a reasonably satisfying answer, Nick was going to demand he get transferred to a proper hospital.

As the guy lifted a small surgical knife off the tray, Ruth approached the bed and leaned to observe him make the small cut.

It stung, but it wasn't as horrible as he'd expected.

Surprisingly, the doctor didn't object to her breathing expectantly over the cut. Nick didn't mind, but it proved to him that they didn't know what they were doing in this crappy clinic. Didn't they care about their patients getting infected by germs from visitors?

Ruth shouldn't have brought him there.

A long moment passed with Julian, the-doctor-in-training, and Ruth hovering over Nick's palm.

At first, the blood welled over the cut and trickled down his palm, but then the bleeding stopped quite quickly. Still, the two kept observing the cut with rapt attention.

The sight of his own blood wasn't something Nick could watch without getting queasy, so he concentrated on Ruth's hair. It had so many shades. He hadn't noticed it before.

"I'm going to clean your palm," the doctor said as he picked up a clean gauze square from the tray.

Gently, he wiped the blood away.

Ruth gasped and put a hand over her mouth.

"Take a look, Nick," the doctor said.

With a grimace, he hazarded a quick glance, but what he saw made him take a closer look.

There was no cut.

Had he imagined the incision? Had they played another hypnotic prank on him like the one Jackson had pulled?

Nah, it didn't make sense. And Ruth hadn't faked the gasp.

"Where did it go?"

"It's healed," the doctor said.

"Impossible."

"Ruth? Do you want to take it from here?"

With the guiltiest expression Nick had ever seen on her face, Ruth nodded. "I will. Thanks, Julian."

"My pleasure." He turned to Nick and offered his hand. "Welcome to Oz, Nick."

"Huh?"

"Ruth will explain. When you're done, call me, and I'll remove the catheter and the IV."

RUTH

*T*he moment of truth had arrived, and Ruth was terrified. Elated, but also so anxious that her hands started trembling and tears misted her eyes. Nick was going to hate her for deceiving him and for orchestrating his transition without asking him first.

He might eventually forgive her, but he would never trust her again.

"Talk to me, Ruth. You're scaring the shit out of me. Am I dying?"

She chuckled. "No, and you never will. Well, provided you stay safe and don't let anyone with a sword anywhere near you."

Nick pushed himself higher on the bed and reached for her hand. "Now I'm worried about you. Did you take something for your nerves?" Then another thought occurred to him. "Maybe it's an allergic reaction. We should call Doctor Julian back. Or better yet, the other one, Bridget."

Fates, where to start? At the end or at the beginning?

"I'm not crazy, and I'm not on anything. I'm an immortal, and now so are you. You weren't sick, Nick. You were transitioning. In a short while, you'll feel a lot of pain in your gums and in your throat because you'll start growing fangs and venom glands."

Nick looked at her with a mixture of worry and pity in his eyes, but then he touched a hand to his throat. "It hurts."

"Julian will have to give you something to manage the pain, but otherwise you can go back to work in a day or two."

He shook his head. "I still don't know what the hell you're talking about."

"Please don't hate me," she whispered, looking away as tears misted her vision. "I didn't have a choice. It was either doing it without your knowledge or risking your freedom."

"Come here," he said softly as he pulled on her hand. "Lie next to me and tell me everything from the start."

Nick's cautious tone implied that he still thought she was insane. Once he heard the whole story, though, he would no longer think that. Instead, he would think of her as deceitful and manipulative and probably kick her out of his bed.

But until then, she was going to enjoy his closeness.

Before, she hadn't dared to climb into bed with him because of all the wires. But now they were irrelevant.

Cuddling up to Nick, Ruth put her head on his chest and threw her arm over his middle. "I know this is hard to believe. I'll start from the beginning, and once you hear the whole story you'll believe me. If not, we can call Julian in here and ask him to show you his fangs."

"So he is an immortal too? Fascinating. And what about the other doctor? The one with the big boobies?" He was mocking her.

Worse, he'd noticed Bridget's cleavage even though he was barely conscious.

Typical man.

"She is Julian's mom." That should cool down his enthusiasm.

"Unbelievable."

Fates, he was starting to annoy her with his 'I'm talking to a crazy woman' attitude. "Shut up, Nick, and listen. Keep your comments and questions until I'm done."

"Okay, no need to get all pissy."

"You would be pissy too if I looked at you as if you were nuts."

"True. I'm sorry. I'm going to keep my mouth shut from now on."

"Thank you."

The longer she talked, the stiffer he became next to her, the hand rubbing small circles on her back falling down to the bed.

When she was done telling him the history of her people, including the secret war they'd been waging with their enemies since antiquity, Nick let out a long breath.

"How long did you suspect that I was a dormant carrier of your godly genes?"

This was the hardest part of the reveal.

Telling Nick about the history of gods and immortals, explaining the biological differences between them and humans, including Dormants and transition, all of that had been relatively easy. But telling him that everyone around him had been keeping secrets and lying to him was going to be brutal.

"Eva suspected that you were special from the moment she met you, same as she suspected Tessa and Sharon. Who, by the way, transitioned before you."

"So she was an immortal even then? Bhathian didn't induce her transition?"

Nick's quick mind had apparently processed all the information she'd fed him over the past hour. He didn't need anything explained twice or simplified, which was a relief.

"Eva knew she was an immortal, but she didn't know how or why. She must've encountered a random immortal who induced her without realizing that she was a Dormant. She met Bhathian sometime after transitioning, but before realizing that she was no longer human. They hooked up for one night, and it resulted in Eva getting pregnant, which is quite miraculous given it was a one-time thing. Nathalie is their daughter from that encounter, not her cousin." Like Sylvia was her daughter and not her sister, but Ruth was saving the biggest shocker for last.

"I get it, and it all kind of makes sense, but I can't believe this was all right under my nose and I didn't notice anything." He rubbed his jaw. "I remember thinking that Eva was an odd bird for babying us even though she was too young for that. I thought she was not that much older than Sharon."

He smiled. "I've also noticed that Tessa looked good, but I thought it was Jackson's doing. He was good to her. And Sharon didn't change at all."

"I think it's normal. You had no reason to look for anomalies."

"Yeah, like your bat hearing and your strength. It was easy to accept your explanations because they fit my worldview."

Ruth was starting to breathe easier. Nick didn't seem angry or even overly shaken up, but then he hadn't heard the punch line yet.

He turned toward her and looked into her eyes. "I just don't understand why you felt like you had to keep all of this a secret from me. Don't you know that I love you? I would've never told anyone about you or the clan. I would never do anything to endanger you."

"Not intentionally. But as long as you were human, information could've been extracted from you. The clan has a very strict policy about this. The only reason I was allowed to have a relationship with you at all was that you were a suspected Dormant."

Turning to lie on his back, Nick appeared to be mulling over all that he'd learned, as long moments passed. When he spoke, his tone was cold. "Is that why you are with me? Because you knew there was a chance I was a Dormant? I must've been quite a catch for you."

Dear Fates, she'd expected Nick to ask a lot of questions, and she'd prepared many elaborate answers while waiting for him to transition, but none included anything about this. The concept was so foreign to her that it had never crossed her mind that Nick might think she didn't really love him.

How could he be so blind? Wasn't it evident that she was crazy about him?

Lifting her head, Ruth cupped his cheek and forced him to look at her. "I'm with you because I love you, you stupid lug. I didn't want to be with anyone, mortal or immortal, but you kept insisting and chipping at my resistance until I gave in, and I'm glad I did. You're the best thing that has ever happened to me."

Well, that wasn't entirely true.

She looked away. "Well, it's the second best thing that has happened to me," she murmured.

Hooking a finger under her chin, he asked the inevitable question, "If I'm the second best thing, who or what is the first?"

"Sylvia."

He arched a brow. "Your sister?"

"My daughter."

In the silence that followed, Nick's mouth fell agape. "Sylvia is your daughter," he said after a long moment.

"Yes."

"How old are you, Ruth?"

"I'm fifty-six."

NICK

*a*lone in the clinic's shower, Nick stood under the spray of water with no intention of getting out any time soon.

Since waking up, he hadn't had a moment's privacy except for the times Ruth could no longer hold it in and had to rush to the bathroom. The rest of the time she'd answered his questions while looking at him with a pair of anxious eyes.

Putting on what he'd hoped was an agreeable expression, Nick had done his best to hide how pissed off he was, mainly because he wasn't sure why he was so angry.

It wasn't as if Ruth had done something harmful to him. He was a fucking immortal thanks to her, or rather thanks to Brundar. It still creeped him out to think the guy had bitten him while he'd been passed out from being drugged, not drunk.

Ruth had organized one hell of a setup to induce his transition without his knowledge. But he shouldn't be mad at her. She had no choice.

He got that.

Turned out that he was immune to thralling, so they couldn't tell him shit before attempting to induce his transition. If Brundar's bite hadn't worked, and Nick hadn't transitioned, they couldn't erase the experience from his brain like they did with other humans. Apparently, he was an anomaly.

Figures, and in more ways than that.

Nick had always been different. No wonder that when he'd fallen in love, it was for the rarest woman possible. An immortal.

Ruth was fifty-six.

That had been the biggest shocker, that and Sylvia being her daughter and not her sister.

Slowly, he was getting used to the idea that his girlfriend was older than his mother, his adoptive one and probably his biological as well. How could he have been so clueless?

There had been a few clues here and there, but mostly Ruth acted the age she looked.

He'd accredited her maturity to the difficult life she'd had, but then she'd never really talked about it. He should've wondered about how Ruth could afford the house she was living in. He knew that before Jackson had given her the job at the café, she'd never worked for a living, and welfare didn't pay enough to cover rent or mortgage payments.

Bottom line, if he knew next to nothing about the woman he'd fallen in love with, and the little he knew was a big fat lie, who the hell had he fallen in love with?

Had he been so desperate for love that he'd convinced himself Ruth was the one? Could he have turned any woman willing to accept him as her boyfriend into the one?

"Nick? Are you okay in there?" Ruth opened the door.

"I'm fine."

"Eva brought you a change of clothes. I'm putting them on the counter."

"Thanks."

Crap, now he would have to face Eva too. Another big fat liar. It didn't help reminding himself that they had no choice. They should've known he could be trusted.

Their lack of faith in him stung. Big time.

When he was done getting dressed, Nick opened the door to his patient room expecting to see Eva, but there was no one there other than Ruth. His boss probably didn't stick around because she felt guilty for lying to him throughout the years. As she should.

"Are you ready to go?" Ruth asked.

"Sure." He cast one last glance at the equipment, regretting not having a chance to check it out.

She lifted a white paper bag. "I have the pain medication Julian prescribed for you. Do you need it now?"

His throat hurt and his gums throbbed, but it was tolerable, and he didn't want to feel groggy. "I'll take some before hitting the sack. Are you taking me to Eva's or to your place?"

His car was parked in Ruth's garage. He needed to get it.

"Actually, I'm taking you to Sylvia's. Julian wants you to stay in the village for at least two days so he can keep an eye on you. Sylvia invited us to stay with her and Roni. Eva and Bhathian are there too, and so are Sharon and Robert and Tessa and Jackson. Everyone wants to congratulate you."

"A party. I'm touched."

He'd meant to sound sarcastic, but Ruth hadn't caught it. "I'm glad you're feeling okay to see people. Some of the transitioning Dormants came out the other side too weak to deal with anyone." She threaded her arm through his. "But my guy is made from tougher stuff."

That made him feel a little better.

He should remember that Ruth loved him. She hadn't been faking it. He believed her when she claimed she'd fallen for him because of who he was and not what he was. His new enhanced senses picked up on many more cues than his old human ones. Maybe now he wouldn't be as clueless.

God, he'd been such a putz.

"It's pretty out here," he said as they walked outside the clinic.

Ruth had told him about the village, and how all the clan members were supposed to eventually move in there. He hadn't expected it to look so park-like. Everything was green, with tall trees that had to have been planted already grown. The village wasn't old enough for trees to mature.

The village. Suddenly he was reminded of Callie's comment from the other dinner. "When Callie said she wanted to open a restaurant in the village, she meant here, not in Woodland Hills."

Ruth smiled. "Yep. Jackson is going to leave managing the café in town entirely to me and take over the one here. That's the other location he was talking about."

So many things that had seemed off in one way or another were suddenly becoming clear. It was as if a fog was lifting and he was seeing the world in a completely different way.

"I can see clearly now, the rain is gone, I can see all obstacles in my way…" he hummed the rest of the tune as they walked down the walkway.

Ruth put her head on his shoulder. "I'm glad your mood is improving." She pointed at a one-story house with rose bushes in the front yard. "That's Sylvia and Roni's house."

"Did you plant the roses?"

"Yes."

The door opened, and Sylvia came out. "Hey, Nick, congratulations. Roni got the barbecue going. Are you hungry for steaks?"

They climbed the three steps to the front porch. "Nick is not supposed to eat solids for the next day or two."

Waving them inside, Sylvia snorted. "As you remember, Roni didn't follow the doctor's orders."

"I also remember that he barfed after that."

As he entered, a roomful of people started clapping. People he'd known for a while, some of them for years, and yet didn't.

Eva heaved herself off the couch with some help from Bhathian. "Come here, Nick, and give me a hug. I've been waiting so long for this."

He embraced her gently, careful of her big belly.

"Now we can finally move into the village and have this baby in a safe place." Bhathian clapped him on the back. "Eva refused to move until you found your *bashert* and transitioned. She wasn't willing to leave you behind."

"Really? You were waiting for me?" He was touched beyond words. And to think he'd been so angry at her.

"Of course. How could I move when you couldn't join

me?" She palmed his cheeks, kissed one and then the other. "You're like a son to me."

Eva's words had melted the last of his anger, leaving Nick emotionally and mentally depleted. "I don't have the words to tell you how much this means to me. I'm really touched."

Eva grinned. "I'm just glad to see you come out okay on the other side. I've been so worried." She smoothed her hand over her belly.

Bhathian wrapped his massive arm around Nick's middle. "You need to sit down, kid. You look pale." He led him to the couch and sat next to him. "Everything good?"

"I guess. What's a bashert?"

"It means a soul mate," Sharon said, then leaned to give him a crushing hug. "Ruth is your bashert, and you are hers."

38

WONDER

"I really don't need to buy anything," Wonder protested as Anandur dragged her through the Cairo international airport duty-free shops.

"We have time to kill and nothing to do, and we need to get some souvenirs for people."

Their flight from Aswan to Cairo arrived a little late, but their connecting flight to Los Angeles was still two hours away. Plenty of time, but she didn't want to spend them shopping. "If we buy a souvenir for everyone you consider a friend, we'll need to get another suitcase. Or two."

Anandur had discovered that Aswan had no shortage of fancy boutiques selling fashionable, western attire, and had insisted on buying her dresses and other stuff she didn't need.

The six days there had been filled with little sightseeing, but mostly lazing on the beach or by the pool, and lots of fabulous sex.

It had been an awesome vacation that had cemented

their relationship. As impossible as it seemed, she was falling in love with him more and more with every passing moment. Not that he hadn't annoyed her at times, because he had, but she was more than willing to work around his little quirks.

Like Anandur's obsessive need to buy her stuff.

Every time she'd refused, saying she didn't need this or that, he had gotten upset, going as far as getting cranky. In the end, she'd let him buy her whatever he wanted just because it made him happy. Already, they'd had to get an additional suitcase to carry all the purchases.

"Come on. I want to check out that jewelry store." He pulled her after him.

They had nice stuff, if a bit on the gaudy side. Big gold pieces that were studded with gems in all kinds of colors. One bracelet in particular caught her eye. It was set with jade stones, and the price tag wasn't overly shocking, which meant that the stones were probably fake and the rest was gold-plated and not solid gold.

Immediately, the sales clerk appeared at her side. "Would you like to see the matching necklace and earrings?"

She started shaking her head when Anandur interrupted, "Yes, we would."

The salesman smiled like a happy shark and rushed behind the counter. A moment later he returned with a box containing the complete set. "Isn't it beautiful? And the color matches your unique eyes, mademoiselle. This was made for you."

"Try it on." Anandur lifted the necklace out of the display box and put it around her neck. "Let me see."

She turned to him, adjusting the center to rest in the hollow of her throat.

"Magnificent." The clerk handed her a handheld mirror.

Moving to stand behind her, Anandur put his hands on her shoulders and peered at her reflection. "I agree."

It was pretty, but not practical. Where would she wear a thing like that? It wasn't the kind of piece one could wear to work or even for a visit to a friend's house.

"It's too much." Taking it off, she held it out to the salesman.

The guy shook his head, put his hands behind his back, and then looked at Anandur for help.

Suddenly, a memory flitted through her head.

A beautiful redheaded girl was offering Wonder a similar necklace, and Wonder was trying to refuse the gift. But the girl would not have it. She seemed like a bossy little thing, and Wonder had a feeling she was just as difficult to say no to as Anandur.

The memory was fuzzy, but also warm. It hadn't tugged at her heart with sorrow like the memory of Esag had.

"What's the matter?" Anandur sounded worried.

"I remembered something. I think that I once had a friend who gave me a similar necklace."

"Another boyfriend?" Anandur grimaced.

"No, a girl. A beautiful little redhead."

He frowned. "Can you describe her?"

"The memory is fuzzy. I just remember thinking of her as beautiful." She smiled. "And bossy."

Anandur nodded. "We are taking the set," he told the clerk. "Wrap it up."

"Yes, sir." The guy rushed to ring the pieces up.

"You didn't even ask what the price was," she whispered. "You know you're supposed to haggle over it."

It was the local custom. A tourist who didn't haggle was thought of as stupid.

"Not in the airport's duty-free." He handed the guy his credit card. "Besides, the price is reasonable."

If the stones were real, then yes. But she was quite certain they weren't.

"Do you know if it's a fake or not?"

"I don't care. It's a key to your memories, or at least some of them, so it's worth the price even if it is fake."

39

ANANDUR

*A*s they got comfortable in their business class seats, Anandur with a shot of scotch and Wonder with a glass of orange juice, he took her hand and put it on his thigh.

Things were going well, even though the trip brought up only two vague memories. At this point, their relationship was strong enough to withstand whatever new memories surfaced.

Wonder loved him, passionately. It was in her eyes as she gazed at him with admiration, in her indulgent smile when she thought he was acting silly, and in her uninhibited laughter when he was telling her the corniest of jokes.

She was like a new woman. Confident and joyful.

He'd loved her before the trip, but now he was consumed by her. Every thought, no matter the subject, circled back to Wonder.

She was the most important person in his life.

Heck, she was his life.

Before, Anandur hadn't been aware that he'd been only marking time while waiting for her.

Lifting his face to the ceiling, he offered his thanks to the Fates. *Thank you for bringing Wonder and me together. I promise you'll never regret it. And if you ever need help with your schemes, I'm your man.* He tapped his chest with the hand holding the scotch. *Forever grateful and willing to serve,* he added for good measure.

He wasn't a freeloader. He was a giver.

The thing was, Wonder was a giver too. Conventional wisdom claimed that partners should not be too similar in character, and that their different qualities were supposed to complement one another instead of overlapping.

Syssi and Kian were a perfect example of that, as were Brundar and Callie.

Opposites were supposed to attract.

Was he missing something? Was their relationship not as perfect as he believed it to be?

Couldn't be. It felt all too right.

"What's wrong?" Wonder asked.

As he lifted her hand to his lips for a kiss, her new jade bracelet jingled. "Stupid rambling thoughts, that's all."

"Maybe I can help. You looked upset for a moment. I don't want to see my invincible knight of cheer turning glum."

Evidently, even when Wonder seemed preoccupied with her own thoughts, she was still highly attuned to him. There was no hiding from her. He'd better get used to that.

"We are very similar, you and me."

"I don't see how. But what if we are? There is nothing wrong with that."

He emptied his glass and put it on the armrest. "We are both givers."

"What do you mean by that?"

"We derive more pleasure from giving to others than from receiving."

Wonder smirked. "I don't know about that." She leaned to whisper in his ear, "I have no problem with you giving me pleasure."

He wrapped his arm around her shoulders and whispered back, "And there is nothing I love doing more, but if you keep talking like that, I'll have to make use of that bathroom." He was just teasing. They were too big to fit in there.

As opposed to the first time he'd mentioned it, this time Wonder didn't seem as appalled by the idea. On the contrary, the gleam in her eyes suggested she was considering it.

However, after giving it a little more thought, she must've arrived at the same realization he had. "It's too cramped in there."

He wasn't done teasing her, though. "When they dim the lights, I'll spread a blanket over both of us, and we can play footsie."

"What's footsie?"

"Wait until the lights are down and I'll show you." He waggled his brows.

"Okay." Wonder didn't look worried. "I don't think we are alike at all." She picked up their previous conversation. "I'm not funny, and you are. You're also more outgoing. You like to fight, and I don't."

"I admit I like a good fight, but mostly it's about having the ability to protect. We have that in common. Others might call it rescuer syndrome, but I call it having what it takes to do the job and not shying away from the responsibility of doing what needs to be done. You won't hear me apologizing for it."

"And you shouldn't." Her brows dipped to form a deep crease. "I can't understand anyone turning a good quality like this into a negative thing." She narrowed her eyes. "A syndrome implies something bad, right?"

As beautiful as she was when content and peaceful, Wonder was stunning when riled. She should let her inner tigress unsheathe her claws more often.

"The negative part, love, is that we are compelled to rescue others even to our own detriment."

Letting out a breath, Wonder slumped into her seat. "I can't argue with that. I was in big trouble before you showed up."

"And yet, if faced with a similar situation again, you would act exactly the same."

"Yeah, you're right. As far as self-preservation goes, it's stupid."

"But admirable." He leaned and planted a quick kiss on her lips. "You see, we think alike. I would've done the same thing."

"But that's good, isn't it? Imagine if one of us couldn't accept the other getting into dangerous situations. It would have strained the relationship."

True. He was just glad that Wonder didn't want to be a Guardian. Dealing with that would've been a nightmare for him.

So sue him if he was a hypocrite. "I'm glad you have no problem with what I do. Not every female can tolerate living with a Guardian."

Wonder turned to face him. "What do you mean by living with?"

"You know, sharing a house."

"But we don't."

"Which is something we're going to fix as soon as we get back. In fact, I'm going to text Magnus right now and tell him to look for a new place." He should've done it before they had left for Egypt, but it hadn't crossed his mind.

Or, if he cared to be honest with himself, Anandur had been a chicken, still afraid Wonder might choose the other guy.

But she had chosen him, and he didn't want her spending even one night away from him. Hell, he was going to have a hard time letting her out of his sight for even an hour, which was a big problem since both of them needed to get back to their jobs.

As he pulled out his phone, Wonder put her hand over his. "You didn't ask me if I wanted to move in with you."

He arched a brow. "Don't you want to?"

"I do, but that's beside the point. You should've asked."

Women were strange. Why ask when it was the obvious thing to do? They loved each other, and he considered her his mate.

Naturally, they needed to live together.

Unless she didn't think of him as hers.

Maybe he was making assumptions he shouldn't?

"Am I your mate, Wonder? Do you accept me as your one and only? Do you want to spend the rest of your life with me?"

A bright smile spread over her beautiful face. "Of course, I do. But was it so difficult to ask?"

40

WONDER

"How are we getting home?" Wonder asked.

The plane was approaching the passenger boarding bridge and some of the passengers were already releasing their seatbelts.

"One moment," Anandur said. "Let me check." He pulled out his phone.

The question she'd really wanted to ask was whose home they were going to. Was she spending the night with Gertrude and Hildegard? Or was she going to move in with Anandur and share his house together with Magnus until the other Guardian found a new place?

She had no problem with that, and, hopefully, Magnus wouldn't mind either.

The truth was that she couldn't imagine sleeping alone in her bed even for one night. Having Anandur right there beside her was how she wanted to fall asleep every night and wake up every morning.

"Apparently, we were dearly missed." Anandur glanced up from his phone, which had started buzzing with text messages as soon as he'd taken it off airplane mode. "Kian sent his driver to pick us up with the limousine, and we have a welcoming party waiting for us when we get back."

"Cool, I've never been in a limo. Is it fun?"

"It has a nicely stocked bar with stuff that doesn't taste like piss."

"I'll take your word for it." Wonder zipped up her purse and put it on her lap. "I hope they don't expect us to go straight from the airport to the party. I want to shower first."

He sniffed at her hair. "You smell fine to me."

She huffed. "I could stink like yesterday's garbage, and you'd think I smelled amazing. I think my pheromones are messing with all of your other senses."

Either that or he lied a lot, but she doubted that. He loved sniffing her hair and nuzzling her neck, and he'd often mentioned how great she smelled, even when she felt less than fresh, which with Egypt's heat and humidity had been an issue. Five minutes after leaving the hotel's air-conditioned interior, her clothes would stick to her body, and she'd have to pull her hair up because her neck was sweaty.

"Where did you come up with that? I've never heard of pheromones working that way. Have you been talking to Bridget?"

"No, but there is no other explanation for your sense of smell getting all wonky."

"I think it's love." He nuzzled her neck. "Do I ever smell bad to you?"

Wonder giggled as he touched a sensitive spot. "No, but that's because you never do. How can you ever get smelly when you shower twice a day?"

He grimaced. "Normally I don't. Egypt was just so damn hot and humid."

Anandur sounded as if he was apologizing for his attention to cleanliness.

She smiled at him. "I love it that you're so clean. I don't think I could've lived with a guy who wasn't. I like things clean and tidy too."

"About that." He scratched his beard. "I'm clean but messy. I may not live up to your standards."

As if a little mess could diminish the pure joy of just being with him. Cupping his cheek, Wonder leaned to kiss Anandur's lips. "I love you, silly. And I don't expect you to be perfect. A little mess is such an insignificant thing. We will find a compromise."

"Oh, yeah? Like what?"

Pretending to think it over, she tapped her chin. "If you keep the living room nice and tidy, I'll let you mess up the bedroom." She winked. "But only for a good reason."

"Define good reason."

She got closer and whispered, "Like throwing the coverlet on the floor to make love to me. That's a good reason. Or putting all the pillows in one big pile to accommodate that position you like so much." She waggled her brows.

"Teaser." He nipped her nose. "You think you're safe from me because we are getting chauffeured home? There is a privacy partition in the limo."

Although the idea sounded exciting for a moment, she soon realized the disadvantages. It would get messy, and Wonder doubted a limo came with a shower.

Making love in a car, even a limousine, didn't appeal to her. Still, if Anandur wanted to be adventurous, she wasn't going to deny him. "In that case, I'll definitely need a shower when we get back."

"It can be arranged."

As the plane stopped and the seatbelt sign was turned off, Anandur got up and pulled down their carryon from the overhead bin. Blocking the aisle for her to get in front of him, he kept reading messages on his phone while holding up the throng of passengers waiting to get out.

"I've gotten some exciting updates."

She turned around. "Good ones?"

"Excellent. Do you remember the guy I told you about who might be joining our community?"

"I assume you're not talking about Eva's baby." He'd mentioned three new additions to the clan. One was her, the other a baby on the way, and the third one was a young guy they believed was a Dormant.

"I'm talking about Ruth's boyfriend. He's finally ready to join, which means that Eva and Bhathian will be moving in soon."

So the guy had transitioned successfully, which according to Anandur wasn't a given. It was a dangerous process, and they'd had a couple of close calls with Dormants who had almost not made it.

"I'm glad he's okay, for him and for his girlfriend. That's very good news."

"It is. We celebrate every new member."

41

ANANDUR

*N*ick transitioning was one less thing to worry about, and Eva moving into the village before her baby's arrival was another.

Life was good.

He and Wonder were moving in together and starting their mated life, Brundar's wounds were finally healing, and the clan was growing. Not by much, but any addition was a blessing.

The thing was, even an optimist like him knew that the calm was temporary. When things were going smoothly, something had to happen to mess them up.

Anandur could only hope that it wouldn't be anything major, like Doomers discovering the village's location and storming it in a way no one had predicted, circumventing all of the clan's defenses.

Leaning toward Wonder's ear, he whispered, "That prickling feeling I got in Luxor, did you experience anything like it during our vacation?"

Wonder looked at him over her shoulder. "Now that you mention it, I did. But it turned out to be nothing."

Anandur tensed. "What was it?"

"When you went to buy us coffee at the airport, an old guy lightly brushed against my arm on his way to the table next to ours. I got that weird feeling for a moment, but it didn't make any sense. He looked like he was in his eighties, stooped back, thick glasses, and a big belly. He sat right next to us the whole time. When you came with the coffees and didn't react to his presence at all, I dismissed it."

"You should have told me. I would've paid more attention."

She shrugged. "I was sure it was nothing. But next time I'll tell you when I sense something off about someone."

"Please do." He wrapped his arm around her middle and pulled her back against his body.

An immortal could've put on a convincing disguise. Eva had done it successfully for years. But then he doubted an immortal could've been sitting right next to him without triggering his alarm. Not unless it was someone he knew and had been exposed to before.

Could it be that someone from the clan was spying on him?

Not likely. The only reason anyone would go to so much trouble would be revenge for one of his pranks. But none of them had been malicious enough to justify such an elaborate plot. Anandur couldn't think of anyone who would put on prosthetics and follow them around the world just to get back at him.

"Thank the gods," Wonder said as the aircraft's door opened and they were let out.

At the passport checkpoint, she fidgeted a little, but

their fake documentation didn't raise any red flags. They retrieved their luggage, passed customs without getting stopped, and headed up the ramp into the waiting area.

They found Okidu standing just outside the roped-off area with a broad smile on his face and a bouquet of flowers in his hands.

"For madam." He bowed and handed it to Wonder. "You look lovelier than ever."

Taken aback, she hesitated before taking the flowers, then put on a fake smile and snatched them from Okidu's hands. "Thank you."

Hadn't she met the Odu before? That would explain her strange reaction to him. He looked too old to be an immortal, and she knew no humans were allowed in the village.

"Who sent the flowers, Okidu?" Anandur asked.

"Master Magnus asked me to stop by a florist and purchase a bouquet. There is a note from him." The butler pulled a small envelope hidden inside the decorative wrapping.

Wonder lifted a pair of puzzled eyes to Anandur. "Do you know what this is all about? No one has ever sent me flowers before."

That was something Anandur planned on fixing as soon as possible. If Wonder liked flowers, he would buy her a bouquet every time he was in town. "Probably congratulations. Magnus is an old-fashioned fellow."

He waited until they were seated in the limo and the partition went up before explaining about the butler. "Okidu isn't human. He isn't an immortal either. He is a kind of hybrid creation of machine parts and flesh. That's why he seemed so strange to you."

She shook her head. "It wasn't that. He said that I looked lovelier than ever, but I've never met him before."

"Think nothing of it. Okidu parrots what he hears on his British television shows. It's probably a phrase he heard and repeated to you."

Wonder didn't look convinced. "Maybe. It's strange, but although I'm sure I've never met Kian's butler, he seems vaguely familiar. I have a feeling I know him from somewhere. Or maybe someone who looks like him." She grimaced. "I don't know why, but I had an immediate aversion to the guy." She waved a hand. "Or cyborg, or whatever."

"That's odd. I've never heard of anyone reacting to Okidu that way. Everyone likes him. He plays the jolly butler role so well that it's easy to forget he's only mimicking stuff he sees on the tube."

Wonder shrugged. "Maybe that's the problem. I don't like the idea of servants. It bothers me when I see someone bend over backward for a person they consider their superior. I don't know if you've noticed, but I'm very big on equality. I don't like that women are discriminated against in some societies, and I don't like places that have different classes of people. A person should be judged based on merit, not based on where he or she was born and to whom."

"That's my girl." Anandur wrapped an arm around her shoulders. "A champion of freedom, justice, and equality."

Her brows dipped, creating deep furrows between her eyes. "Are you making fun of me?"

"Not in a million years. I meant it as a compliment. Now tell me what Magnus wrote."

"Okay." She pulled the folded note out of the envelope, and as she read it, a big smile spread over her lovely face.

"What does it say?"

"He says that he's already moved out and is very happy with his new roommates who are neat and tidy and don't leave their boots in the living room. He wishes us best of luck and advises me to hide the pillows if we ever get into a fight." She looked up at him. "Should I ask, what is he talking about?"

Anandur humphed and crossed his arms over his chest. "You can do a thousand favors for a buddy, but does he remember that? Nay. But you kill one pillow…" He shook his head.

"What happened to the pillow?"

He'd better tell her or she'd keep bugging him until he fessed up. "Remember the night of our first kiss?"

"How can I forget?" She blushed and looked away. "I'm so sorry about that."

He uncrossed his arms and wrapped one around her shoulders. "It's in the past, lass. You're mine now. Anyway, I was a tad upset, and I couldn't sleep. I kept punching the pillow into the shape I thought would make it comfortable, but I used a little too much force. The thing exploded, and even though I vacuumed as much of the fallout as I could, Magnus and I have been chasing tiny feathers ever since."

WONDER

"Oh. My. Gods." Wonder threw a hand over her mouth.

Amanda's living room was packed with people, everyone clapping and hooting as if Anandur and Wonder had returned from Egypt holding the World Cup trophy between them.

To dispel any doubts as to what the celebration was all about, a large banner hung over the fireplace, with their names bisected by a large red heart.

"Consider this an engagement party." Amanda pulled Wonder into her arms for a quick hug, then transferred her to Carol, who was jumping up and down awaiting her turn.

"You look amazing!" Carol squealed.

"Come here, big guy." Amanda hugged Anandur. "I'm so happy you guys found each other. Although, I'm a little bummed that I had nothing to do with it."

Next was Brundar, who shocked Wonder by giving her

a one-armed one-second embrace. "Thank you for making my brother a happy man." He stunned her again.

"Stop gaping," Callie whispered as she hugged her.

"Sorry. I didn't mean to. It's just that…"

"I know. It's okay." Callie kissed her on one cheek and then on the another. "I'm overjoyed to have you as a sister. Not in law, mind you, because neither of us is married yet, but in spirit."

Wonder swallowed the big lump that had formed in her throat. Having a sister, if only in spirit, filled some missing part in her heart that she hadn't even known existed until Callie brought it up.

"Thank you. I would love to have you as my sister. And Brundar as my brother, if he'll have me, that is."

"He already does. Just don't expect him to act any differently. It takes time to learn his tiny, nearly invisible tells. When you get to know him better, you'll see what I mean."

"I can't wait."

The hugs and kisses and congratulations went on for a while, overwhelming Wonder with emotion and gratitude for her new family, but also with a tinge of anxiety.

Everyone was taking it for granted that she and Anandur were a mated pair, and they were probably right, but Wonder thought it was too soon for an official celebration. Perhaps in a few months, when they settled into a routine, and she decided what she wanted to do with her life, she and Anandur could throw an official engagement party.

Maybe even set a date for a wedding.

Wonder shook her head. Here she was, anxious about

an unofficial engagement party, and at the same time thinking about a wedding.

Talk about not making sense.

Things were moving light-speed fast, and she was still playing catch up.

"Okay, everyone." Amanda clapped her hands. "Let's take this party out into the yard. Dalhu says the steaks are about ready."

Wonder was curious to meet the ex-Doomer who'd won Amanda's heart. He'd never visited the café, and this was the first time she'd been invited to their house. From the little Carol had hinted at, the circumstances of Amanda and Dalhu's meeting had been similar to Wonder and Anandur's, just in reverse.

One day she was going to ask Amanda about it.

"Come on, love." Anandur took her hand. "Let's eat. I'm starving."

"I bet. Me too. The portions on the airplane were tiny."

Out in the backyard, she spotted Dalhu easily. He was the biggest guy there, and she would've added the meanest if not for the way he looked at Amanda. It was obvious the guy worshiped her.

Still, if Wonder had met Dalhu in the back alley of her club, she would've thought twice about capturing him.

Catching her staring at her guy, Amanda walked over and threaded her arm through Wonder's. "Come and meet Dalhu. You haven't met yet, right?"

Wonder shook her head. "He never comes to the café."

"I know." Amanda sighed. "Did I tell you that Dalhu is a talented artist?"

"You mentioned a paintbrush."

"Right. Anyway, my Dalhu is not only talented, but he is

very passionate about his art. Which means that it's next to impossible to pry him away from his canvases. The moment he's done with one, he starts the next."

"That's actually enviable. I would've loved to have an all-consuming talent. As it is, I don't even know what I want to do with my life."

"Yes, well. Passion is fine, but obsession is not. Right, darling?"

Dalhu dropped another steak on the big platter that was already heaped with a mountain of them. "It's a fine line." He wiped his hands on a dishrag and then offered one to Wonder. "I heard a lot about you, Wonder."

"I hope good things."

He gave her a once-over, but there was nothing sexual about it. "I would like to paint a portrait of you. You have a very interesting face."

"Thank you. I think." What did he mean by interesting?

"You're beautiful, darling," Amanda immediately caught up. "Dalhu is thinking like an artist. Beauty on its own doesn't interest him. He paints the soul."

That sounded poetic, but Amanda was probably just being nice, and exaggerating to make Wonder feel good. Which was sweet.

"I would love to see some of his work."

"Did you see his landscapes in the living room?"

"Sorry, but with everyone congratulating us, I didn't really pay attention."

"That's okay. First get something to eat, and then I'll show you some of his work. Most of the portraits he's done are hanging in other people's houses, but there are several works in progress you can take a look at. Did Anandur show you his?"

"No." Wonder glanced at Anandur, who was smiling sheepishly. "Where is it?"

"In my bedroom."

Not the one in the keep because she'd been there and hadn't seen Anandur's portrait. It was probably in his house in the village, which they hadn't even stopped by, heading straight for Amanda's house.

"It's a nude," Amanda whispered loudly in Wonder's ear.

"Oh, my. I'd love to see that."

"It's not a nude. I had my pants on. Do you think this dude would've agreed to paint a naked guy? The only one he paints full nudes of is Amanda."

The woman didn't even bat an eyelash at that. "I would've never allowed my Dalhu to look at naked models. So naturally, he has to use me as his nude muse." She kissed his cheek and then wrapped her arm around his middle.

Wonder didn't think Amanda had anything to worry about. Dalhu could've had a bunch of naked beauties parade in front of him, and he would've regarded them with the same dispassionate eyes as he had her.

"I brought vegan burgers." Syssi handed Dalhu a container. "Can you grill them for Kian and me? There is enough in there for Amanda and Bridget too. If they are in the mood for a veggie burger, that is."

"No problem. I'll make them once I'm done with the steaks."

"I'd love one. Thank you for thinking of me." Amanda patted Syssi's shoulder.

"You're welcome."

After loading her plate with corncobs, potato salad, and French fries, Amanda asked, "And where is my brother?"

"Take a guess." Syssi put two corncobs on her plate.

"Working."

"Right. Some last minute details on a deal that was supposed to close yesterday." She added potato salad.

"The guy doesn't know when to quit." Amanda started walking toward the table.

Syssi waited for Wonder to finish loading her plate with steaks, which was a little awkward to do in front of a vegetarian, but she didn't make any comments about the poor animals, which Wonder was grateful for.

"Tell us all about Egypt," Syssi said when they started walking toward the table. "Did any new memories surface?"

"Not really. I remembered a little bit more about Esag. He'd been the one who'd trained me. And I also had a brief memory of a girl I knew. Well, more than knew. I think we were friends. But other than her being a beautiful redhead and the impression that she was bossy, there was nothing more. Her facial features were hazy, and then I forgot even that."

Syssi frowned. "Do you remember what either of them was wearing?"

"Unfortunately, I don't. I know that Esag was tall and smiled a lot and that the girl was short and bossy. That's about it."

43

ANANDUR

"*I*'m so full." Wonder rubbed her tummy. "Dalhu, you're a man of many talents. The steaks were so tasty that I ended up eating three."

"Thank you. I'm glad you enjoyed them."

"Next barbecue in our house." Anandur wrapped his arm around Wonder and pulled her closer.

He didn't like her giving Dalhu compliments. It might have been petty of him, but he wanted her admiration all for himself. He couldn't compete with the Doomer in art, but he could grill steaks just as well if not better.

"Which reminds me," Amanda said. "I still didn't show you Dalhu's work. Are you ready to see it now? Or do you need a few more moments to digest?"

"I'm ready." Wonder glanced at Anandur. "Do you want to come?"

"Sure." He wasn't going to stay out in the backyard while she gushed over Dalhu's incredible talent.

"I'll come with you." Syssi pushed away from the table.

"What about you? Want to come and present your work?" Amanda asked.

"I'll stay and make sure we are not running out of food."

Amanda chuckled. "My guy doesn't like it when people compliment him. He's shy."

Dalhu tilted his head as if to say, really?

Anandur didn't think the dude was shy. He was too critical of his own work and didn't think it was as good as everyone was saying it was.

As they entered the living room, Amanda pointed at a large landscape picture hanging over the fireplace mantel. "This is Dalhu's latest work. He's been into landscapes lately." She waved her hand around the room and the many landscapes covering its walls. "I think they are beautiful, but Dalhu is not happy with them yet. He says he needs more practice before he offers them for sale."

Wonder stopped in front of one of the smaller paintings. It was a close up of a rose bush, with colors so vivid that the roses seemed to be sticking out of the canvas. "I would buy this. How much is he charging for a painting?"

Amanda shook her head. "He wouldn't hear about selling something he is not completely happy with. His portraits go for a thousand each."

That was a lot of money. He'd only charged Anandur five hundred. But that was before he'd gotten famous and every immortal wanted a portrait.

"It's a bit rich for me." Wonder moved to look at another picture. It was of a meadow surrounded by trees. A swath of light cut through the dense foliage, illuminating a wooden bench. "I like this one too."

Anandur was going to have a talk with Dalhu and have the dude part with some of his 'imperfect work.' With payment or without. If Wonder liked the landscapes, Anandur was going to get them for her.

"Let's go to Dalhu's studio. That's where he keeps what he calls his works in progress." Amanda huffed. "He's such a perfectionist."

They followed her down the hallway to one of the bedrooms that had been converted into Dalhu's workspace. She pushed the door open and flicked on the light switch.

Two easels held big canvases. One was a portrait of Phoenix reaching with a chubby hand for a toy, her eyes glowing with mischief. The other was of Turner, the way he looked before his transition.

Anandur walked over to stand in front of it. "Did Turner commission this before he transitioned?"

"No." Amanda stood next to him. "He didn't commission it at all. Dalhu decided that the guy looked more interesting before."

"I agree. There was hardness in him that is gone now. His eyes, though, I never noticed how intense they are."

"Right? I didn't either, but Dalhu did." There was a note of pride in her tone.

"What's under there?" Wonder pointed at the largest canvas in the room. At least five feet by two and a half, it was leaning against the wall and wrapped in brown packing paper.

"Oh, this." Amanda sauntered over and started to unravel the twine wrapped around the canvas. "He painted this one while we were still living in the keep and hasn't touched it since. I think he is afraid to finish it." She pulled the paper away to reveal Annani's portrait.

"Oh, my gods." Anandur heard Wonder exclaim from behind him.

Smiling, he started to turn around. "Isn't she stunn…" He stopped.

Wonder's face was paler than a ghost's.

"What's wrong?" He rushed to her side.

"It's her…" She pointed with a violently shaking hand. "The goddess…"

"Yes, this is Annani, our Clan Mother."

Wonder shook her head. "My lady, the princess…" Her eyes rolled back in her head, and her knees buckled.

Catching her before she hit the floor, Anandur absorbed Wonder's fall and sat with her cradled in his arms. "Quick, call Bridget over here," he told Amanda.

"I'm on it." She rushed out of the room.

"Wonder recognized Annani," Syssi said quietly. "She fainted from the shock."

"That's impossible. She could never have seen her. Do you think she dreamt of her? Like in one of your prophetic dreams?"

"It could be. Did she ever mention having precognition?"

"No, but she talked about dreaming of gods and goddesses and immortals."

"Maybe those weren't dreams. Maybe those were memories."

A chill ran down Anandur's spine. "What are you suggesting, Syssi?"

"Maybe her coma lasted much longer than any of us suspected. Perhaps she spent a very long time in stasis."

Syssi's suggestion was ridiculous. "She couldn't have survived for thousands of years. That's impossible."

"Why not? Is there a limit on stasis?"

"Other than Annani and those in Mortdh's stronghold, no one survived the cataclysm."

Syssi crouched next to him on the floor. "What if Wonder was in Mortdh's stronghold when the bomb detonated in Sumer? She could've escaped somehow and traveled all the way down to Egypt. Something must've happened there that put her in stasis. Maybe she got accidentally buried when a building collapsed."

Wonder stirred in his arms, groaned, but didn't open her eyes.

"Wonder? Can you hear me, lass? Say something."

As she turned her face and pressed her nose into his midsection, Anandur let out a sigh of relief. If Wonder was moving, she was okay.

"What's going on?" Bridget rushed in.

"She fainted. But I think she's awake and just refusing to communicate."

The doctor knelt next to him on the floor. "You need to lay her down on her back and elevate her legs."

Wonder lifted one arm and wrapped it around Anandur's middle, holding on tight.

"I don't think she wants to move."

"I saw that. We will give her a minute." Bridget glanced at the open door where a crowd was starting to gather. "I'm sure Wonder would appreciate some privacy. Dalhu, bring me a glass of water and a glass of juice. Amanda, go get a blanket for Wonder. Everyone else, please go back outside."

No one argued with Bridget when she used her doctor's tone. Immediately, the corridor emptied of people, and several moments later Amanda came back with the blanket, and Dalhu returned with two full glasses. He put them down on the floor next to Bridget, then stepped back.

The doctor touched Wonder's arm. "Wonder, honey, can you tell us what happened?"

Clinging even harder to Anandur, Wonder shook her head almost imperceptibly.

As she tucked the blanket around her, Amanda glanced at the painting that had started it all. "She took one look at Annani's portrait, gasped and fainted."

"Did she say anything?" Bridget asked.

Anandur didn't remember what it was, but Syssi did. "She said my lady, the princess."

Bridget looked up at Syssi. "That's all?"

"Yes. I think Wonder recognized Annani and it jarred some of her buried memories free. She fainted from the shock."

"How could it be possible?" Amanda asked. "There is no way she could've met Annani. My mother routinely goes on excursions among humans, but what are the chances of her bumping into Wonder and leaving such a profound impression as to make the poor girl faint from taking one look at her picture?"

44

WONDER

*W*onder felt like throwing up. Or crying. Or both.

Fragments of memories were swirling in an uncoordinated dance around her head, making no sense.

And as much as she tried, she couldn't get rid of them either.

Go away, leave me alone, she screamed on the inside. *I don't want to remember.*

"Gulan, get me my blue dress," the beautiful girl with the massive red hair commanded.

"Gulan, where are my new sandals? Can you check under the bed?"

"Gulan, come do my hair."

"Gulan…"

It took Wonder a few moments to realize that the girl had been addressing her.

Her name was Gulan, not Wonder, and she was a servant.

Or had been.

The fragments of images her memories were hurling against the barrier that her brain was desperately trying to keep up didn't look like anything she was familiar with.

Two things were clear to her, though. First, the stunningly beautiful girl was the goddess Annani, the princess. Second, Annani hadn't been Wonder's friend, she had been her employer.

Gulan's boss.

Except, Wonder didn't feel as if Gulan had resented the bossy teenager from her memories. She'd felt protective of the tiny goddess. Had she been Annani's bodyguard?

That would explain the training she'd received and her natural inclination to step in when her superior strength could be of use.

How and when, though, Wonder still couldn't tell. It was messy in her head, the distorted fragments refusing to coalesce into a solid picture. Or maybe she was purposefully preventing them from doing so.

People were talking around her, their worried and perplexed voices clear, but not the words they were saying.

Except, she didn't care about what was coming out of their mouths, or what they were thinking of her for clinging to Anandur like a baby to its parent. While the crazy turmoil in her head was threatening to annihilate her and everything she'd believed about herself, he was the one solid thing she could hold onto.

There was no way she was letting anyone pry her away from Anandur. She would unleash the full extent of her power and destroy whoever tried. Because if she let go of him, she would be letting go of Wonder as well.

"Wonder? Can you hear me?" Anandur asked again.

He sounded worried. It was her fault. But all she could do in response was tighten her arms around him.

"If Wonder would only turn around, I could snap a picture and text it to my mother, see if she recognizes her."

No, no, no. Annani would come for her and take her away from Anandur, or send a servant to retrieve her.

"I don't want to go," she murmured into Anandur's stomach, digging her fingers into his flesh.

He stroked her hair. "You're not going anywhere, love. I've got you."

"She sounds terrified," the doctor said. "Wonder, honey, you need to talk to us and tell us what's wrong. I promise you that no one is going to make you leave. You don't have to go anywhere you don't want to."

The doctor could promise whatever she wanted, but once the goddess learned of Gulan, no one could stop her from claiming her. Anandur and the doctor and even Kian couldn't protect her if the goddess decided she wanted Gulan back. No one said no to Annani.

"You can't keep me here. She'll come for me."

"Who will come for you, lass?"

"Annani."

The room hushed, and Wonder realized that she'd given herself away. That was the confirmation they'd all been waiting for.

"Why would she come for you?" Anandur asked.

"Because I'm hers."

"You're not making any sense, love."

"Okay, Wonder, that's enough," Bridget said sternly. "I want you to sit up, drink the orange juice, and tell us what's going on."

There was no avoiding it. She could hide for a few

more moments, but eventually, she'd have to tell them who she was. Or rather had been.

Wonder wasn't Gulan.

Wonder didn't want to be Gulan.

Wonder didn't even want to remember Gulan.

Unfortunately, with every passing moment more and more of the fragmented memories solidified, painting an unflattering picture of a subservient life.

That girl had been miserable. She'd been a lowly servant who lived for the whims of her lady. Gulan had been a graceless young woman who men had ignored. Her only chance of having a family had been accepting a position of a concubine or mating a human.

Esag, she remembered now, hadn't loved her. He'd liked her enough to offer her a position as his concubine, but not enough to break his engagement to a girl he couldn't stand.

Now that Wonder knew what love was, she realized that she hadn't loved him either. It had been only an infatuation.

Her love for Anandur burned as bright as a midday sun. Compared to that, what she'd felt for Esag was like the glow of dying embers.

Gulan had been a nobody who had no one.

Wonder was a free, confident, and capable woman who could make her future into whatever she desired.

Wonder had Anandur, an immortal male who loved her passionately.

Gulan had had nothing.

45

ANANDUR

he studio's door burst open, and Kian strode in. "I was told that Wonder fainted. What's going on?"

"She was about to tell us," Bridget said. "But maybe we should move this somewhere more comfortable."

"We can use the master bedroom, and we don't even have to go out into the corridor. I had a door installed between the rooms," Amanda said. "We have a sitting area with a couch and two armchairs in there. Wonder can lie down on the couch." She glanced at Kian. "But maybe we should let Bridget and Anandur talk to her alone. Whatever it is has scared the crap out of her. She's quite shaken up."

If he weren't holding Wonder in his arms, Anandur would've kissed Amanda on both cheeks. This was probably the most selfless gesture she'd ever made. The princess loved gossip as much as the next woman, and he was sure she was dying of curiosity, but she'd offered to leave in order to make Wonder more comfortable.

"Nice try," Kian blew Amanda off. "I need to hear this. Especially after the interesting talk I had with Okidu."

Amanda arched a brow. "Okidu? What does he have to do with Wonder?"

"I'd rather hear it from her."

Why the hell did Kian sound so hostile? Wonder was holding it together by a thread, and then the jerk had to barge in and make a scene because it always had to be about him.

The girl was trembling in Anandur's arms.

"Watch your tone, Kian," he hissed through rapidly elongating fangs.

The good thing about his boss was that he wasn't stupid. Taking one look at Anandur's face and then at Wonder's, he nodded and continued in a much more amiable tone. "Let's move this to your bedroom, Dalhu. Lead the way."

Anandur carried Wonder to the couple's spacious master bedroom and sat down with her on the couch, while Kian took one of the armchairs and pulled Syssi to sit on his lap. Bridget sat in the other one.

Lifting the footboard bench, Dalhu carried it over to the front of the fireplace, put it down, and then motioned for Amanda to take a seat but didn't join her. "Coffee or alcohol?" he asked. "I'm not sure what the protocol is for something like this."

"Bring both, darling," Amanda said. "A bottle of scotch and a carafe of coffee."

"Got it. What should I tell the people outside?"

Good question.

"Tell them that Wonder was dehydrated and exhausted from the trip," Bridget suggested. "That's probably the real reason for why she fainted. If she were in better shape, she could've handled the emotional shock."

"Sounds good, doc." He opened the studio door.

"You're the best." Amanda blew him a kiss.

When the door closed behind Dalhu, Bridget leaned forward and braced her elbows on her knees. "Are you ready to talk, honey?"

Wonder took a shuddering breath and nodded.

"That's a brave lass." Anandur stroked her arm gently. "Take your time. No one is in a hurry."

Kian cleared his throat.

The bastard.

Leaning her back against his chest, Wonder started talking. "My real name is Gulan, and I was Annani's maid."

"Her maid?" Amanda exclaimed. "My mother doesn't have maids. She has butlers, her Odus."

"I was her maid before she got the Odus." Wonder chuckled sadly. "They kind of put me out of work. Once she got them, Annani didn't need me anymore. They took over my job."

Anandur was still trying to wrap his head around what Wonder was saying, but Kian looked as if he'd known that already.

He narrowed his eyes at the guy. "You don't look surprised, Kian. How come?"

"Because Okidu came back from the airport and reported that he'd delivered Master Anandur and Lady Gulan safely to the party. When I asked him who Lady Gulan was, he said that she used to be the Clan Mother's companion, and now she was Master Anandur's mate. So I asked when did she serve as the Clan Mother's companion, and he said before the goddess became the Clan Mother, when she was still known as Princess Annani."

Anandur leaned back against the couch cushions. "Where have you been during all these years, Wonder?"

She sighed, the scent of her tears increasing his sense of alarm. "For reasons I don't want to talk about right now, I ran away after Annani and Khiann's mating ceremony. I dressed as a man and joined a caravan headed for Kemet, or Egypt as it's called nowadays. It was a very long journey, and everything went well. I thought I'd made it safely and could start a new life, but a massive earthquake put an end to my journey."

Lifting her arm, Wonder wiped her tears away with her sleeve. "That's all I remember."

Bridget pushed to her feet and started pacing the room. "You must've gotten buried alive and gone into stasis." She turned to look at Wonder. "You are a real miracle, a wonder. Theoretically, I knew immortals could survive in stasis indefinitely, but I never expected to find a live survivor after five thousand years."

Wonder stiffened in his arms. "Did you say five thousand years?"

The doctor stopped her pacing. "How many years did you think passed since you left Sumer with that caravan?"

"I don't know. I haven't studied history. I thought it was maybe a few centuries ago. But five thousand years?"

"Not exactly, but more or less."

She shook her head. "Wow, I can't believe it. I'm ancient."

"Well, not really. How old were you when you ran away?"

"Eighteen and seven moon cycles."

Bridget nodded. "Then that's how old you are plus the time since you've awakened. Your body went into stasis, and your brain didn't accumulate any new experiences. You're about nineteen and a half."

Anandur chuckled. "So I was right. I'm an old lecher who's seduced a teenager."

Wonder wasn't amused. "You said that Annani was the only goddess. What happened to the others? Did the boat of a million years pick them up?"

He was tempted to say yes, but he had no idea what the boat of a million years was.

"I'm afraid not," Bridget said. "They are all gone.'

Wonder's hand flew to her chest. "Gone?"

"I'm afraid so."

WONDER

"*T*ell me what happened. Where did the gods go?"

Anandur's strong arms coiled around her. "Maybe we should talk about it some other time. You've had enough of a shock."

Instead of calming her down, his words had added to her anxiety. "Tell me what happened. I need to know."

The door between the studio and the bedroom opened, and Dalhu walked in with a tray. "Who wants scotch and who wants coffee?"

Wonder was tempted to ask for the scotch, the entire bottle of the disgusting stuff. Anything to numb her frayed nerves and prepare her for what was about to come. Nothing she was about to hear was going to be good. She could tell that by the pinched expressions on Syssi and Kian's faces, and the deep sorrow in Bridget's eyes.

Hiding her discomfort better than the others, Amanda got up to help Dalhu. "Okay, people, let's take a coffee break from the drama. Who wants what?"

Once the drinks were distributed, Amanda ducked into

the bathroom and returned with a box of tissues. "You're gonna need it." She handed the box to Wonder, then crouched on the floor next to her. "Just remember. Everything you're going to hear happened a really long time ago. It's very tragic, but you've survived. Not only that, you've survived for a reason. The Fates have a plan for you."

Was that supposed to cheer her up?

"Why are you telling me this? You're just scaring me more."

Amanda put a hand on Wonder's arm. "Because I know how it feels to lose people you love. You'll feel guilty for being alive while they perished, and you'll wish you could join them beyond the veil. What I'm trying to say is, don't give in to despair. You're a strong woman, Wonder. Never forget that. And you're loved by one of the best men I know. If nothing from what I told you makes sense to you, just remember that Anandur is worth living for."

That actually helped. And the cup of strong black coffee Dalhu had put in her hands had a curiously grounding effect. "I'm ready. Which one of you is going to tell me what happened?"

"I will," Bridget said. "Kian probably knows our history better than any of us, but his delivery leaves a lot to be desired." She cast him an apologetic glance. "You can correct me if I get something wrong."

"I'm sure you know as much as I do. Go ahead."

"What was the last major event you remember, Wonder? Or do you prefer me to call you Gulan?"

"Please call me Wonder. Gulan is dead." She hadn't meant to sound so vehement, but she meant what she'd said. "And the last major event was Annani and Khiann's wedding."

"Well, Mortdh didn't take it as well as Ahn thought he had. He decided to kill Khiann and take Annani for himself."

"Did he succeed?"

"Unfortunately, yes."

"Poor Annani." Wonder couldn't imagine the pain. They had been so in love. When the tears started flowing, she was grateful for Amanda's foresight and pulled out a bunch of tissues. "What did she do?"

"Luckily for us and for all of humanity, she didn't wait for Mortdh's trial to end and escaped to the north with her seven Odus. Mortdh had no plans to submit to the gods' verdict. Instead, he loaded a nuclear bomb on his plane and dropped it over the large assembly while they were deliberating how to bring him to justice."

"He killed all the gods?"

Bridget nodded. "What we know, we pieced together from human records. Annani was hiding somewhere in the area of today's Norway when he struck, so there wasn't much she could tell us because she heard about it much later. It must've been a small bomb, and Mortdh probably believed the damage would be restricted to the immediate area of the assembly building, but he didn't take into account the wind. He himself got caught in it and died along with the other gods. But it didn't end with that. The easterly wind swept over the entire region, killing everything in its path. The devastation was so widespread that Sumer never recovered."

"What about the immortals? Did any of them survive?"

Gulan's family, her little sister Tula, were they all gone?

"Most of them perished. If any survived, they must've hidden among the human population and stayed in hiding to this day. We couldn't find any even though we searched and followed every rumor. Mortdh's stronghold was up north in the area of today's Lebanon, so it escaped the deadly wind. Whoever was there at the time is probably still alive. Unless they fell out of Navuh's favor. Right, Dalhu?"

Dalhu nodded. "There were a number of executions over the years, but not many."

Wonder pulled more tissues from the box and blew her nose. They couldn't have all perished, she was proof of that. If she'd survived, others must've as well. Perhaps there were more immortals scattered around the area, buried under rubble, waiting for someone to find and revive them from their stasis.

"I can't be the only survivor. There must be more gods and immortals buried in the ground. We just need to find a way to recover them."

Bridget cast her a pitying look. "The gods are gone for sure because the assembly hall, where they were all present at the time, was hit with a nuclear bomb. None of them could've survived that. And if there are other immortals in stasis somewhere out there, they would be impossible for us to find."

Desperately searching her mind for how some could've survived, Wonder could think only of those who joined Navuh's caravan as Areana's escort. If Navuh still lived, any immortals who'd been with him at the time should still be alive as well. "What about Areana and her entourage?"

"Who's Areana?" Anandur asked.

"Annani's half-sister who was supposed to mate Mortdh. She traveled up north to his stronghold on Navuh's caravan. If he survived, so should she."

ANANDUR

*T*he room fell silent once more.

Annani had a half-sister no one had ever heard about? As far as they knew, the goddess was an only child.

Maybe Wonder's memories had gotten entangled with her dreams, and after so long she couldn't tell the difference. It wasn't an unreasonable assumption. Anandur had had dreams so vivid that later on, he hadn't been sure whether he'd lived through the experience or had dreamt it.

The first one to recover from Wonder's explosive revelation was Amanda. "My mother never mentioned having a half-sister. I assume she was Ahn's daughter and not Nai's, right?"

Wonder nodded. "She was much older than Annani. Ahn had fathered her many years before he met Nai."

"Was her mother an immortal?" Kian asked.

"No, she was a goddess. Not one of the important ones, but still a goddess."

"I can't believe it." Amanda threw her hands in the air. "I know our mother is vain, but to hide the fact that there might be another goddess out there, and not any goddess but a half-sister? Areana might still be languishing as Navuh's prisoner."

Kian rubbed his jaw. "Which begs another question. How the hell is he holding a goddess captive? She should be able to thrall him and anyone else who stands in her way, and just walk out."

Wonder shook her head. "Areana was a very weak goddess. So much so that Ahn was ashamed of her. She was less powerful than some of the immortals."

Taking Wonder's hand, Anandur gave it a little squeeze before voicing his doubts. "You might be confusing dreams with real-life experiences, lass. It doesn't make sense for Annani never to mention having a sister who might still be alive."

When Wonder's chin started quivering, Anandur felt like an ass for questioning her lucidity. She needed him to support her, and not further undermine her.

"Maybe Areana didn't survive, that would be a good reason for Annani not to mention her. I ran away right after the wedding, so I don't know what happened between then and the bomb. It's possible that Areana changed her mind, or that Mortdh decided he didn't want her, and instead of continuing with the caravan, she might have returned home."

A pitiful sob escaped Wonder's throat. "No one survived. They are all dead."

Bridget put down her coffee cup and leveled her gaze at Wonder. "I know you're afraid of the consequences of us letting Annani know that you've survived, but we must do it, and we must do it now. I'm sure you have nothing to worry about. She would be overjoyed to find out that you're alive. But if we drag it out any longer, she will get angry that we didn't let her know right away. I don't know about you, but personally, I don't want to provoke the goddess's wrath."

Wonder sighed. "You're right. And it's not like I don't want to see her. I do. I'm just afraid that she would want me to come with her and resume my duties as her maid or her bodyguard. Not that I mind that either, work is work. But I don't want to leave Anandur, and I don't want to leave the village. I love it here."

Wrapping his arms around her, Anandur pressed a kiss to Wonder's forehead. "You're not leaving me. If Annani demands that you go with her, she'll have to take me too." He looked at Kian. "I'm officially requesting a transfer to the sanctuary."

Kian nodded. "I'd hate to lose you, but I understand. Except, I think that both of you are getting ahead of yourselves. No one can predict Annani's responses."

Wonder grimaced. "I can. I've known her since she was a little girl, and the more memories I'm regaining of her, the more convinced I am that she would want me to accompany her."

"That's as may be, but you knew her five thousand years ago. A lot has happened since. She's not the same girl you used to know."

"Right." Amanda snorted. "I don't think our mother has changed much at all. On the inside, she is still the same person. We all are. You were always an overbearing stick-in-the-mud, Kian, who never knew how to take it easy and have fun, and you still are." She put a hand over her heart. "And I say it with love."

"And you were always a spoiled brat, and I say it with love too."

Amanda shrugged. "I don't deny it."

"Who is going to call Annani?" Bridget asked.

Kian pulled his phone out of his pocket. "I'll do it."

"No, let me." Amanda put a hand on his arm. "I'll deliver the news in a gentler manner. I'm sure it's going to be a shock for Mother as well."

"I think it's best for Amanda to do it," Syssi said.

"Agreed." Kian put the phone back. "Now if we are done here, I want to grab something to eat."

Kian never argued with Syssi, which Anandur found endearing. The bossy, arrogant bastard deferred to his wife in anything she voiced her opinion on.

"I made veggie burgers for you," Dalhu said.

"Thank you. That's very thoughtful of you." Kian lifted Syssi off his lap and stood up.

"Don't thank me. Syssi brought them."

"But you made them."

It was time to take Wonder home. "Are you okay to stand on your own, lass? I can carry you."

Wonder shook her head. "No, I'm fine. I can walk." She glanced at Amanda. "Is there a way we can leave without going through the living room? I don't feel like answering people's questions right now."

"Of course." Amanda walked over to the master bedroom's sliding doors and opened them. "You can leave through here. The doors lead to a side yard. Just go around to avoid the back."

"Thank you."

As Wonder rose to her feet, Anandur helped her up and wrapped his arm around her middle. If she got unstable, he would just lift her up.

"Call me if you need anything," Syssi said.

"Thanks." He looked at Amanda. "After you talk to Annani, let me know how it went."

Amanda nodded. "You got it."

As they walked out, Wonder trembled in his hold. Bravely, she kept the tears at bay until they were halfway between Amanda's and their house, and then the dam broke. Doubling over, she let out a wail Anandur was sure was heard all the way to Amanda's backyard.

His heart breaking for her, he scooped her up and held her tight as she sobbed uncontrollably. No words were going to take her pain away, but he mumbled them in her ear anyway while rubbing small circles on her back.

"I love you, lass. You're never going to be alone because I will always be at your side."

Then he listed the names of all the people who cared about her and even some she hadn't met yet.

He told her his family was hers.

And still she cried.

"Everything is going to be okay, sweetheart, I promise."

Wonder shook her head. "How can you say that? They are never coming back. They are gone forever."

Hugging her tighter, he kissed the top of her head. "Please don't cry. You're breaking my heart."

With a loud sniff, Wonder wiped her face with her sleeve, then clutched his shirt and pressed her cheek to his shoulder. "I'm trying. It's just so hard."

As another choked sob escaped her throat, Anandur felt

like an ass for asking her to stop crying. She needed to let it all out, and he needed to be there for her.

"Oh, lass, don't mind me and let the tears flow. I've got you."

ANNANI

*W*ith a shaking hand, Annani put the phone away.

Fortunately, she had taken Amanda's call in her private chamber, so there were no witnesses to her moment of weakness.

Gulan was alive.

The mysterious immortal named Wonder, the woman who had overpowered two of the most formidable Guardians and then joined their clan, was none other than her old friend.

Annani had heard the story, but she had not made the connection.

Maybe she should have. The exceptional physical strength was a rare talent for an immortal female. It should have at least aroused her suspicion.

Except, it was so out of the realm of possibility that the thought had never crossed her mind. How could she have conceived of anyone surviving in stasis for over five thousand years?

The details of how this had come to pass were not clear yet.

According to Amanda, Wonder had fainted as soon as she had laid eyes on Annani's portrait. The shock of recognition had then triggered the return of her memories, but not all of them, and the ones she retained had been all jumbled. The girl had been unable to tell them what had happened to her.

However, the part of Amanda's account that troubled Annani the most was that the initial return of memory had terrified Gulan. As more of them had trickled back, she had calmed down significantly, but still had not seemed happy to remember her past.

Why had her memories scared her so?

Perhaps she had been reminded of her family perishing in the disaster?

Annani would not have been surprised if the cause of Gulan's initial memory loss was the shocking news of the fate that had befallen Sumer.

It was easier to forget than live with the pain. The guilt over surviving while others perished was not easy to live with either.

Annani was well familiar with both. Except, she had found the motivation to keep on living—the most worthy goal of preserving her people's traditions and saving humanity from the fate that Mortdh's followers had in mind for them.

She could share her vision with Gulan, giving the girl hope for the future, and the sooner the better.

There were so many questions Annani wanted to ask Gulan, and so many stories she wanted to tell her—five thousand years' worth of experiences.

Reuniting with her best friend would no doubt make it to the very top of them, right after the births of her children.

It was nine-forty in the evening local time, which meant ten-forty at night in Los Angeles. If she boarded the plane in the next half an hour or so, she could arrive at the village at around five o'clock in the morning.

First things first, though, she needed to call Kian and let him know she was on her way. He would need to prepare for her visit.

Perhaps he could also tell her a little more about Gulan. She had asked Amanda for the girl's phone number, but Amanda had advised against calling. Wonder was probably asleep, she had said, recovering from her shock, and the girl needed time to calm down and process everything.

Annani agreed. It had been quite a shock to learn of Gulan's survival, she could only imagine what the girl was going through.

Her hands still shook as she chose Kian's contact from her list of favorites.

He picked up the call on the first ring. "Mother, I've been expecting your call."

"I am coming over."

"I've expected that too."

"I am glad you know me so well. It was quite a shock to learn my old friend is still alive. I cannot wait to see Gulan. Can you tell me about her? I asked Amanda, but for some reason, she seemed reluctant to talk about her. Did she turn unpleasant?"

"Not at all. She is a lovely female. But you have to realize that while you've lived and matured over the past five thousand years, Wonder hasn't. She is still a very young woman."

Annani chuckled. "Gulan is older than me by a year."

"Not in life experience."

"Yes, that is true. Tell me more about her."

"Do you know that she and Anandur are a couple now?"

"Yes. Amanda told me that they went on a trip together and have just returned."

"They are very much in love."

"Yes, I assume they are—" There was a knock. "Hold on one second. Someone is at the door."

"It's me, Mother," Alena said. "Can I come in?"

"Yes, of course."

"I just got off the phone with Amanda, and she said you might be distraught and need me by your side."

Eyes misting with emotion, Annani patted the spot next to her on the couch. "Come sit with me. I have Kian on the line."

She had wonderful children who cared deeply for her. Whatever else she achieved in her life, she would always consider them her greatest success.

"I am going to put you on speakerphone, Kian." She pressed the microphone icon. "Where were we?"

"I said that Wonder and Anandur are very much in love."

"Oh, yes. Well, this is how it is supposed to be. Do you think they are fated mates?"

"I don't know, Mother. It's up to them to discover whether they are or not. It's still a very new relationship. I would advise against separating them, though. I don't think either of them would tolerate it well."

It finally dawned on her what Kian was trying to communicate in his not so subtle way.

Was he afraid she would take Gulan away from Anandur?

"I would never do that, son. Naturally, I want to spend time with my dear friend, but if I invite her to come back with me to the sanctuary, I will invite Anandur as well. Are you okay parting with him, though? He has served as your bodyguard for nearly a thousand years. He is like a brother to you."

In fact, Kian and Anandur were probably closer to one another than she and Gulan had ever been. They had certainly spent many more years together.

But Annani was a selfish goddess, and she wanted her long lost friend back. Kian had Brundar and the other Guardians to keep him company, and most importantly he had Syssi.

Annani had only Alena to talk to without having to put on her queenly persona, and she was lonely.

Kian sighed. "I'm not happy about it, but as a leader, I need to put my people's needs before my own. Anandur will be miserable without Wonder."

"And she will be miserable without him."

"Exactly."

"We will have to figure out how to make it work for everyone. But now I need to get ready."

"Call me when you're an hour away. I'll send Okidu to pick you up. Are you bringing your Odus with you? Or should I send a couple of Guardians to escort you?"

"I'll bring two, which should suffice."

"Figure that you'll need two more seats on the way back. You might want to take the larger jet."

"An excellent suggestion. Thank you. Good night, Kian."

"Good night, Mother."

Annani ended the call and let the phone drop on the couch next to her. The past hour had left her emotionally drained. "Can you take care of the arrangements, Alena? I feel exhausted after all this excitement."

"I can imagine. It's such wonderful news. I'm excited too. I can't wait to meet Wonder."

Annani turned to her daughter. "Do you want to come with me? I dread the thought of spending the flight alone. I do not think I would be able to sleep, and I could use someone to talk to."

Alena's eyes brightened. "I would love to."

"Then it is settled. You are coming with me."

49

KIAN

*I*t was still dark outside when Kian carefully lifted Syssi's arm and crawled out of bed. Annani hadn't called yet, but he'd been lying awake for hours, and he craved a cigarette.

Not to disturb Syssi, he crept around his own house like a thief, grabbing clothes from the master's walk-in closet and then ducking into one of the guest bathrooms. Syssi hadn't slept much either, tossing and turning and sighing until finally quieting a couple of hours ago. She needed to get some rest before Annani's arrival.

Kian wondered whether she couldn't sleep because he'd been awake, keeping her up with his own tossing and turning, or because she'd been bothered by the same thoughts that had made sleep impossible for him.

His mother's visits always stressed him out.

The goddess's presence was tiring. Or maybe she had this effect only on him. Kian loved her unconditionally, but Annani was a handful, and as glad as he was to see her, he would be just as glad to see her go.

The problem was that this time she would be taking Anandur with her.

Things wouldn't be the same without the guy—not for Kian and not for the rest of the local clan.

The village would lose its heart.

Outside in his backyard, Kian lay down on one of the chaise lounges and pulled out a cigarette from the pack of his new, special-order custom-made brand.

One drag, two drags, the tobacco helped reduce his elevated stress level.

It didn't last long, though.

Bundled in a floor-length sweater, Amanda walked into his backyard. "I knew I'd find you here." She sat sideways on the other chaise, facing him. "Couldn't sleep either, eh?"

He shook his head. "Nope. Mother's arrival always stresses me out."

"It's not about Mother. It's about Anandur. You can admit to hating the idea of letting him go."

"I admit it. Did you come up with some clever way to keep him here?"

"That's what I was doing all night long, trying to come up with a solution that would make everyone happy, but there is none. The goddess gets what the goddess wants, and she wants Wonder aka Gulan by her side. So unless you convince Mother to move into the village, she'll take Wonder and Anandur will have to follow."

Kian took another drag from his cigarette. "Believe it or not, I offered. She refused."

Amanda chuckled. "I can imagine how relieved you were."

"As if you would've wanted her here permanently. She would've stolen your spotlight."

"True." Amanda lifted her legs and lay down. "It's so quiet and peaceful out here. For now…"

They spent the next several minutes in silent companionship, which was out of character for Amanda. Not that Kian was complaining, but she hadn't even commented on the cigarette stink. Maybe she liked the smell of this new custom-made brand—pure tobacco, with no additives, hand wrapped in a tobacco leaf instead of paper.

As he put it out in the ashtray, the call from Annani came.

"I am an hour away, and I cannot wait to see Gulan. I have Alena with me, and she cannot wait to meet my old friend as well."

"I'll see if she can be here when you arrive."

"If she is sleeping, do not wake her up. I can wait."

Right, Annani had made it obvious she wanted Gulan waiting for her. "I'll check with Anandur."

"Thank you. We will see you soon." His mother ended the call.

After sending Okidu to the airstrip, Kian put the phone on the side table, lit another cigarette, and then palmed his phone again to type a message to Anandur.

Annani is an hour away from the airstrip, and she wants Wonder waiting for her when she arrives. Can you make it to my house by six?

Fortunately, it had taken the goddess longer than she'd estimated to get ready for her trip. Five in the morning was a decent hour to start the day, but six was more comfortable.

A moment later his phone pinged with a return text. *Got it. We will be there at six.*

Kian hadn't expected a different answer. It wasn't as if

Anandur had any choice. Refusing the goddess or informing her that Wonder needed more sleep and would get there later wasn't really an option.

Annani was a diva, but she was also the Clan Mother and deserved their respect. Until a few hours ago, he would've added that she was also the only goddess on earth, but that might no longer be true.

Areana, Annani's half-sister, might've survived the catastrophe and been held captive by Navuh ever since.

The thing was, if Navuh had her, he was keeping her a secret. Dalhu and Robert had never heard of Areana, or any goddess for that matter. Navuh's harem was rumored to have several immortal females, but not a goddess.

Then again, Navuh wouldn't have wanted that known.

What's more, Kian wouldn't be surprised if the despot had disposed of Areana.

A full-blooded goddess would've undermined his position. Except, according to Gulan, Areana's powers were insignificant, so Navuh could've passed her off as an immortal.

The last and least likely possibility was that Areana wanted to be with Navuh. He'd probably kept Annani's existence a secret from her and had convinced the goddess that there were no other gods or immortals left in the world. Lacking Annani's guts and tenacity, Areana might have stayed because she believed there was nowhere for her to go.

Amanda stretched and yawned. "Do you want coffee?"

"I could use some. Do you know how to work the cappuccino machine?"

"Pfft." She waved a dismissive hand. "It's easy. Press the

on button, let it heat up, and then press one of the little buttons with the coffee cup picture on them."

Yeah, operating it was simple, but setting it up to produce good coffee was anything but. The device needed constant adjustments. Syssi tinkered with it endlessly.

"On second thought, use the coffeemaker in the kitchen. With the noise the machine makes as it thumps the coffee, there is no way Syssi won't wake up. I want her to get at least another hour of shuteye."

"What's the matter, she couldn't sleep either?"

"None of us wants to see Anandur go. Syssi loves the guy."

A smirk on her lovely face, Amanda put a hand on her hip and struck a pose. "I'm surprised you're not throwing a jealous hissy fit because your woman loves another guy who is not her brother."

A lot had changed, him included. "Anandur is like a brother to her."

In retrospect, Kian realized that his jealousy had been more about his own insecurities than anything Syssi had done. He hadn't been sure of her love for him because he hadn't thought he was lovable. Syssi had changed all that.

"But he isn't her brother, is he?" Amanda goaded him.

"It's not going to work. I no longer suffer from that affliction."

50

WONDER

"*I* can't believe Annani flew all night to see me." Wonder applied peach lipstick and took a step back from the mirror to appraise her appearance.

She'd showered and washed her hair, styled it, put on the most flattering outfit she owned, and covered the dark bags under her eyes with lots of makeup. The redness she could do nothing about.

After crying herself to sleep, then again every time she'd woken up throughout the night, and also this morning in the shower, her eyes were all dried up and itchy. Hopefully, by the time they got to Kian's house, they would be back to normal. Provided she didn't succumb to tears once again.

"That's because you mean a lot to her." Anandur put his hands on her shoulders and looked at their reflection. "You were much more than a servant to her."

"I know that. I overreacted yesterday because I was shocked and scared and didn't know how to deal with who

I used to be. I like the new me much better. Gulan was a nobody."

"You were Annani's companion. That's an important position."

"I guess." She turned around and wrapped her arms around Anandur's middle. "I love you. Wherever you are, that's where I want to be."

"Same here. Wherever you go, I go. So don't worry about a thing. If Annani wants you in the sanctuary, that's fine. I already asked Kian for a transfer, and I'm going to join the Guardian force there. Annani will have no problem with that. She is a romantic with a soft heart and would never stand in the way of love."

"But what about your brother? You're going to miss him."

"I will, but so what? I know he's in good hands, and I no longer need to watch over him. Besides, we can come to visit." He hooked a finger under her chin. "Everything is going to work out fine. You have nothing to worry about."

She nodded. "Thanks for the pep talk. It helped."

"I'm glad. Now let's get moving. Annani is not known for her patience."

Wonder rolled her eyes. "Tell me about it."

"Right. What was she like as a girl?" He closed the door behind them.

"Trouble. She would come up with the craziest of schemes and expect me to take part in them. I had no choice but to do what she told me to, but I was living in a constant state of fear. The princess could get away with anything, but the same wasn't true for me. If we had gotten caught, I would've been blamed for not keeping her safe, and would've either been punished or fired or both."

"Did you ever get caught?"

Wonder chuckled. "No. She was very thorough in planning her stunts."

"Did you like her?"

"Are you kidding me?" She lifted her face to him. "I loved her. I worshiped the ground she walked on. There was no one like her, not even among the gods. She was like sunshine. Everyone wanted to bask in her presence."

"Did she return your love?" Anandur asked quietly.

"She called me her best friend. But then she met Khiann, and I got replaced."

"That's a natural progression of things when people mature. He was her true-love mate."

"I know." Wonder sighed. "I knew it back then too, but I didn't internalize it. Without experiencing this kind of love myself, I couldn't understand how all-consuming it was, and I was somewhat resentful. I feel so guilty now. Poor Annani, she lost him so soon."

Crap, she was tearing up again, including the chin quivering and the choking sensation in her throat.

"Quick." Wonder waved a hand. "Distract me with something. I don't want to start crying again."

"Well." He puffed out his chest. "I'm very pleased that you consider me your true-love mate."

She had said that, hadn't she? In a way.

"I don't really know what the difference between love and true love is."

He wrapped his arm around her. "They are one and the same. In the past," he chuckled, "In your days, many of the matings were arranged, and not the natural outcome of two people falling in love and wanting to spend the rest of their very long immortal lives together. Many of those couples eventually grew to love each other. But it wasn't the same as the all-consuming fire of falling in love with a person, and realizing that she is the one and only for you."

That made sense. "I can't think of being separated from you for more than a few hours." Wonder touched her belly. "I get this uncomfortable feeling in here. It's as if my body is telling me that it's wrong to be away from you, and that I shouldn't do it."

He kissed the top of her head. "When immortals fall, they fall hard. And there is the addiction component. It's a chemical thing that is the result of repeated venom bites, but I suspect that it works much faster on true-love couples."

"Why would you think so?"

"Because I think I'm addicted to you, and it's not supposed to work this fast on males."

"I remember that Annani and Khiann couldn't keep their hands off each other." Her eyes misted again.

"Hey." Anandur stopped and gripped her chin. "No more sad thoughts. Leave the past where it belongs and concentrate on the future, meaning you and me." He dipped his head, at the last moment kissing her cheek instead of her lips. "Damn lipstick. I don't know why you bother. Your lips are beautiful without any enhancements."

"I wanted to look sophisticated, you know, like Amanda. Elegant clothes, makeup, hairdo. I don't want Annani to think of me as a servant. I can't go back to that role. It's no longer who I am."

Anandur shook his head. "Am I Kian's servant?"

"No. You're his bodyguard."

"True, but if he sends me to get him coffee, I go. I basically do whatever he tells me to do. Does that make me his servant?"

"He's your employer."

"Yes, he is, and he is also the leader of this branch of the clan. But that's not all he is to me, and I'm much more than an employee to him as well. We play different roles in different circumstances. During work hours I defer to him and treat him with respect. But off duty, we are best buddies, and I don't hesitate to call him out on all his bullshit. Sometimes I even do it when I'm on the clock."

She wished things could be as simple as Anandur was making them sound, but the truth was that the authority carried into personal life and a subordinate could never be real friends with a superior. There could be appreciation, admiration, and even love, but not real friendship.

"Do you want to tell me that off-duty you treat Kian exactly the same as your Guardian friends?"

"More or less."

"In what way less?"

"When he's acting like a sanctimonious prick, and I feel like punching him in his too pretty face, I don't act on it. But that's because he's Annani's son. Not because he's my boss."

Wonder shrugged. "Same difference. You always think of Kian as a superior, and that precludes real friendship."

"I disagree."

She shrugged. "Then we agree to disagree."

"Is this our first official fight as a couple?"

"Oh, no!" Wonder affected a mock-horrified expression. "I didn't hide the pillows!"

ANNANI

*E*xcitement bubbling inside her, Annani did not wait for her Odu to open the door for her. Rushing out of the limo, she flew into Kian's waiting arms. "Where is Gulan?"

Amusement danced in his eyes. "What? No hello? No how are you, my son?"

"Yes, yes, hello, I love you, now take me to Gulan."

Annani started walking toward the elevators when she remembered Alena. Turning around, she waved a hand. "Hurry up, child. You can hug Kian all you want later."

The small entourage of her two children and three Odus followed her, the latter carrying her and Alena's luggage.

Fortunately, the elevator was big enough for all six of them, including the suitcases. As soon as the bunch of them spilled out into the pavilion, Annani kept going at a fast clip.

Kian, having long legs, caught up to her. "Slow down,

Mother. Wonder is probably not there yet. I told Anandur to come over around six in the morning. It's a quarter to."

How disappointing.

Annani slowed down to her usual regal glide. "You should have said so before."

"You didn't give me a chance."

Alena joined on her other side and threaded her arm through Annani's. "I've just spent five hours listening to stories about Gulan and the stunts the two of them pulled, or rather Mother pulled and dragged the terrified Gulan along. I'm surprised the girl even wants to meet with her after what she put her through."

Annani waved a dismissive hand. "We had fun. If not for me, Gulan would have never done anything interesting. She was such a timid girl, despite her size and her strength." Annani put a hand over her heart. "Spunk comes from here. Not here." She flexed her arm.

"You're in for a surprise," Kian said. "Wonder is a very different person than Gulan, even though they are one and the same."

Was he referring to Gulan capturing Anandur?

Annani remembered Amanda telling her about it. The girl had thought he was a Doomer and about to hurt a human female.

"Gulan, Wonder, she is still the same person. My Gulan was timid most of the time, but when riled she found her courage."

Heroism did not mean a lack of fear. It meant doing what needed to be done despite it. Annani had been afraid at times and discouraged at others, but it had never stopped her forward movement. Gulan's normal state had been fearful, but Annani had never doubted the girl would protect her if needed.

As they reached Kian's house, Syssi and Amanda were waiting for them on the front porch.

"Welcome, Clan Mother." Syssi bowed, her hair falling forward and covering her face. Nevertheless, Annani had caught the mischievous smirk before the hair hid it.

It had become a game between the two of them. Syssi teased her with the official greeting to get a similar one in response. Only hers was much more ridiculous.

"Good morning, she who is my son's mate," Annani said with a straight face, bursting into laughter a split second later. "Come here and give me a hug." She beckoned her daughter-in-law.

Next was Amanda, and then they stepped inside, her two Odus following Okidu with the luggage to the guest rooms, and the rest of them getting comfortable in the living room.

"Can I offer you cappuccinos?" Syssi asked. "Something to snack on?"

"Yes, and yes," Alena said. "With all the rush we forgot to tell the Odus to restock the jet. All we had were pretzels and chocolates. I need some real food."

"I'll have Okidu prepare breakfast. But coffee first." Syssi walked over to her machine.

Reaching into a hidden pocket in her gown, Annani pulled out her phone and glanced at the time. "It is two minutes to six. They should be here already."

Unable to stay still, she pushed to her feet, walked over to the front door, and threw it open. Scanning the pathways leading to Kian's house, she spotted Anandur's red hair as soon as he and Gulan rounded the curve.

"Oh, my dear Fates." Her hand flew to her heart. There she was. Her Gulan, looking all grown up with her face made up, wearing contemporary clothes and her hair in a loose, modern style.

She looked beautiful, and not as huge as Annani remembered her. In fact, she looked about the same height as Amanda, only more solidly built.

A moment later, they were both running toward each other with tears streaming down their cheeks.

Mindful of her superior size and weight, Wonder stopped first and opened her arms, catching Annani as she flung herself at her old friend.

Embracing for long moments, they clung to each other and sobbed, their joyous reunion tinged by grief for all of those they had lost.

"Fates, Gulan, to see you alive and well…" Annani was about to wipe her face with her hand when someone handed her a bunch of tissues.

"I thought you would need them," Syssi said as she handed another bunch to Gulan. "Would you like to continue inside?"

"Yes, that is a very good suggestion." Annani blew her nose as gently and as quietly as possible.

She had not allowed anyone to see her fall apart like this in forever. As a leader, it was not a luxury she could indulge in.

Except, at that moment she did not feel like the five-thousand-year-old head of a clan, and she did not feel the weight of responsibility for humanity's fate resting on her shoulders. At that moment she felt like an eighteen-year-old girl who had found her best friend after grieving for her death.

WONDER

*A*nnani hadn't changed in the slightest. She looked exactly the same as Wonder remembered her.

Except for the eyes.

Now, she understood better what Anandur and Bridget had tried to explain about immortal age tells. There was an ocean of wisdom in Annani's eyes, which made her gaze seem ancient. It was a flickering effect, because sometimes they reverted to the mischievous gleam of her youth, especially when she laughed. But at other times Wonder could see the weight of the world reflected in those old eyes, and in those moments she felt both proud and sad for her friend.

After breakfast, the others had excused themselves to the backyard, leaving her and Annani alone in the living room to sit on the couch and hold hands like a couple of teenage girls which neither of them was.

"I don't know where to start," Wonder said. "I have so many questions, but each of them is going to bring both of us pain."

Annani smiled sadly and reached for the box of tissues Syssi had left on the coffee table. "We have these to wipe our tears and our noses. The others were kind enough to give us some privacy, so we can cry if we want to. Fates know we have plenty to cry over."

Wonder nodded. Her biggest sorrow was her little sister Tula, followed by their parents, and then by Esag. She'd cared for him even if she hadn't been really in love with him. It must've been so much more devastating for Annani.

She'd lost Khiann.

How had she survived that?

Wonder still remembered the desolate expression on Areana's face, even decades after Annani's sister had lost her truelove mate. There was no recovering from that, and yet Annani somehow had. She'd always been strong. That was why her father had adored her so. Ahn had been so proud of Annani.

"I hate to ask, but how did you recover from losing Khiann?"

"I never did, I still miss him with every fiber of my soul. I cried for years, but at some point, I realized that wallowing in my grief was selfish. I had the fate of humanity to think of. There was no one but me to counteract Mortdh's legacy of hatred. Navuh was following in his father's footsteps, and with his influence humanity was regressing instead of progressing. I had to stop that trajectory because I was the only one who had the means to do that."

"How? You were just one young and inexperienced goddess."

Annani smiled sheepishly. "Do you remember Ekin's tablet?"

"What about it?"

"I stole it before I ran off. I thought it would help me establish a new civilization up north, but it ended up helping save humanity at large. We still do not understand all that is stored on it. I certainly do not. But thankfully some of my progeny are smart enough to reverse engineer the information little by little. It is the foundation of all technological progress."

"Then it's a good thing that you stole it."

"I believe the Fates were guiding my actions."

Wonder frowned. "If the Fates were real, they should've stopped Mortdh, and not just saved one goddess and whispered in her ear to steal a tablet."

Annani sighed. "I pondered the same question many times, and I reached the conclusion that the Fates are not all powerful. There are larger forces at play. They do what they can to salvage the situation."

"What forces? Like the God humans believe in?"

Annani shrugged her slender shoulders. "I do not know. Call it nature, or call it God, or call it the underlying principles of the universe, or the balance between good and evil. Whatever it is, the Fates cannot counteract this force. They can only work in the periphery, making tiny little changes in the fabric of reality."

"When did you become so smart?"

Annani laughed, the sound raising goosebumps on Wonder's arms. It carried an otherworldly beauty Wonder hadn't heard in a very long time.

"I am not any smarter than I used to be. All of that might be total nonsense. I am just musing out loud."

"It sounds smart."

Annani laughed again. "I know. I have to appear smart to justify my title. Clan Mother implies wisdom."

Wonder looked down at their entwined fingers and sighed. "The hardest part for me is thinking of Tula perishing before she had the chance to live."

Rearranging the folds of her silk gown, Annani crossed her legs. "I do not want to give you false hope, but there might be a slight chance that Tula survived."

Despite Annani's preface, hope leaped in Wonder's chest. "How?"

"Do you remember my half-sister Areana? The one who was supposed to mate Mortdh in my stead?"

"I meant to ask you about her. When I mentioned Areana, your children didn't know she existed. How come you didn't tell them about her?"

"I told them very little about my lost family. First, it was too painful, and second, I always thought that one day I would write down our people's history. But I never got around to actually doing so." She looked down. "Whenever I think that it is time, I find an excuse to postpone it. Even after all this time, the memories are still too painful."

Wonder could empathize. She would have rather not talked about the past either.

"Anyway." Annani lifted her chin and continued. "Areana convinced Navuh to let her stay for the wedding."

Which meant that she hadn't left with Navuh's caravan and had probably perished with the rest of the gods. "I don't remember seeing her there."

"Well, you were distraught over Esag and hardly paid attention to anything."

"That is true."

"Navuh headed out without Areana, and Ahn's warriors escorted her to Mortdh's stronghold after the wedding. Then you ran away, and we assumed that you headed that way as well."

"Why would I?"

"Because it was the only other settlement of immortals outside of Sumer."

"I wasn't looking for other immortals. I wanted to get away from them."

"Well, we could not have known that. Khiann sent Esag to look for you on that route, and Tula begged Areana to take her on as her maid. She wanted to accompany her to Mortdh's stronghold, believing that she would find you there."

"So if Areana survived, so did Tula."

"Right. But I have no way of knowing whether they did or not. Shortly after that, Mortdh murdered my Khiann. The big assembly sentenced him to entombment, but they could not figure out how to bring him to justice, and there were rumors of him amassing forces and planning an attack."

Poor Annani. Not only had her beloved been murdered, but she'd feared Mortdh would attack and capture her, which would have been a worse fate than death. "So you decided to run."

"Exactly. Hiding out in the far north, isolated and living among savages, I did not find out about the disaster until a long time after it happened. It took months for the rumors to start trickling in. And because they were told by humans, who could not comprehend the existence of a weapon so destructive, it all sounded like a myth. It took me a while to realize what they had been talking about."

"How awful." As tears started running down her cheeks again, Wonder reached for the tissues, pulled out a few and handed them to Annani before taking some for herself.

Annani dabbed at her eyes and took a deep shuddering breath. "Esag might have survived as well. He had not returned before I escaped."

"He would not have joined Navuh's camp."

"Perhaps he had no choice."

ANANDUR

*A*fter more than two hours of talking, Wonder and Annani had still barely acknowledged Anandur and Kian's departure. Syssi and Amanda had stayed in the backyard, but eventually they too had probably left.

They all had work to do, and as much as Anandur was curious to hear all about the reunion, he had to patiently wait for his lunch break.

Frankly, hearing all about Wonder and Annani's rekindled friendship was not as interesting to him as hearing all about Esag. He hadn't had a chance to ask Wonder about her five-thousand-year-old crush yet, and he was burning with an unhealthy curiosity.

Except, the dude was dead, so why dig out what should stay buried?

Because.

Because Wonder was his mate and he wanted to know everything about her, and especially about what had made her fall for Esag. Had he been better looking than Anandur? Wittier? More charming?

Not likely, but he wanted to hear Wonder confirm it. Hell, he needed her to tell him that he was better in every way.

Petty?

Sure.

Childish?

You bet.

So what.

"Do you think they are done?" Anandur asked Kian when they returned to his village office. "I don't want to text Wonder in case she is still with Annani."

Kian had only one morning meeting in the city, so they were back before lunch, and Anandur could take a break to be with his girl.

"I'm positive that they are not done yet. But Okidu is on his way with lunch, so he can fill us in. You're welcome to join. I told him to make enough for three."

Brundar rose to his feet. "I'd rather head home and eat lunch with Callie."

Anandur would have gladly gone with him, but first of all his brother hadn't invited him, which was a bit of a disappointment, and secondly, on the remote chance that Wonder was done with Annani, he'd rather head home as well. He could always heat up some frozen dinners for them.

As the door closed behind Brundar, Kian leaned back in his chair and crossed his arms over his chest. "I'll be sorry to see you go."

That was nice to hear. "I'm touched." Anandur put a hand over his heart. "Are you going to miss me?"

Kian nodded. "That's because I'm used to seeing your

ugly puss every day. And an old-timer like me doesn't take well to change."

"Yeah." Anandur scratched his beard. "Same here. I had a hard time moving out of the keep and seeing humans living in our old apartments. Especially your and Amanda's penthouses. But change is inevitable, true?" He turned around as the door opened and Okidu walked in.

"I brought lunch, master." The butler walked over to the conference table and started unloading his big thermal carrier.

"Are Wonder and the Clan Mother done talking, Okidu?"

"No, master." The Odu kept pulling items out of the bag and arranging them neatly on the table.

"What are they doing?"

Okidu never volunteered extra information. Every bit required a direct question.

"They are eating lunch with Mistress Alena."

"Could you let me know when they are done? Anandur would like to know when Wonder leaves."

The butler straightened up. "Wonder?"

"Lady Gulan."

"Oh, yes. I will let you know as soon as the Clan Mother's companion departs."

"Thank you."

"You are most welcome."

"I guess they have a lot to talk about," Anandur said once Okidu was done, and they sat at the table.

It would've been nice to be included in that lunch, but apparently Annani didn't think Anandur should be part of their conversation. She wanted Wonder all to herself. Was that going to be a problem?

Probably.

If the goddess decided to hog all of Wonder's time, she would. Anandur and his wishes were of no consequence.

Suddenly what Wonder had said on the way to Kian's house made much more sense to him. There was a big difference between working for Kian and working for his mother.

Kian was his superior, that was true, and he was a smart guy, way smarter than Anandur, but Anandur never felt subservient to him, or considered himself beneath him. After all, he could beat Kian in the wrestling match any day, and as charm went, Kian's was nonexistent while Anandur's was abundant.

Annani was another story.

Wonder was right. Working for the goddess entailed a level of subservience that working for Kian did not.

54

WONDER

*A*s much as Wonder was fascinated by all the things Annani had been telling her, it was already evening, and the goddess didn't show any signs of being ready to dismiss her.

In her previous life, Wonder, or rather Gulan, would've said nothing and waited patiently for Annani to be done. This time around, however, she was going to assert herself. Politely, of course, and with as much deference as Annani deserved, but she wasn't going to jump and obey the goddess's every whim with no regard for her own needs and wishes.

If she were to resume her post as Annani's companion and bodyguard, she'd better define the new rules of engagement from the start.

Rule number one, Wonder hadn't addressed Annani as 'my lady' even once.

At first, she'd had to force herself to squeeze out the goddess's given name, but with each subsequent utterance, it had become easier, until it felt completely natural.

On her part, Annani seemed delighted by it.

"Okidu is about to serve dinner," Syssi said. "He is asking that we take our seats at the dining table."

Kian's wife had returned from work more than an hour ago, but she'd gone to her bedroom to give them privacy.

It was time to go home.

"Thank you for inviting me, but I need to get going. Anandur must miss me." Wonder rose to her feet.

Annani didn't try to stop her, which was a relief since Wonder wasn't sure she had the guts to insist.

Following her to the door, the goddess pulled Wonder into a quick hug. "Are you ready to leave tomorrow?" She glanced back to see if Syssi was still there. "I do not wish to outstay my welcome," she whispered. "Kian is stressed enough as it is, and playing host to his mother does not contribute to his peace of mind. I should let him and Syssi return to their routine."

Wonder had been expecting that, just not so soon. Only she should've known better. Once Annani set her mind on something, she didn't wait. It was full speed forward from the get-go.

"I need to check with Anandur. He said that he'd already asked Kian for a transfer, but I don't know if he can leave by tomorrow."

Annani smiled. "And I guess that you are not willing to leave without him."

"I can't. The thought of not seeing him for more than a few hours makes me feel physically uncomfortable."

With a sigh, Annani put a hand over her heart. "Love. I still remember how it feels." She patted Wonder's arm. "I kept you long enough. Go to your guy." She gave her a gentle push out the door. "Just let me know when the two of you are ready to leave."

"I will."

Wonder didn't walk home, she ran, crossing the distance which usually took ten minutes at a leisurely stroll in less than three.

She halted at the door, deliberating whether she should knock or just walk in. Officially, she'd moved in, but it had been only yesterday. She hadn't even moved her things here or said goodbye to her roommates.

Not that her meager possessions were a problem.

Last night, Okidu had delivered her trip suitcase to Anandur's, and most of what she owned was inside it, but she still had a few things at her old place, and she needed to say thank you and goodbye to Gertrude and Hildegard.

In fact, she would have to say goodbye to a lot of people she'd grown to care for.

With a sigh, Wonder reached for the handle, but the door opened before her hand made contact with it.

Without saying a word, Anandur crushed her against his bare chest and kissed her like he hadn't seen her in weeks. She rubbed against him, feeling the same urgency to get as close as possible to her mate.

Talking could wait, as could dinner. Right now Wonder had only one thing on her mind. "Take me to bed."

"Yes, ma'am!" Anandur lifted her up, turned around, kicked the door closed, took two long steps into the living room, and deposited her on the couch. "This is closer."

He had her naked in seconds.

At first, Anandur tried to slow down, kissing and caressing to prepare her.

But Wonder lost patience in moments. She didn't need

the foreplay, she was as ready as a female could get, throbbing with the need to be filled.

"I want you inside me now."

Between one breath and another, Anandur pulled off his jeans and cast them aside. Fisting his shaft, he positioned it at her entrance.

"Yes!"

As the tip touched her wetness, he groaned. "You're so ready for me, lass."

She was. So what the hell was he waiting for?

Like a lioness in heat, she arched up with a harsh growl.

Eyes glowing and fangs dripping venom, Anandur looked mindless with need as he surged inside her, filling her with one hard thrust.

They both groaned, their arms tightening around each other like they were never letting go.

At the back of Wonder's mind, a thought skittered by. Was this the result of the addiction Anandur had been talking about?

If it was, she saw nothing wrong with it.

Their lovemaking wasn't tender.

The ferocity of need made their coupling more explosive than ever. Wonder welcomed the total abandon, the lack of rational thought, the bruising hold they had on each other. Even the animalistic growls coming out of her own throat didn't alarm her.

Consumed by lust for her mate, she gave herself up to the pleasure.

55

ANANDUR

*A*s they lay spent on the too narrow couch, wrapped in each other's arms, Anandur felt at peace. He had all he needed right there. As long as he had Wonder by his side, he could weather out whatever else life threw at him.

Moving to Alaska? No problem.

Saying goodbye to his brother and his friends? A problem, but he could live with that. A five-hour flight in each direction wasn't that bad. He could come home on weekends.

"Annani wants to leave tomorrow," Wonder said.

"I assume she wants you to join her in the near future."

Wonder snorted. "Apparently, you don't know your Clan Mother well. She wants us to fly back with her tomorrow."

"Damn."

"Yeah, I know. On the other hand, there is no reason to delay. We have to go, and the longer we drag it out, the harder it's going to be on everybody."

He stroked her arm. "Do you want to go?"

"I don't have a choice. But even if I did, I would've accepted Annani's offer."

"Why?" He chuckled. "Do you remember all your why questions?"

"Yes, and I also remember how patiently you answered them." She lifted her face and kissed the side of his jaw. "Annani needs me."

"That's all? She needs you? What about what you need?"

Resting her cheek on his chest, Wonder sighed. "In a way, I need to be with her too. Not permanently, though. I like it here too much. I'd miss everybody."

"So would I." He stroked her back. "What does she need you for anyway?"

"Officially, I'm to be her companion and bodyguard. When she goes on her excursions among humans, she takes the Odus with her, but they are not the same as a companion she can share her experiences with."

"What about Alena?"

Wonder chuckled. "The excursions Annani refers to are not the kind a mother takes her daughter on, if you catch my drift."

"Oh." For some reason, he'd never given much thought to the goddess's day to day life. In his imagination, she sat on an elevated dais all day and issued commands to her underlings. Except, Annani was also flesh and blood and had needs like any immortal female.

A goddess, he corrected himself. Which meant that she was probably more lustful than the lustiest of immortal females.

"I don't want you going with her on hunting trips. You're mine."

She raked her fingernails through his sparse chest hair. "I'm just the bodyguard. I'm not going to watch or partake. Besides, this is what Annani wants, so this is what Annani gets. Right?"

"Doesn't mean that I have to like it."

"No, it doesn't."

"Tell me about Esag." That was another thing Anandur wasn't going to like but needed to hear about.

"What do you want to know?"

"Everything. Who he was, what he did, what kind of a male he was, how you felt about him, how he felt about you. Those kinds of things."

Wonder shifted, turning to her back. Her head resting on his arm, she took his hand and threaded her fingers through his. "Esag was Khiann's squire. He was tall, not like you, but taller than me, which was very important to me back then. I always felt too big, and no one treated me like a girl, assuming I was manly."

Cupping one ample breast, Anandur humphed. "There is nothing manly about you, lass. You're all woman to me."

"Thanks. Anyway, as I told you before, he was also very charming, smiling a lot and flirting constantly. He was the first guy to show me any attention and treat me like a girl, so naturally, I fell for him."

Anandur's heart sank. "So you loved him after all."

"At the time, I thought I did, but it was only an infatuation. Or maybe not even that. I was probably only attracted to him physically and mistook it for something more. Now that I know how real love feels, I realize it was only a youthful crush."

"Did he love you?"

"He liked me, and he desired me, but he didn't love me

enough to break off his engagement to a girl he didn't even like. His family needed the connection with his intended's, and Esag believed that by breaking the engagement he was going to ruin his family's business and his sisters' chances of good matings."

"He didn't love you. If he did, nothing and no one would've stood in the way of his claiming you for himself and pledging himself to you."

"That's exactly what I thought."

"Is that why you ran away?"

She shook her head. "It's too embarrassing to repeat. Let's just say that he did something I found offensive."

Anandur felt his fangs punch out, which was a testament to how angered he was because after biting Wonder twice, his venom glands should've been spent. "Tell me what the bastard did."

It was good the dude was dead. Otherwise, Anandur would've had to do something about that.

Wonder hesitated for a moment. "Annani didn't think it was so horrible, so maybe I overreacted a little. Although I still feel it was an offensive proposal." She sighed. "Since he couldn't break the engagement without ruining his family, but he still wanted to be with me, he asked me if I was willing to be his concubine."

Anandur knew what a concubine was, but maybe the term implied something else in ancient Sumer. "Like a mistress?"

"Kind of. He said that it would be in name only, and that he would take care of me and treat me as if I was his official wife. He promised to spend most of his time with me."

"How old was he?"

"Nineteen."

Anandur wanted to hate the dude for hurting Wonder's feelings, but he could understand a young guy like that not having the guts to go against his family and trying to find a solution that would make everyone happy.

"Esag was a coward. But it seems to me that he really cared for you. I understand that you didn't want to accept his proposal, and I'm glad you didn't, but I don't think you should've been offended by it either. He didn't mean it as an insult."

"I know he didn't mean it. But what you don't understand is that he expected me to accept the proposal because a girl like me wouldn't have gotten a better one. That was what I found so offensive. Also, at the time I thought that a concubine was just a step above a prostitute, but that was a misconception which Annani later corrected."

Anandur hadn't heard much after the "Girl like me wouldn't have gotten a better one."

"What do you mean, you wouldn't have gotten a better proposal? Why not? You're beautiful and smart and kind. What more can a guy ask for?"

Turning to her side, Wonder threw her arm over his chest and kissed his cheek. "I love you so much."

"I love you too, but you didn't answer my question."

She sighed again. "I was the daughter of an immortal mother and a human father. Back then it meant a lower status than those born of two immortals. There was a hierarchy. The gods were on top, the direct offspring of gods with immortals was second, the children of two immortals third, the children of immortals with humans fourth, and humans were the lowest. I was also a head taller than most men and had the shoulders to match. Add to that my freakish strength, and most guys, even the nice ones, thought of me as one of them and not as a girl, let alone a prospective mate."

He pulled her closer and kissed the top of her head. "Their loss is my gain. I think you are as perfect as a woman can get. And I think that any guy who fails to see that is a fool. How about that?"

56

WONDER

*E*ven after Annani's thorough descriptions, the sanctuary was more beautiful than Wonder could've imagined. It was a slice of paradise hidden in the icy wilderness of Alaska, the dome enclosing it ensuring that it was always pleasantly warm inside.

"Since the dome is covered in ice and snow, the sunlight is artificial too," Annani explained. "That and the enclosed air filtration system are the only complaints I have. They still need some work. Can you feel the difference in the air quality?"

Anandur took in a deep breath. "It smells fine to me. After living in Los Angeles and breathing in smog, this smells fresh."

"But it does not smell authentic."

He took another sniff. "Yeah, you're right. But it's very subtle."

"Come." Alena threaded her arm through his. "I'll take you to our Guardian chief. He's expecting you. Quite eagerly, I might add. It seems your reputation precedes you."

He shrugged. "I'm so old that most of the guys have served with me at one time or another. They know first-hand what I can do."

Wonder left Annani's side to give Anandur a quick peck on his cheek. "I'll see you in the evening."

Her stomach churned uncomfortably at having to separate from him even for several hours. Tomorrow was going to be even worse. She'd have to spend an entire workday without him. How did the other couples manage?

"You will get used to that," Annani said as if guessing her thoughts. "It is most difficult in the beginning."

"Am I so obvious?"

The goddess laughed. "You looked at Anandur's retreating back with such sorrow that it was not hard to guess what was going through your mind." She continued walking. "The Odus are preparing your suite of rooms. You'll have your own living room and bedroom. No cooking facilities, though. In the sanctuary, we take our meals together in the dining hall."

"That's nice."

"I think so too. It brings us together as a community. Naturally, you can keep snacks and drinks in your suite. There is a bar with a refrigerator and cabinets to store non-perishables."

As they reached Annani's personal quarters, one of her Odus rushed to open the double doors for them.

"Your place is very pretty," Wonder said. It looked nothing like Annani's mated quarters in the palace, but that was to be expected. Fabrics and furniture designs had changed a lot over five thousand years.

"Yes, I think so too. I also have a reception room for conducting official meetings. This is my private area." The goddess glided toward a huge fish tank, pulled out a food container and sprinkled some over the top. A flurry of activity started as the little fish rushed to grab the tiny food flakes.

"Do you like fish?"

"I like their beautiful colors, and I find it relaxing to watch them swim around."

"How do you entertain yourself? Do you spend a lot of time with Alena?"

Annani motioned for Wonder to follow her and sat down on a comfortable-looking couch. The thing was covered with plush down-filled cushions in several colors. "Come sit with me, Gulan."

She'd been meaning to tell the goddess to call her Wonder, but it had never seemed like a good time for it until now. She joined Annani on the couch. "If you don't mind, I'd rather you call me Wonder. I like it better than Gulan."

"What is wrong with your given name?"

Wonder lifted one of the smaller cushions and put it in her lap. "I'm no longer that girl. When I woke up from stasis, I didn't know who I was, or where I came from. It was as if I were born right there in that underground cavern. I had to learn everything from scratch, and that included learning about myself."

She stopped, trying to find the right words to articulate the way she felt. To her credit, Annani waited patiently for her to continue.

"I adopted the name Wonder, which I later discovered was the title of a fictional comic character, and I kind of grew into it. The way I feel about myself, the way I think about myself now is very different from how I felt as Gulan. I like myself as Wonder much better."

Annani took Wonder's large hand and cupped it between her delicate ones.

"You always had it in you. I remember thinking that I should rile you more often because you found your voice only when you got angry. I think that in time, you would have grown into the person you are now even without losing your memory and starting over. We are who we are. We do not really change much."

Wonder arched a brow. "Really? Do you still pull pranks and cause mischief?"

Annani laughed. "Of course. Maybe not as often as I used to, but I would have perished from boredom if I had to act stately and refined at all times."

"It's a drag, I suppose."

"You have no idea. I am the Clan Mother. I have to act like a queen."

"Your mother trained you well for that role."

The smile melted off Annani's beautiful face. "She did. I remember resenting her for insisting I always look regal. I wish I could go back in time and give her a hug and tell her that I love her and appreciate all that she did for me. I was such a spoiled, ungrateful brat." A tear slid down Annani's cheek. "I do not think I cried as much since grieving for Lilen."

"Who's Lilen?"

"My son. He was killed in battle."

"I'm so sorry."

"I am too. It happened a long time ago, but the pain never goes away."

Poor Annani. She'd suffered so much sorrow throughout her life. It was a miracle she managed to keep such a positive attitude. The goddess was so brave.

"I bring back painful memories that make you sad. Maybe it's not such a great idea for me to serve as your companion again."

Annani waved a dismissive hand. "That is ridiculous. I just found you, and I am not letting you go. There is nothing wrong with having a good cry now and then. If I wanted to laugh all of the time, I would have hired a clown as my companion."

"Funny that you would say that. You might have one right here under your nose. Anandur loves to make people laugh."

"Then you are very fortunate to have snagged him. He reminds me a lot of Esag. Esag loved to clown around too."

Wonder huffed. "I don't want to speak ill of the dead, but Esag wasn't half the man Anandur is. The resemblance is only superficial."

The smile returning to the goddess's face prompted Wonder to continue. "Anandur is a real man who is willing and able to stand by my side no matter what. He loves me and is dedicated to making me happy. Esag only thought of himself and what would make him happy."

57

ANNANI

*A*nnani's eyes misted again. Her Khiann had been the same, always mindful of her wellbeing and doing everything in his power to make her happy. In return, he had received her eternal love and dedication.

Tragically, she had had such a short time to shower him with love. What he had given her, however, had been sustaining her throughout the millennia.

"Why are you sad again?" Wonder asked.

Annani loved that the girl no longer felt like a servant and was treating her like a friend and not a boss. If a name switch had achieved that, Annani had no problem sticking with Wonder. In fact, it had a nice sound to it.

"You are correct. Your Anandur sounds more like my Khiann than like Esag."

"I think so too. When I captured Anandur, he could've gotten free with ease. The only reason he didn't was that he wanted to earn my trust. He was willing to stay locked up in a cage with three Doomers and cause his brother needless worry to do so."

Annani knew what the comparison was all about. Both her and Wonder's mates had sacrificed for love. Except, her Khiann had sacrificed more than a few days of freedom.

"My Khiann was willing to risk his life to be with me." Tears started running in rivulets down her cheeks. "And he paid the ultimate price. I cannot help but feel responsible. Not only for his death but for that of my entire people. If I had gone willingly to Mortdh, none of that would have happened."

Wonder regarded her with eyes that were much more mature than her age suggested. "Do you really believe that? Because I don't. Mortdh was crazy. He was obsessed with becoming the ultimate leader of the gods. I still remember what you told me. You said that he would not wait for Ahn to step down and that he would try to seize power by force. Ahn would've fought back, and Mortdh would've dropped the bomb. Maybe it would have happened several years later, but the outcome would have been the same. Only in this version, you would've died along with the other gods. Imagine the world with humanity at the mercy of Mortdh or Navuh."

A shiver ran down Annani's spine. "I do not want to imagine that."

"Neither do I." Wonder handed her a napkin to wipe her tears away. "As you explained to me yesterday, the Fates had done what they could and saved you for a reason. They could not have stopped the events from unfolding the way they did, but they could change one little thread." She pointed at Annani. "You are that thread. And by doing so they altered the course of history."

"I would like to think that you are correct, and most

days I do. Except, from time to time doubt assails me, especially when I feel down. Then I think about my children and my love for them. It never fails to fortify my resolve."

Wonder nodded, but then shook her head. "I don't know how it's possible, but now that I think about it, Kian reminds me of Khiann. You named your first-born son after him and just changed the spelling a little."

"I did. It is a bad omen to name a child after someone who died tragically. But it was my way of honoring Khiann's memory. And you are right, he does look a little like Khiann. Especially the determined expression."

"Khiann was much more mellow than Kian."

Annani smiled. "Khiann was nineteen. His namesake is nearly two thousand years old. Kian was not always as grumpy and as intense as he is now. The mantle of responsibility did that to him."

"How do you explain the resemblance? Did you choose lovers who reminded you of Khiann?"

"Naturally. I have a thing for tall, handsome men, with commanding personalities. You, on the other hand, prefer the charming, easy-going types."

Wonder laughed. "I also have a thing for wide shoulders and big muscles."

"And apparently you like redheads."

"I do. But it seems like you don't have a particular hair color you favor. Kian's hair is light brown, Amanda's is black, but I know it's fake and that her real hair color is red. Alena is blond. What about Sari?"

"Sari has chestnut hair."

Hugging the decorative cushion to her chest, Wonder leaned back. "I might be imagining it, but I see some of Khiann in Amanda and Alena as well."

Annani nodded. "I do too." She smiled. "As you have guessed, I do like a certain type of man."

As much as she wished she could, Annani couldn't share with Wonder the prophecy she had received after Khiann's murder.

The human soothsayer had prohibited it.

It might have been total nonsense, something the old human had invented to lift Annani's spirits from depths of despair. But true or false, it had helped her when hope had deserted her, and she had nothing else to cling to. For that, Annani was grateful even if it were a lie.

In her darkest moments, and she had had quite a few of those, she had recited the prophecy in her mind, and it had given her strength to claw her way out of an otherwise uncontrollable downward spiral.

Over the millennia, she had rearranged some of the words and the sequence of its lines so they would rhyme even when translated into another language. By now, she could recite the prophecy in eight or nine of them.

Do not despair, my lady. Not all is lost.

True love cannot die, its warmth cannot turn to frost.

Your beloved's love floats in the ether searching for a new baby to be born.

Khiann will find a way to come back to you in some form.

Seven children will be born to you, all different, but his spirit will shine through their eyes warm and bright.

And one day, thousands of years from now, he will come back to you, and you will know him at first sight.

I saw it all with my blind eyes, my lady, and everything I see with my second sight comes to pass.

. . .

After delivering the prophecy, the human soothsayer had made Annani swear she would never repeat it to anyone. If she ever did, the old crone warned, Khiann would never return.

Out of the promised seven, Annani had given birth to five children. Which for a goddess was nothing short of miraculous. But after sweet Lilen had been taken away from her, only four remained.

The soothsayer had failed to forewarn Annani about that. Losing her son was just as bad as losing Khiann had been, maybe even worse. By then, though, Annani was well acquainted with grief. Perhaps that was why it had subsided sooner.

The thing about grief was that it never went away. The pain lurked under the surface, waiting for a moment of weakness to hijack her mind and leach away her strength.

At those dark moments, she thought of her children and all of her grandchildren and their children. It was comforting to think that the spirit never died and that sparks of it found their way into the souls of her progeny.

If she believed the prophecy, there were two more children in her future, but Annani did not put much faith in that.

The prophecy was just a crutch, something to cling to and find solace in when she felt all alone on her proverbial throne, and in moments of gloom.

58

ANANDUR

*A*nandur was going to die a slow death by boredom.

There were only three other Guardians at the sanctuary, old timers who wanted to take it easy and still get the cushy Guardian pay.

There was nothing to do.

When going out on excursions, Annani took her Odus as bodyguards. The three Guardians were more of a precaution in case the sanctuary was invaded by a polar bear. Other than those, there was nothing around for miles upon miles of desolate, frozen wilderness. Thanks to William's genius, the place was undetectable by plane or satellite or any other conventional means.

Anandur didn't know how it worked, but it was something about obscuring or disturbing signals to make it look like a natural phenomenon.

Whatever. The important thing was that it worked.

"We are in charge of the deliveries," Boogie said. "We

pick them up in town, bring them to the transport plane, and then the Odus carry them in."

Boogie's real name was Bowen, but everyone had called him Boogie for as long as Anandur could remember, and it had nothing to do with dancing.

"What else?"

"Sometimes we escort the Clan Mother when she takes a few people with her on her trips. We keep the others safe."

"What about training?"

Boogie grimaced. "With just the three of us, it gets boring to spar. We mainly lift weights and run on the treadmill."

Anandur had a feeling they didn't do that often.

Maybe he should seek a new career. "Do they need an extra cook in the kitchen?"

"No, why do you ask?"

"Because there isn't much for me to do here, and I'm going to go crazy if I sit on my ass all day and stare at the three of you."

Roland lifted up a tattered book. "You can catch up on your reading."

"Yeah, I think I will." He pushed to his feet. "I'm going to check on my lady and see if she's ready to retire for the day."

"Lucky bastard," Roland murmured.

"I know. See you guys tomorrow."

He found his way back to Annani's quarters with ease and knocked on the door. Hopefully, he wasn't breaking protocol. But he'd forgotten to ask the other Guardians about it.

Wonder opened the door with a big smile spreading over her face. "Did your ears twitch?"

"Why would they twitch?"

"Because we were gossiping about you. My mother used to say that if you talk about someone a lot, their ears start to twitch and they know you're talking about them."

"That's nonsense."

She shrugged. "I know. But my sister and I believed her."

"Are you ready to go?"

"Hold on." She looked over her shoulder. "Are we done for today, Annani?"

"Yes, we are. I will have Oridu show you to your suite." The goddess got up from her couch and glided toward the door. "How was your day, Anandur? Did you get along with the other Guardians?"

She sounded like a mother asking him if he had had fun at school with his new friends.

"There isn't much to do."

"I am sure you will find something to keep yourself occupied."

Surprising the hell out of him, Annani stretched on her tiptoes and put her hand on his shoulder, signaling that she wanted him to bend down. When he did, she kissed his cheek. "Thank you for being good to Wonder."

"I'm doing my best. She's my mate."

His answer seemed to satisfy the goddess. "I will see you both tomorrow morning. I'm in the mood for shopping in Paris, and I could use an extra bodyguard."

Now, that sounded exciting. Anandur hadn't been to Paris in ages, and he knew Wonder would love the city.

Annani smirked. "I see that whetted your appetite." She kissed Wonder on both cheeks. "Tomorrow at eight."

As they followed Oridu across the central portion of the dome, the light dimmed to mimic evening. People were strolling through the lush landscape, and they stopped for brief hellos and introductions. The sanctuary was home to only seventy-two immortals, one goddess, and three Odus. Getting to know everyone wasn't going to take long.

"Here we are." Oridu pushed the door open and bowed. "Your luggage is inside the closet. Enjoy your evening." He bowed again and left.

"Finally." Wonder let out a breath as Anandur closed the door behind the Odu. "I'm exhausted." She took a look around. "This is almost as nice as Annani's suite. I'm surprised they gave us such a spacious place. The sanctuary isn't big."

Anandur took Wonder's hand, led her to the couch, sat down, and pulled her into his lap. "I missed you." He cupped her nape and kissed her long and hard.

"I missed you too."

"How was your day with Annani?"

"Fine."

"Define fine."

"We talked a lot. There are things she cannot talk about with anyone else but me. With everyone else, she needs to act as the Clan Mother. I'm her only friend. But it's hard for both of us to deal with the past. I think having me around is not good for her. She said she hadn't cried as much since grieving for Lilen."

Wonder shook her head. "Yeah, talk about sad." She plastered a smile on her face. "And how was your day?"

"Let's just say I've considered switching careers and becoming a cook."

"That bad?"

"There is nothing to do. The three Guardians assigned to the sanctuary are out of shape old-timers. I don't have anyone to train with."

"Poor baby." She kissed his cheek. "Let's give living here a try. Maybe things will get better." She smirked. "Perhaps they need a librarian?"

"I'd rather cook."

"I don't think heating up frozen dinners counts."

"Then perhaps I can take up gardening."

"There sure is a lot of greenery to take care of here."

WONDER

"*E*very time I see this," Wonder waved her hand at the lush tropical gardens she and Annani were strolling through, "I'm amazed that all of this is hiding under tons of snow and ice."

Waterfalls, vivid green trees, bushes, flowerbeds—the garden was a feast for the senses. The sanctuary's residents called it the Central Park, after the one in Manhattan, which Annani had taken her and Anandur to see.

It had been a fun-filled week.

Annani had made sure of that, taking them first to Paris under the pretext of a shopping excursion, and then to New York under the pretext of showing Wonder Central Park, which Wonder thought looked nothing like the one in the sanctuary. It was much bigger, but not nearly as lush.

Except, she knew it was sort of like a honeymoon, and once things settled into a routine, Anandur would be miserably bored and so would she.

There was only so much she and Annani could talk

about without bringing up the past and making each other sad.

"It is even lovelier here when we have little ones," Annani said. "I love hearing their squeals of joy as they splash in the ponds or go down the slides. Those are my happiest times."

"How come there aren't any here now?"

"We had a couple until recently. But it is hard for the new mothers to be here for an extended period of time, away from their homes and their jobs. As soon as they think the children are old enough to be safe in the outside world, they leave."

"Do all of them come to have their babies here?"

"Most do. Nathalie and Andrew decided against it, which was very disappointing. I adore that little girl. But Andrew could not leave work, and Nathalie refused to leave him behind, which I can understand. It is different for the single mothers. We did not have mated couples until recently."

"So I guess Eva is not going to have her baby here."

"I do not think so. I will extend the invitation, of course, to her and to Bhathian. Perhaps having his old friend here would make Anandur happy. He will have someone to train with."

That wouldn't solve the problem. Anandur missed the village, he missed his brother, and he missed his friends. He even missed working for Kian.

Wonder missed everyone too.

In time, they might make new friends in the sanctuary, but the new ones couldn't replace the old ones, and they would still miss their friends.

Besides, before the return of her memories and the

move to the sanctuary, Wonder had aspirations that hadn't included going back to her old job as Annani's companion slash maid. She'd had dreams of doing more for herself, even though she hadn't decided yet what that more was.

She could become a teacher, or a fitness instructor, or a nurse. There were so many possibilities. In the sanctuary there were none. It was isolated, and a daily commute to town was not practical. Which precluded school. She could do what Amanda and Syssi had suggested and study online, but the idea didn't appeal to her. After spending five thousand years in the ground, she didn't want to resume her life in isolation.

"What do the people here do?" she asked. "They can't work outside the sanctuary."

Annani shrugged. "All the things that can be done remotely, which nowadays is almost everything. We have a fashion designer, a couple of jewelry designers, games and software designers, poets, writers, philosophers, and screenwriters. Some do book editing and several offer translation services. Immortals absorb new languages with ease."

None of the occupations Annani had listed appealed to Wonder. She had no artistic talent, be it fashion design or poetry. Besides, all of those jobs were done in solitude. She preferred working at the café and meeting people to sitting alone in a room all day and doing whatever.

"Why do you ask? Are you not happy spending time with me?"

Gods, how was she going to answer that without hurting Annani's feelings? Her old friend had done every-thing she could to make Wonder and Anandur's time in the sanctuary as pleasant as possible.

"I love spending time with you. But I want to do more with myself." She lowered her head. "I also miss the new friends I made. But if I go back, I'm going to miss you. I wish you could come live in the village. That would've been perfect. We could hang out together whenever we want, and I could pursue whatever career I decide on. Kian said the clan would fund my education. Naturally, I will only accept it as a loan and repay it as soon as I can."

Annani nodded and pointed at a bench. "A serious talk needs to be done while sitting down."

What did the goddess mean by a serious talk? Should she worry?

Once they were seated, Annani took Wonder's hand in hers. "I cannot move into the village. It will create strife between Kian and me that I would rather avoid. He would try to restrict my freedom because he worries for my safety, and I would have to put my foot down because I love to travel and visit different places around the world. Also, having me there would undermine his authority, which is something I would rather avoid as well. I love my children, and they love me, but we all have strong personalities. Living in close proximity to each other we would be stepping on each other's toes."

"What about you and Alena?"

"Alena chose a different path than Kian and Sari's." Annani chuckled. "The official reason is that she loves children and wants to manage the sanctuary, which she does wonderfully. But the truth is that she is here to keep me in check, so I do not go overboard with my stunts and take crazy risks."

"Kian and Amanda seem to get along just fine."

"They do, but that is because Amanda does not seek a

leadership position and is very happy to see Kian shoulder the responsibility. That is the only reason she defers to him."

"I guess I have a lot to learn about politics."

"It is not about politics at large. We are a family. But even within a family there are power struggles. I do not want mine to squabble. That is why we have three locations and two centers of power. Sari and Kian are leading their people independently from each other, and they have me as a figurehead, so neither is tempted to boss the other because officially I am still the head of the clan."

"You're very clever."

Annani smirked. "Thank you. But mostly I learned by trial and error. I had five thousand years to perfect it. Which brings me back to you." She sighed. "We are not the same girls we used to be. I have lived for a very long time and followed the path I was destined to follow. You are still a nineteen-year-old girl who needs to figure out what her path is. The truth is that you cannot do that here as my companion. I would have loved for you to stay, but as selfish as I am, I would be a lousy friend if I prevented you from becoming all that you can be."

Tears pricking her eyes, Wonder wrapped her arms around Annani's shoulders and hugged her gently. The goddess's appearance was so misleading. Her delicate features and compact size hid a powerhouse of inner strength and wisdom.

"I'm honored you call me a friend."

For a long moment, they stayed in each other's arms, but then Annani pulled away and took Wonder's hands in hers. "There is something you can do to make it up to me for leaving."

"Name it."

Annani waggled her brows. "I love presiding over weddings."

"You mean Anandur's and mine?"

"Who else's?"

"He hasn't proposed yet. Not in so many words."

"Pfft. As far as Anandur is concerned, it is a done deal. A wedding is just a party to celebrate your union, and I do love parties."

ANANDUR

"We are going home!" Wonder called out as soon as she entered their suite.

"Is Annani planning a trip to the village?" Anandur hadn't expected the goddess to go visit Kian again so soon. Usually, months passed between one visit and the next. Was she doing it for Wonder and him?

That was nice of her.

Wonder crossed the room in several bounding steps and flung herself into his arms. "We are going home to stay, not for a visit. Annani will come later to preside over our wedding."

"When?"

She tilted her head back. "The going home or the wedding?"

"Both. And I accept."

"Accept going home? Of course, you do."

"Your proposal. The answer is yes."

Wonder's cheeks reddened. "I'm sorry. I should've asked. Would you be my mate?"

Anandur laughed and twirled Wonder around, not because it was funny, but because he was so happy. "I'm already your mate. But I'd love us to celebrate with a big party and with Annani presiding."

A grin spread over Wonder's beautiful face. "We can leave tomorrow morning. Annani will have her Odu fly us back. And as to the wedding, it's whenever we decide, but I kind of want to do it sooner rather than later because it will make Annani happy. I feel guilty for leaving her."

Plopping on the couch with Wonder in his arms, he shifted her so she was sitting sideways on his lap. "How did you manage to pull it off? I thought we were stuck here for the long haul."

"Annani is a much better friend to me than I've given her credit for. The moment she realized I wanted more out of my life than being her companion, she immediately accepted that I had to leave. She was also well aware of you being unhappy here."

"I didn't keep it a secret."

"I know. But she is Annani, the Clan Mother, and I didn't expect her to pay attention."

"In short, you underestimated her."

Wonder rolled her eyes. "Big time. I feel so ashamed. Annani is amazing. With her diva attitude and her impetuous nature, it's easy to overlook that she is so incredibly brave and smart and insightful."

"Well, she is a goddess."

Wonder waved a dismissive hand. "You think so because you only know one goddess. I knew many gods. Just like humans and immortals, some were brave, and others were not. Some were smart and others not so much. Some were hard-working and others were lazy. Some wanted to do good and improve the lives of everyone, including that of humans, while others couldn't care less and were only interested in their own luxury and comfort. Trust me when I say that Annani is special. She has her father's leadership ability and her mother's compassion and her uncle's smarts. If the gods were still with us, Annani would have been the best among them."

"Then we are doubly fortunate that the Fates chose for her to survive and not another god or goddess."

Wonder nodded. "I believe Annani was chosen for a reason. She is the one tiny thread the Fates pulled out of the burning tapestry, saving it to start a new one."

WONDER

*E*yes red and puffy from a tearful goodbye, Wonder boarded the small jet with Anandur and waved at Annani until the door lifted and closed.

"That was hard." She puffed out a breath.

"Annani told you that whenever you want to visit, she'd send the plane for you."

"I know, and that makes it a little easier. But I still feel so bad for abandoning her."

He took her hand and gave it a squeeze. "Tell me about Annani's parents and her uncle. You said that she has her mother's compassion, her father's leadership ability, and her uncle's smarts. That made me curious to hear more about them."

If Anandur was trying to distract her, Wonder was all for it. He was doing her a favor. She didn't like the guilty feelings churning in her gut. Talking about the past would take her mind off that, and maybe it would help her forget Annani's tear-filled eyes and clinging embrace.

"Ahn, Annani's father, was a good leader, and he loved

Annani, but then he did a stupid thing by promising her to Mortdh. He was willing to sacrifice her happiness for a promise of peace that was as flimsy and as worthless as dried out, crumbling leaves."

The next five hours went by quickly as Wonder told Anandur story after story about gods, immortals, and humans, and how they had all lived together peacefully.

More or less.

She didn't know much about Mortdh and his northern camp, other than what Annani had told her. Things had been different up there. Mortdh had not followed the gods' rules of engagement with humans or with immortals, and his hateful attitude toward women had been well known.

"I have an idea for you," Anandur said as the limousine's windows turned opaque, which meant they were almost home. "Have you thought about becoming a historian?"

"What's a historian? Someone that tells stories from the past?"

"Something like that. Let me read you the definition." He pulled out his phone and typed the word into the search bar. "Here it is. A historian is a person who studies history and writes books and or articles about it."

That sounded interesting. But all the history she knew was from an ancient civilization that no longer existed.

"What do I need to do to become one? Is there a school for that?"

"Of course. You can go to college and study history. But first, you'll have to get your high school equivalency diploma."

"I'll think about it."

On the one hand, Wonder knew it would be interesting to learn about what had happened in the world over the millennia of her stasis. On the other hand, it didn't sound like the kind of job that involved working with people. Sitting alone in a room full of books wasn't fun.

"I prefer working with people. I don't want to spend my days alone."

"You can become a history teacher."

That sounded much better. One of the careers she'd been considering was teaching. Why not history?

"I like your idea."

"Good." He kissed the top of her head. "You can chronicle the clan's history, which is something that should've been done a long time ago, and I will sleep better knowing you have a safe job that doesn't put you in harm's way."

She wanted to come back with a retort about his double standard attitude, but they had arrived at the village's underground parking and Okidu was already opening her door.

"Madam." He bowed and offered her his hand.

A sound of chattering greeted them as they exited the pavilion, and it soon became clear what it was all about.

It seemed as if the entire clan was there to welcome Anandur and her home. And if she had any doubts as to the reason for the party, a big banner hanging from the second-story windows of the office building dispelled them.

It said in big bold lettering, "Welcome home Wonder & Anandur."

Her name was first, but Wonder didn't have any illusions as to whom everyone was so happy to welcome home.

They'd got their mascot back.

Carol was the first to pull her into her arms, but she

wasn't the last, and as people kept smiling and hugging and kissing her cheeks, Wonder realized that they were genuinely glad to see her too.

As if she hadn't shed enough tears already, Wonder felt her eyes mist, but this time not because she was mourning her loved ones, but because she was happy.

She'd found a home with these people and a promising future, maybe as a historian, or maybe not. There was plenty of time to decide about that. But most importantly, she'd found the best possible man ever to build that future with.

"Quick! Get Bridget!" someone hollered over the noisy crowd.

Murmurs started immediately, people clearing a path for the doctor as she rushed toward Eva, who was standing over a small puddle and holding up her enormous belly.

Anandur wrapped his arm around Wonder's shoulders. "And that's number three."

She lifted her eyes to him. "Number three?"

"First you, then Nick, and now this little fellow. Three new members joining our clan."

The end...for now...

Dear reader,

Thank you for reading the **Children of the Gods series.**

If you enjoyed the story, I would be grateful if you could leave a **short review** for *Dark Survivor Reunited* on Amazon. (With a few words, you'll make me very happy. :-))

COMING UP NEXT
THE CHILDREN OF THE GODS BOOK 23
DARK WIDOW'S SECRET
MAGNUS & VIVIAN'S STORY

(Read 3 chapters on VIP portal)

&
THE CHILDREN OF THE GODS ORIGINS BOOK 2
GODDESS'S HOPE
AREANA & NAVUH'S STORY

(READ 3 CHAPTERS ON VIP PORTAL

FOR EXCLUSIVE PEEKS AT UPCOMING RELEASES

JOIN MY *VIP CLUB* AND GAIN ACCESS TO THE **VIP** PORTAL AT

ITLUCAS.COM

CLICK HERE TO JOIN

(OR GO TO: http://eepurl.com/blMTpD)

If you're already a subscriber and forgot the password to the VIP portal, you can find it at the bottom of each of my emails.

You can also email me at isabell@itlucas.com

THE CHILDREN OF THE GODS ORIGINS

1: GODDESS'S CHOICE

When gods and immortals still ruled the ancient world, one young goddess risked everything for love.

2: GODDESS'S HOPE

Hungry for power and infatuated with the beautiful Areana, Navuh plots his father's demise. After all, by getting rid of the insane god he would be doing the world a favor. Except, when gods and immortals conspire against each other, humanity pays the price.

But things are not what they seem, and prophecies should not to be trusted...

THE CHILDREN OF THE GODS

1: DARK STRANGER THE DREAM

Syssi's paranormal foresight lands her a job at Dr. Amanda Dokani's neuroscience lab, but it fails to predict the thrilling yet terrifying turn her life will take. Syssi has no clue that her boss is an immortal who'll drag her into a secret, millennia-old battle over humanity's future. Nor does she realize that the professor's imposing brother is the mysterious stranger who's been starring in her dreams.

Since the dawn of human civilization, two warring factions of immortals—the descendants of the gods of old—have been secretly shaping its destiny. Leading the clandestine battle from his luxurious Los Angeles high-rise, Kian is surrounded by his clan, yet alone. Descending from a single goddess, clan members are forbidden to each other. And as the only other immortals are their hated enemies, Kian and his kin have been long resigned to a lonely existence of fleeting trysts with human partners. That is, until his sister makes a game-changing discovery—a mortal seeress who she believes is a dormant carrier of their genes. Ever the realist, Kian is skeptical and refuses Amanda's plea to attempt Syssi's activation. But when his enemies learn of the Dormant's existence, he's forced to rush her to the safety of his keep. Inexorably drawn to Syssi, Kian wrestles with his conscience as he is tempted to explore her budding interest in the darker shades of sensuality.

2: DARK STRANGER REVEALED

While sheltered in the clan's stronghold, Syssi is unaware that Kian and Amanda are not human, and neither are the supposedly religious fanatics that are after her. She feels a powerful connection to Kian, and as he introduces her to a world of pleasure she never dared imagine, his dominant sexuality is a revelation. Considering that she's completely out of her element, Syssi feels comfortable and safe letting go with him. That is, until she begins to suspect that all is not as it seems. Piecing the puzzle together, she draws a scary, yet wrong conclusion...

3: DARK STRANGER IMMORTAL

When Kian confesses his true nature, Syssi is not as much shocked by the revelation as she is wounded by what she perceives as his callous plans for her.

If she doesn't turn, he'll be forced to erase her memories and let her go. His family's safety demands secrecy – no one in the mortal world is allowed to know that immortals exist.

Resigned to the cruel reality that even if she stays on to never again leave the keep, she'll get old while Kian won't, Syssi is determined to enjoy what little time she has with him, one day at a time.

Can Kian let go of the mortal woman he loves? Will Syssi turn? And if she does, will she survive the dangerous transition?

4: Dark Enemy Taken

Dalhu can't believe his luck when he stumbles upon the beautiful immortal professor. Presented with a once in a lifetime opportunity to grab an immortal female for himself, he kidnaps her and runs. If he ever gets caught, either by her people or his, his life is forfeit. But for a chance of a loving mate and a family of his own, Dalhu is prepared to do everything in his power to win Amanda's heart, and that includes leaving the Doom brotherhood and his old life behind.

Amanda soon discovers that there is more to the handsome Doomer than his dark past and a hulking, sexy body. But succumbing to her enemy's seduction, or worse, developing feelings for a ruthless killer is out of the question. No man is worth life on the run, not even the one and only immortal male she could claim as her own...

Her clan and her research must come first...

5: Dark Enemy Captive

When the rescue team returns with Amanda and the chained Dalhu to the keep, Amanda is not as thrilled to be back as she thought she'd be. Between Kian's contempt for her and Dalhu's imprisonment, Amanda's budding relationship with Dalhu seems doomed. Things start to look up when Annani offers her help, and together with Syssi they resolve to find a way for Amanda to be with Dalhu. But will she still want him when she realizes that he is responsible for her nephew's murder? Could she? Will she take the easy way out and choose Andrew instead?

6: Dark Enemy Redeemed

Amanda suspects that something fishy is going on onboard the Anna. But when her investigation of the peculiar all-female Russian crew fails to uncover anything other than more speculation, she decides it's time to stop playing detective and face her real problem—a man she shouldn't want but can't live without.

6.5: My Dark Amazon

When Michael and Kri fight off a gang of humans, Michael gets stabbed. The injury to his immortal body recovers fast, but the one to his ego takes longer, putting a strain on his relationship with Kri.

7: Dark Warrior Mine

When Andrew is forced to retire from active duty, he believes that all he has to look forward to is a boring desk job. His glory days in special ops are over. But as it turns out, his thrill ride has just begun. Andrew discovers not only that immortals exist and have been manipulating global affairs since antiquity, but that he and his sister are rare possessors of the immortal genes.

Problem is, Andrew might be too old to attempt the activation process. His sister, who is fourteen years his junior, barely made it through the transition, so the odds of him coming out of it alive, let alone immortal, are slim.

But fate may force his hand.

Helping a friend find his long-lost daughter, Andrew finds a woman who's worth taking the risk for. Nathalie might be a Dormant, but the only way to find out for sure requires fangs and venom.

8: Dark Warrior's Promise

Andrew and Nathalie's love flourishes, but the secrets they keep from each other taint their relationship with doubts and suspicions. In the meantime, Sebastian and his men are getting bolder, and the storm that's brewing will shift the balance of power in the millennia-old conflict between Annani's clan and its enemies.

9: Dark Warrior's Destiny

The new ghost in Nathalie's head remembers who he was in life, providing Andrew and her with indisputable proof that he is real and not a figment of her imagination.

Convinced that she is a Dormant, Andrew decides to go forward with his transition immediately after the rescue mission at the Doomers' HQ.

Fearing for his life, Nathalie pleads with him to reconsider. She'd rather spend the rest of her mortal days with Andrew than risk what they have for the fickle promise of immortality.

While the clan gets ready for battle, Carol gets help from an unlikely ally. Sebastian's second-in-command can no longer ignore the torment she suffers at the hands of his commander and offers to help her, but only if she agrees to his terms.

10: Dark Warrior's Legacy

Andrew's acclimation to his post-transition body isn't easy. His senses are sharper, he's bigger, stronger, and hungrier. Nathalie fears that the changes in the man she loves are more than physical. Measuring up to this new version of him is going to be a challenge.

Carol and Robert are disillusioned with each other. They are not destined mates, and love is not on the horizon. When Robert's three months are up, he might be left with nothing to show for his sacrifice.

Lana contacts Anandur with disturbing news; the yacht and its human cargo are in Mexico. Kian must find a way to apprehend Alex and rescue the women on board without causing an international incident.

11: Dark Guardian Found

What would you do if you stopped aging?

Eva runs. The ex-DEA agent doesn't know what caused her strange mutation, only that if discovered, she'll be dissected like a lab rat. What Eva doesn't know, though, is that she's a descendant of the gods, and that she is not alone. The man who rocked her world in one life-changing encounter over thirty years ago is an immortal as well.

To keep his people's existence secret, Bhathian was forced to turn his back on the only woman who ever captured his heart, but he's never forgotten and never stopped looking for her.

12: Dark Guardian Craved

Cautious after a lifetime of disappointments, Eva is mistrustful of Bhathian's professed feelings of love. She accepts him as a lover and a confidant but not as a life partner.

Jackson suspects that Tessa is his true love mate, but unless she overcomes her fears, he might never find out.

Carol gets an offer she can't refuse—a chance to prove that there is more to her than meets the eye. Robert believes she's about to commit a deadly mistake, but when he tries to dissuade her, she tells him to leave.

13: Dark Guardian's Mate

Prepare for the heart-warming culmination of Eva and Bhathian's story!

14: Dark Angel's Obsession

The cold and stoic warrior is an enigma even to those closest to him. His secrets are about to unravel...

15: Dark Angel's Seduction

Brundar is fighting a losing battle. Calypso is slowly chipping away his icy armor from the outside, while his need for her is melting it from the inside.

He can't allow it to happen. Calypso is a human with none of the Dormant indicators. There is no way he can keep her for more than a few weeks.

16: Dark Angel's Surrender

Get ready for the heart pounding conclusion to Brundar and Calypso's story.

Callie still couldn't wrap her head around it, nor could she summon even a smidgen of sorrow or regret. After all, she had some memories with him that weren't horrible. She should've felt something. But there was nothing, not even shock. Not even horror at what had transpired over the last couple of hours.

Maybe it was a typical response for survivors--feeling euphoric for the simple reason that they were alive. Especially when that survival was nothing short of miraculous.

Brundar's cold hand closed around hers, reminding her that they weren't out of the woods yet. Her injuries were superficial, and the most she had to worry about was some scarring. But, despite his and Anandur's reassurances, Brundar might never walk again.

If he ended up crippled because of her, she would never forgive herself for getting him involved in her crap.

"Are you okay, sweetling? Are you in pain?" Brundar asked.

Her injuries were nothing compared to his, and yet he was concerned about her. God, she loved this man. The thing was, if she told him that, he would run off, or crawl away as was the case.

Hey, maybe this was the perfect opportunity to spring it on him.

17: DARK OPERATIVE: A SHADOW OF DEATH

As a brilliant strategist and the only human entrusted with the secret of immortals' existence, Turner is both an asset and a liability to the clan. His request to attempt transition into immortality as an alternative to cancer treatments cannot be denied without risking the clan's exposure. On the other hand, approving it means risking his premature death. In both scenarios, the clan will lose a valuable ally.

When the decision is left to the clan's physician, Turner makes plans to manipulate her by taking advantage of her interest in him.

Will Bridget fall for the cold, calculated operative? Or will Turner fall into his own trap?

18: DARK OPERATIVE: A GLIMMER OF HOPE

As Turner and Bridget's relationship deepens, living together seems like the right move, but to make it work both need to make concessions.

Bridget is realistic and keeps her expectations low. Turner could never be the truelove mate she yearns for, but he is as good as she's going to get. Other than his emotional limitations, he's perfect in every way.

Turner's hard shell is starting to show cracks. He wants immortality, he wants to be part of the clan, and he wants Bridget, but he doesn't want to cause her pain.

His options are either abandon his quest for immortality and give Bridget his few remaining decades, or abandon Bridget by going for the transition and most likely dying. His rational mind dictates that he chooses the former, but his gut pulls him toward the latter. Which one is he going to trust?

19: DARK OPERATIVE: THE DAWN OF LOVE

Get ready for the exciting finale of Bridget and Turner's story!

20: DARK SURVIVOR AWAKENED

This was a strange new world she had awakened to.

Her memory loss must have been catastrophic because almost nothing was familiar. The language was foreign to her, with only a few words bearing some similarity to the language she thought in. Still, a full moon cycle had passed since her awakening, and little by little she was gaining basic understanding of it--only a few words and phrases, but she was learning more each day.

A week or so ago, a little girl on the street had tugged on her mother's sleeve and pointed at her. "Look, Mama, Wonder Woman!"

The mother smiled apologetically, saying something in the language these people spoke, then scurried away with the child looking behind her shoulder and grinning.

When it happened again with another child on the same day, it was settled.

Wonder Woman must have been the name of someone important in this strange world she had awoken to, and since both times it had been said with a smile it must have been a good one.

Wonder had a nice ring to it.

She just wished she knew what it meant.

21: DARK SURVIVOR ECHOES OF LOVE

Wonder's journey continues in *Dark Survivor Echoes of Love*.

22: DARK SURVIVOR REUNITED

The exciting finale of Wonder and Anandur's story.

23: DARK WIDOW'S SECRET

Vivian and her daughter share a powerful telepathic connection, so when Ella can't be reached by conventional or psychic means, her mother fears the worst.

Help arrives from an unexpected source when Vivian gets a call from the young doctor she met at a psychic convention. Turns out Julian belongs to a private organization specializing in retrieving missing girls.

As Julian's clan mobilizes its considerable resources to rescue the daughter, Magnus is charged with keeping the gorgeous young mother safe.

Worry for Ella and the secrets Vivian and Magnus keep from each other should be enough to prevent the sparks of attraction from kindling a blaze of desire. Except, these pesky sparks have a mind of their own.

24: DARK WIDOW'S CURSE

A simple rescue operation turns into mission impossible when the Russian mafia gets involved. Bad things are supposed to come in threes, but in Vivian's case, it seems like there is no limit to bad luck. Her family and everyone who gets close to her is affected by her curse.

Will Magnus and his people prove her wrong?

25: Dark Widow's Blessing

The thrilling finale of the Dark Widow trilogy!

26: Dark Dream's Temptation

Julian has known Ella is the one for him from the moment he saw her picture, but when he finally frees her from captivity, she seems indifferent to him. Could he have been mistaken?

Ella's rescue should've ended that chapter in her life, but it seems like the road back to normalcy has just begun and it's full of obstacles. Between the pitying looks she gets and her mother's attempts to get her into therapy, Ella feels like she's typecast as a victim, when nothing could be further from the truth. She's a tough survivor, and she's going to prove it.

Strangely, the only one who seems to understand is Logan, who keeps popping up in her dreams. But then, he's a figment of her imagination—or is he?

27: Dark Dream's Unraveling

While trying to figure out a way around Logan's silencing compulsion, Ella concocts an ambitious plan. What if instead of trying to keep him out of her dreams, she could pretend to like him and lure him into a trap?

Catching Navuh's son would be a major boon for the clan, as well as for Ella. She will have her revenge, turning the tables on another scumbag out to get her.

28: Dark Dream's Trap

The trap is set, but who is the hunter and who is the prey? Find out in this heart-pounding conclusion to the *Dark Dream* trilogy.

29: Dark Prince's Enigma

As the son of the most dangerous male on the planet, Lokan lives by three rules:

Don't trust a soul.

Don't show emotions.

And don't get attached.

Will one extraordinary woman make him break all three?

30: Dark Prince's Dilemma

Will Kian decide that the benefits of trusting Lokan outweigh the risks?

Will Lokan betray his father and brothers for the greater good of his people?

Are Carol and Lokan true-love mates, or is one of them playing the other?

So many questions, the path ahead is anything but clear.

31: Dark Prince's Agenda

While Turner and Kian work out the details of Areana's rescue plan, Carol and Lokan's tumultuous relationship hits another snag. Is it a sign of things to come?

32 : Dark Queen's Quest

A former beauty queen, a retired undercover agent, and a successful model, Mey is not the typical damsel in distress. But when her sister drops off the radar and then someone starts following her around, she panics.

Following a vague clue that Kalugal might be in New York, Kian sends a team headed by Yamanu to search for him.

As Mey and Yamanu's paths cross, he offers her his help and protection, but will that be all?

33: Dark Queen's Knight

As the only member of his clan with a godlike power over human minds, Yamanu has been shielding his people for centuries, but that power comes at a steep price. When Mey enters his life, he's faced with the most difficult choice.

The safety of his clan or a future with his fated mate.

34: Dark Queen's Army

As Mey anxiously waits for her transition to begin and for Yamanu to test whether his godlike powers are gone, the clan sets out to solve two mysteries:

Where is Jin, and is she there voluntarily?

Where is Kalugal, and what is he up to?

35: Dark Spy Conscripted

Jin possesses a unique paranormal ability. Just by touching someone, she can insert a mental hook into their psyche and tie a string of her consciousness to it, creating a tether. That doesn't make her a spy, though, not unless her talent is discovered by those seeking to exploit it.

36: Dark Spy's Mission

Jin's first spying mission is supposed to be easy. Walk into the club, touch Kalugal to tether her consciousness to him, and walk out.

Except, they should have known better.

37: Dark Spy's Resolution

The best-laid plans often go awry...

38: Dark Overlord New Horizon

Jacki has two talents that set her apart from the rest of the human race.

She has unpredictable glimpses of other people's futures, and she is immune to mind manipulation.

Unfortunately, both talents are pretty useless for finding a job other than the one she had in the government's paranormal division.

It seemed like a sweet deal, until she found out that the director planned on producing super babies by compelling the recruits into pairing up. When an opportunity to escape the program presented itself, she took it, only to find out that humans are not at the top of the food chain.

Immortals are real, and at the very top of the hierarchy is Kalugal, the most powerful, arrogant, and sexiest male she has ever met.

With one look, he sets her blood on fire, but Jacki is not a fool. A man like him will never think of her as anything more than a tasty snack, while she will never settle for anything less than his heart.

39: Dark Overlord's Wife

Jacki is still clinging to her all-or-nothing policy, but Kalugal is chipping away at her resistance. Perhaps it's time to ease up on her convictions. A little less than all is still much better than nothing, and a couple of decades with a demigod is probably worth more than a lifetime with a mere mortal.

40: Dark Overlord's Clan

As Jacki and Kalugal prepare to celebrate their union, Kian takes every precaution to safeguard his people. Except, Kalugal and his men are not his only potential adversaries, and compulsion is not the only power he should fear.

41: Dark Choices The Quandary

When Rufsur and Edna meet, the attraction is as unexpected as it is undeniable. Except, she's the clan's judge and councilwoman, and he's Kalugal's second-in-command. Will loyalty and duty to their people keep them apart?

42: Dark Choices Paradigm Shift

Edna and Rufsur are miserable without each other, and their two-week separation seems like an eternity. Long-distance relationships are difficult, but for immortal couples they are impossible. Unless one of them is willing to leave everything behind for the other, things are just going to get worse. Except, the cost of compromise is far greater than giving up their comfortable lives and hard-earned positions. The future of their people is on the line.

For a FREE Audiobook, Preview chapters, And other goodies offered only to my VIPs,

JOIN THE VIP CLUB AT ITLUCAS.COM

TRY THE SERIES ON

AUDIBLE

2 FREE audiobooks with your new Audible subscription!

THE PERFECT MATCH SERIES

Perfect Match 1: Vampire's Consort

When Gabriel's company is ready to start beta testing, he invites his old crush to inspect its medical safety protocol.

Curious about the revolutionary technology of the *Perfect Match Virtual Fantasy-Fulfillment studios*, Brenna agrees.

Neither expects to end up partnering for its first fully immersive test run.

Perfect Match 2: King's Chosen

When Lisa's nutty friends get her a gift certificate to *Perfect Match Virtual Fantasy Studios*, she has no intentions of using it. But since the only way to get a refund is if no partner can be found for her, she makes sure to request a fantasy so girly and over the top that no sane guy will pick it up.

Except, someone does.

Warning: This fantasy contains a hot, domineering crown prince, sweet insta-love, steamy love scenes painted with light shades of gray, a wedding, and a HEA in both the virtual and real worlds.

Intended for mature audience.

Perfect Match 3: Captain's Conquest

Working as a Starbucks barista, Alicia fends off flirting all day long, but none of the guys are as charming and sexy as Gregg. His frequent visits are the highlight of her day, but since he's never asked her out, she assumes he's taken. Besides, between a day job and a budding music career, she has no time to start a new relationship.

That is until Gregg makes her an offer she can't refuse —a gift certificate to the virtual fantasy fulfillment service everyone is talking about. As a huge Star Trek fan, Alicia has a perfect match in mind—the captain of the Starship Enterprise.

FOR EXCLUSIVE PEEKS AT UPCOMING RELEASES & A FREE COMPANION BOOK

Join my *VIP Club* and gain access to the VIP portal at
ITLUCAS.COM

CLICK HERE TO JOIN
(OR GO TO: http://eepurl.com/blMTpD)

INCLUDED IN YOUR FREE MEMBERSHIP:

- FREE CHILDREN OF THE GODS COMPANION BOOK 1
- FREE NARRATION OF GODDESS'S CHOICE—BOOK 1 IN THE CHILDREN OF THE GODS ORIGINS SERIES.
- PREVIEW CHAPTERS OF UPCOMING RELEASES.
- AND OTHER EXCLUSIVE CONTENT OFFERED ONLY TO MY VIPS.

Made in the USA
Columbia, SC
17 September 2020